The First Gentleman of America

By Branch Cabell

His Life and Letters:

THESE RESTLESS HEADS
SPECIAL DELIVERY
LADIES AND GENTLEMEN

The Nightmare Has Triplets:

SMIRT
SMITH
SMIRE

Heirs and Assigns:

HAMLET HAD AN UNCLE
THE KING WAS IN HIS COUNTING HOUSE
THE FIRST GENTLEMAN OF AMERICA

By James Branch Cabell

Biography of the Life of Manuel (21 vols.)
Preface to the Past

THE FIRST GENTLEMAN

OF AMERICA

★　　★

A COMEDY

OF CONQUEST

★

BY BRANCH CABELL

"My country, 'tis of thee."

WILDSIDE PRESS: MMIII

Published by
Wildside Press
P.O. Box 301
Holicong, PA 18928-0301 U.S.A.
www.wildsidepress.com

With this chronicle is completed the Trilogy of Inheritance, called *Heirs and Assigns*, of which the earlier volumes have been issued under the titles HAMLET HAD AN UNCLE and THE KING WAS IN HIS COUNTING HOUSE.

Inasmuch as the characters and happenings of this book are all pilfered from fact, any incidental resemblance to fictitious events, or to imaginary persons, is unintentional.

CONTENTS

Part One

Part One

The Grandchild of
the White Cloud Serpent

It is a country that may have the prerogative over the most pleasant places knowne; heaven & earth never agreed better to frame a place for man's habitation, were it fully manured and inhabited by industrious people. Here are mountaines, hils, plaines, valleyes, rivers, and brookes, all running most pleasantly into a faire Baye, compassed, but for the mouth, with fruitfull and delightsome land.

—Captain John Smith

★ 1 ★

It is a tale told in the Northern Neck of Virginia, between the Potomac River and the Rappahannock River; and the teller of it says it is the same story he got from his grandfather, who got it from his own grand-father, and so on back to that instant when English ears first heard this same story, about the doings of Nemat-tanon, not very long after forthright Anglo-Saxons came into this part of Virginia, to bring with them double-dealing and firearms and alcohol and yet other amenities which aid the civilized in dealing with the owners of a backward country such as one might plun-der with profit. But it was an old story even then; for it concerns a people who had lived in the Northern Neck of Virginia, reasonably and simply, for an un-recorded while, before the English overran all that great and fertile peninsula with the superior simplicity and the destructiveness of a race of reformers.

These people used to call their country Ajacan. Their country extended from about the present station of Stratford Hall along the south bank of the Potomac, and from about Leedstown along the north bank of the Rappahannock, even unto Reedville and Whitestone,

3

where nowadays these thriving centres of the fertilizer industry affront Chesapeake Bay with stenches of rotting fish and of fish oil. The Ajacans were so untutored in modernity as to believe all this quite valuable waterfront property their own heritage, merely because, ever since time's beginning, it had belonged to their fathers and their forefathers. They did not know about Rodrigo Borgia, or the part which his open-handedness was to display in their living.

Now all this, I repeat, was a large while and a half ago, before the Northern Neck had got modern blessings. The land was then an unperturbed sylvan corner of earth in which simple people lived happily, with quietude. Downing Bridge had not been builded at Hobbs Hole (or as the more modish now call it, Tappahannock) so that even if the inmate of any madhouse had as yet imagined automobiles and their increment, no touring car could well have entered the wide heron-haunted marshes of Richmond County, and have blustered thence, hooting and evil-odored, into the spacious, rolling, very lovely lowlands of Northumberland or the broad fens of Lancaster. There was no court house or bank or general merchandise store, there was not even a jail, in the Northern Neck. As the criminal law and the allied operations of finance languished, so likewise did the excitement of literature, among unmorbid surroundings, for the *Northern Neck News* had not yet begun to give to mankind information as to who was dead since last Thursday, or who was critically ill, or who was about to brave the dangers of marriage, or how very backward were all the crops, or disastrous the fishing season, whether at Weems or at Nuttville or at Morattico or at Lively.

Romance had not, as yet, made out of the Northern Neck an improbable place with billboards rhapsodic as to the miraculous merits of soft drinks, of gasoline, and of cigarettes. In not any roadway of Ajacan did a black and yellow announcement of "Slow Men Working" epitomize cynically the activities of democracy. In the villages of Ajacan were no casual looking post offices, or slatternly service stations, or emaciated trim churches (builded in accord with the more hazy Rutherford B. Hayes conception of Gothic architecture and relieved intrepidly with white lattice work of a Chinese nature), nor did you encounter in Ajacan very many small moving-picture theatres flamboyant with much magnified portrayals of a young man about to kiss a young woman. The homes of Ajacan did not bristle, as do the farm houses of the Northern Neck, like indignant porcupines, with five lightning rods apiece. The people of Ajacan breathed, untaxed and freely, a pure air which stayed not poisoned all during every day by the greasy genialities of good salesmanship, nor did the high-minded imbecility of pre-eminent statesmen make yet further obscure the twilights of Ajacan, for this people

had not any radios. The Northern Neck had contentment, under the rule of Quetzal.

Now Quetzal, so the tale says, was the only son, by
a second marriage, of Iztac, the White Cloud Serpent;
the mother of Quetzal was Xochi; she patronized the
well-being of flowers and of strumpets; and Quetzal had
come out of the heaven which is called Tapallan bringing with him his own son, who at the time of this ex-
odus was an infant. In this way did Quetzal become the
God of Ajacan, to the immediate improvement of local
affairs.

—For whereas the gods of other tribes were bad-
gers or rabbits or turtles, or it might be a giant raven,
which lived, inaccessibly, somewhere up in the sky, this
Quetzal was a visible god, shaped like a pale-colored
human being, who condescended to make his home
where the village called Burgess Store now stands, at
the junction of State Highways Number 200 and Number 360, and with whom a devout adorer might, thus,
consult at need as to religious or legal or personal matters.

"A god of this intimate kind"—it was remarked
by the more thoughtful element of Ajacan society—
"connotes a distinct advancement both in convenience
and in tribal dignity."

This statement had in it more truth-telling than is
with the well-thought-of an habitual form of indulgence; for Quetzal taught to his chosen people many ac-

complishments and devices which were unknown to their neighbors. Their neighbors, such as the Monnakans or the Kecoughtans or the Powhatans, strayed about almost at random, in search of food or of weaker tribes with whom they could fight enjoyably; and they lived, with discomfort, in tents which had been patched up, by their women, out of poles and tree-bark; but the men of Ajacan had been taught by wise Quetzal how to build for themselves their stout, square, solid timber houses, with chimneys, in villages which had each its counsel hall and its storeroom for dried meats and fish and its granaries, and which was exceedingly well guarded with strong oaken palisades. The Ajacans had been taught also how to cultivate fruit-trees and vegetables; and how to treat with respect the laws of Quetzal. This last, above all, had the son of the White Cloud Serpent taught them.

"My chief law," said Quetzal, when he first took charge of affairs, "is for you to avoid fighting with other tribes, because there is no special sense in it."

The Ajacans answered him: "All-gracious Lord, very long ago came to this earth the serpent called Maskanako. This strong black snake prompts magnanimity among humankind; and because of his advice they are embroiled continually, hating one another with an exalted heroism. It is Maskanako who compels us to fight

and to despoil our neighbors, and not ever to be at any
sort of negotiated peace with them, so that our names
may become famous all during this month and known
among persons who live as much as ten miles away.
From Maskanako comes glory; he incites, he makes
dauntless, the need of every brave warrior to kill complete strangers quite completely."

"Perhaps," said Quetzal; "for patriotism is a strong
malady. Yet it is not beyond cure; the times change; and
with them, snakes also are made mutable. For the future
it is I, the son of the White Cloud Serpent, and not any
out-of-date, black serpent like Maskanako, who must
be master during this present crisis and under the man-
date which you are about to give me. I do not like war.
You will let it be known, therefore, that from this day
onward, all such misguided imbeciles as attack Ajacan
will be overcome."

"By what force, O indispensable person?" asked
the Ajacans.

"They will be overcome," Quetzal returned,—after
he had thought about this matter for a moment,—"by
the force of the Charm of Belshaddar, which does not
come out of Babylon, but from Babel; because of which
charm they will walk, as though in a mist, babbling; because of which their knees will fail them; because of
which they will let fall their weapons. Whereafter they
will flounder about at random; and will be made prisoners."

"Aha!" said the Ajacans: for they used to get a great deal of good clean fun out of a prisoner, and their medicine men had learned how to keep a prisoner conscious until, virtually, the final moment of their amusement.

"Then after an impressive ceremony," says Quetzal—"which, upon reflection, it might be better to enliven with a brief musical program,—the heart of each prisoner will be removed. His heart will be ripped out of his body with this same very holy stone knife which I carry here at my girdle. His heart will be made an offertory to me, who am Lord of the Ninth Wind."

This news was proclaimed. Before its inconceivable stark terror, the Monnakans, the Kecoughtans, the Powhatans, and all other tribes trembled, because, inasmuch as their medicine men had not ever heard of the Charm of Belshaddar before today, the scholars and the leading scientists of these tribes had no notion how to oppose this secret strange weapon.

So they took refuge in self-respect.

"The Ajacans," said the medicine men, "are beneath contempt; for they employ unauthorized adjuncts such as we ourselves have not ever used in killing even our most near and intimate enemies. There is such a thing, after all, as a nation's being too proud to provoke an adversary who is thus ignoble. For this reason, let us ignore Ajacan."

It came about, in this manner, that Ajacan was left unmolested. Under the sedative influence of not beginning a new war every week, its people progressed. They advanced from the quaint barbarism of believing in the Black Earth Serpent, to the point of speaking upon all occasions with awe, and quite as if they almost understood themselves, about the White Cloud Serpent; and to the point also of being governed by his son and his grandson. For Quetzal became the God of the Ajacans; and the son of Quetzal (who was named Nemattanon) was by-and-by their chieftain, or as they called it, their Werrowance.

★ 2 ★

—So AFFAIRS sped handsomely in Ajacan, and all prospered in the land, and its people believed that every
beach and wide estuary and tall woodland of Ajacan belonged to Quetzal. As has been told to you, they did not
take into account (for the reason that they had never
heard of any such personage) the Bishop of Rome. They
did not know about his generosity in giving the present
Commonwealth of Virginia, along with all the other
United States of America, to the King of Spain, as a
part of the West Indies. Nor for a long time did the
King of Spain ever hear that among his other provinces
beyond the Atlantic was Ajacan.

Lord Philip knew only that all the west, which,
overnight as it were, through a felicitous combining of
statecraft and of bribery and of Divine favor, had been
made a fief of Spain, was exceedingly full of heathen
perils and wonders and of gold. The Spaniards held
Mexico: that was a prospering colony nowadays, and
the ways of Mexico were commendable. Lord Philip
would not, indeed, have been the most opulent of Christian monarchs were it not for Mexico, where four times
a year the gold taken away from the caziques (as people

called the Indian chieftains of Mexico), or wrung out
of the enslaved natives' labor, was melted down and
cast into large bars, which were then fetched oversea
to Lord Philip, either at Cadiz or at Seville, by the West
Indian Fleet. Lord Philip in this way got every year
some 460,000 pesos, with which to maintain his omnipotence in each known part of the world and the
temporal glories of the Holy Catholic Church in a full
half-dozen kingdoms. So he thought about Mexico at
all times with benevolence.

Yet he remembered also that, northward of Mexico, remained unclaimed those other countries which
had been presented to Spain by the Holy Father of
Christendom; and he thought about how much more
huge they were than Mexico, and more important, and
more amply teeming with gold. It was known that
every sort of marvel and of opulence flourished in the
magic regions north of Mexico; for in those days the
chief scientists and the leading scholars of Europe had
found out a vast deal about the lands which are now the
United States of America, and they had this information duly set down in their books and their maps.

They knew, for example, that when the Moors
took Spain, about eight hundred years before this time,
seven enterprising bishops had sailed away into the sunset, where, but a little distance north of Mexico (either
in Arizona or it may have been in Clara County, or in
Lincoln County, in the southern part of Nevada) each

one of these pioneering prelates had established a rather
large four-square city completely builded out of gold,
and paved also with gold, even in the lesser alley ways
where stood its golden stables and its golden privies,
upon a fine firm foundation of several layers of precious
stones, so as to afford, upon earth, a devout copying of
the New Jerusalem just as the ultimate home of zealous
Catholics had been revealed to St. John at Patmos.
These seven sanctified cities had still to be conquered,
and to be looted lawfully, by their right owner, the
King of Spain.

Besides that, the King knew, to the north of Mexico arose the moonstone and beryl and chrysolite mountains of Appalachia, which shone so bright in the
daytime, on account of the higher peaks' being each an
unflawed single diamond, that they made men blind, and
so would compel a night attack upon the inhabitants
before the pious labor of your troops could despoil these
uplands of your illegally detained chattels. Among your
other fiefs, not very distant from these mountains, was
the kingdom of Cibola, over which reigned, as yet, a
wicked usurper in the form of a prince of the Mon-
tezumas. This heathen thief had so far violated the rules
of honorable war as wickedly to retain, and to carry off
with him, many of the most important crown jewels of
Mexico (even after his family had enjoyed possession
of them for hundreds of years) in the very moment
that the Holy Virgin was collaborating with Cortés to

abash and to starve and to batter Mexico into a surrender, to Spain, of these trinkets. Spain could not afford
to endorse such impiety.

Spain could not afford to be cheated out of Cibola,
because, as all well educated Spaniards knew, the great
flat-topped palaces of Cibola were encrusted completely
with turquoises and emeralds; and the people of Cibola
were put to the inconvenience of making even their
most common tools and household implements, such as
their garden spades and their chamber pots and their
pen-knives and their saucepans, for instance, out of un-
alloyed soft gold, because in Cibola there was not any
other metal. Nor in Quivera, standing a little north-
eastward from Cibola in the lands which Pope Alexander the Sixth had granted to Spain—and by the find-
ings of more modern scientists, about where Topeka
now stands in Kansas—were the inhabitants any more
widely favored as concerned metallurgic resources.
There was in Kansas, in those days, not any kind of
metal except only an unlimited supply of virgin gold,
the chief scientists of Europe assured you during the
heyday of Lord Philip.

Such then were the official reports as to North
America; and all stalwart Spain delighted to hear about
the miraculous kingdoms which belonged by rights to
Spain, and about the unstinted gold which a fair marks-
man could get in the west, so very easily, without any
awkward twinges of conscience, by shooting down, like

partridges, a few hundred unarmed infidels. So, in most cases, it was gold of which the brave adventurers who went to America dreamed high-heartedly. It was gold for which they sought, and gold which they demanded from the Indians, and gold which they got hourly, by one means or another, now that the heathen west had begun to allure all hardy Christians who hungered for wealth, or who loved adventure, or who needed to escape from the unwelcome attentiveness of the police. Into the west trooped well-born gentlemen who were penniless and too proud to work, and impetuous young- sters from every condition in life, and bankrupts, and professional thieves, and murderers who had killed in- judiciously, each one of them duly furnished with a passport to prove him a sound Catholic—which in most instances had been properly forged and sold to him by the Imperial Board of Trade,—and each seeking after the gold of New Spain.

They found, it is true, after reaching Mexico, that the King got most of the gold, nor was gold quite so plentiful in fact as it had been in rumor; yet there was a great deal of gold in the shape of stray windfalls to be picked up, quietly, by the unprudish; and at worst, now that most of the native Mexicans had been reduced to slavery, those Spaniards who had been vagabonds or petty criminals in the Old World could live in the New World as luxurious and well attended grandees without any tiresome need to labor.

Such was one aspect of the patriotic, fine-sounding and rather sordid invasion of the west—the desire to obtain wealth and luxury; and it stays the special aspect which a more thoroughly enlightened era can most readily comprehend, now that to our own scholars and scientists, and to well-educated persons in general, any talk about religion has become a politely condoned outbreak of superstition. But in that day, you must let me remind you, was raging all over Europe a quaint but quite violent plague of faith and of magnanimity. Very many persons, and even persons of high repute, during that dark backward time, were so credulous as to believe alike in the existence of God and in the nobility of serving Him.

So besides those Spaniards who hunted after opulence, came others who aspired differently. The west they knew to be peopled with heathen tribes who worshipped demons. In the archaic phrasing of these out-of-date zealots, the people of New Spain were lost sheep beguiled by hell's cunning very far astray in quagmires of heresy; and these wanderers must be led back, at all costs, into the fold of the True Faith. For that reason, side by side with the roisterers, the cut-throats and the pickpockets, came the missionaries also, in a swarm of devout, great-hearted simple champions of Christ who were seeking to plant the Gospel in the West Indies; who went forth to battle against Satan no less impenetrably armed with supreme love than with supreme narrow-mindedness; and who demanded poverty rather than gold, so that, without any worldly distractions, they could enlighten their strayed fellow creatures as to those things which the Mother Church of Rome had taught to be requisite for human salvation.

★ 3 ★

I WILL now tell you how the magnificent Señor Pedro
Menéndez de Avilés, who at this time was Captain General of the West Indian Fleet, went into Mexico to fetch
back with him a shipload of gold. He found that the
special galleonful of King Philip's income for which
Don Pedro had come into New Spain had been des-
pátched to Seville and must have passed him at sea un-
noted. There was left only the choice for Menéndez to
return empty-handed or to bestow himself idly upon
the wharves of Yucatan, while the Viceroy (who at this
period was the first Don Luis de Velasco to hold that
office) was extorting, by due process of law, enough
opulence to make up another shipload.

Menéndez could not ever abide idleness; and so,
while the flurried Viceroy set about enslaving two more
tribes, of Toltecs and of Nahau, for labor in the gold
mines, and redoubled his own untiring labors, in his torture chambers, to induce ten caziques to pay their just
tribute to the King of Spain somewhat more cheerfully,
Menéndez sailed northward—passing Florida, and continuing northward, along the present coasts of Georgia
and of the two Carolinas. He took with him just enough
cut-throat communicants in armor to keep Spain re-

spected, and four Jesuit Brothers (since a full-fledged Father was not, at the moment, available) to uphold and to disseminate the True Faith.

You must not try to think about Don Pedro as wasting these weeks in a pleasure jaunt. With an habitual knack for making every moment useful, he was looking for the broad navigable straits which the scientists and the map-makers of his day knew to run slantingly across the United States of America, from a bit north of Virginia Beach to the magic City of the Cæsars (which then stood not far from Seattle), and thus gave you a convenient and speedy route into China and Crim Tartary. When his caravel had reached the harbor which Norfolk and Portsmouth now confront, it became evident that Don Pedro Menéndez de Avilés had found, as he usually did find, what he sought.

So did it happen that, at long last, the Spaniards passed between Cape Charles and Cape Henry, which the Spaniards named otherwise, in honor of Mary Magdalen and John the Beloved Disciple. They went up the broad Bay of Chesapeake, which they christened St. Mary's Bay, out of deference to the Mother of God; and they turned westward, a little distance into the Potomac River, which because of their continuing piety they called the River of the Holy Ghost. Since they could now see Point Lookout, upon the Maryland side, they perceived this was not an arm of the ocean but a river. This is a fact which no few historians have overlooked: but the Spaniards (not being extremely learned persons, with a theory to establish) did not overlook it. They landed forthwith at Hack Neck, in Ajacan, upon the Virginian side, about two miles distant from the post office at Ophelia, on their foiled journey into China.

The first thing they did in Ajacan was to raise up the banner of the two castles and the two lions, to show that all these West Indies belonged to King Philip. They sounded trumpets in the King's honor. After that, they more quietly put up a cross, as a sign that Christ likewise ought to be respected everywhere, at the Pope's discretion; and the four Jesuits offered praise and the correct prayers to Heaven.

It was then that a tall young man, in the prime of youth, wearing about his body only a breech-clout of fringed deer-skin, came down to the river bank. Upon his head he had a fillet of bright beads adorned with an eagle's feather. He carried no arms, but he walked with a queerly carved and colored reed cane; and he asked, in surprisingly sound Spanish, what was their need in this place?

Menéndez answered. He looked first at the young savage man in a perturbed way, and the weather-tanned face of Pedro Menéndez, above his short curly beard, became more nearly pallid than was usual, because of the likeness between this tall West Indian and the lost son of Menéndez. Don Pedro said,—

"It is our first need to proclaim here, as in every other place, the loving-kindness of God."

"My people have already a God," was the young man's answer, "and except only when he becomes thoughtless about keeping the Ninth Wind under control, his loving-kindness contents them well enough."

"And how, señor,"—inquired Menéndez, recalling his courtesy,—"do you name this God?"

"He is called Quetzal. He is Lord of the Ninth Wind. I am Nemattanon of the One Reed,"—and the speaker now lifted his strange cane. "I am the only son of Quetzal. Yet you need not be much afraid of me, señors, because—for all that I am also a grandson of the great White Cloud Serpent—I am mortal like you. I am merely a demigod."

"You speak nonsense, my poor Nemattanon: for there is only one true God, and His sole son is Christ Our Redeemer."

The young man answered, reasonably: "Such, señor, may very well be the case in your country; but hereabouts, every tribe has its own God. A tribe which did not have its own special God would be poorly thought of; it would not be respected by anybody. For the rest, I am of course a demigod. Even before I became a werrowance I was a demigod. So there is no least need to dispute the matter. And about this other demigod whom you call Christ Our Redeemer I have not ever heard."

Said one of the Jesuits, whose name has not been recorded:

"It is concerning Christ that we bring glad tidings,

Nemattanon; for I and my fellows here are the un-worthy servants of Christ. We bring with us the truth, that supreme truth which will drive Quetzal out of this place and demolish his wickedness and thrust down his worshippers into everlasting fires."

"I infer," replied Nemattanon, after he had looked for some while at this Jesuit, "that your notions of glad-ness are not the same as are my notions of gladness. At any rate"—the West Indian said, to Menéndez—"we had best wait until we have eaten our dinner before we talk any more about this Christ Our Redeemer and about the big fire into which he is going to put me on account of his loving-kindness."

"In fact," Menéndez agreed,—as, with a pang of recollection, his smile answered that meditative slow smiling which was so very like the demure mirthfulness of his son,—"in fact, the more painful points of theol-ogy do not always rest quietly on an empty stomach."

"Come then, my friends," said Nemattanon.

Thus speaking, he conducted them to his home; he presented them to the attention of his young wife Leota; and he made a feast in honor of these pale-colored foreigners, bringing out red mats for each one of them to sit upon, and feeding the Spaniards very handsomely, with fine fresh vegetables and berries, and with venison and fish and squirrels, and with the meat of land tortoises.

★ 4 ★

RUMORS as to the Spaniards had reached Ajacan, before them, like unamiable heralds. These Wapsinis (or East-people) had come out of the sunrise, said report, in very large canoes which had wings, brightly colored; and the East-people had conquered the Azteca confederation of tribes about Tenochtitlan, in the Valley of Anahuac, a great distance to the south. The East-people had done this through not fighting, self-respectingly, in a civilized manner, with arrows and stone-headed axes, but with unlegalized weapons which spat out fire and death from beyond bowshot. Moreover, the Wapsinis were so treacherous as to make war in hard metal clothing, which your arrows could not easily penetrate. They were so unlike human men that hair grew freely all over their faces; and indeed, some of the older East-people even had quite long beards, like an irreverent parody of the divine white beard of Quetzal. The East-people were altogether a suspicionable tribe.

At any rate, it was in a number so few as to be harmless that these barbarians now had come into Ajacan—hoping to get profit, no doubt, from observing a civilization so much farther advanced than was

theirs. As yet, they had not provoked the fatal Charm
of Belshaddar by disturbing the law and order of Ajacan
with their savageness. So, if but as the favored guests of
our native land's Werrowance—behind whom every
good citizen ought to rally with an especial ferocity
when he was quite plainly in the wrong, because it was
then he most needed moral support—the East-people
had to be treated with indulgence. Thus spoke all
Ajacan, with charity, from the south bank of that same
river of which the north bank is now graced with a
nation's Capitol.

But Nemattanon had become rather more acutely
interested than mere charity required by the ways of
these East-people, whose main faults, after all, as it
seemed to him, were that they held to unpolished ideas
about demigods, and religion in general, and told impossible lies as to the countries from which they came.
The quiet, humor-loving young demigod gave to this
nonsense a demure encouragement; and he liked, in
particular, to stir up such extravagance in the conduct
of the East-people's leader, this Don Pedro Menéndez
de Avilés.

Now it must be told more fully of Don Pedro why
he, who in all his life was not ever afraid of anything
except dishonor, had changed color at his first sight of
Nemattanon. It was, as I have said, because the young
savage man so much resembled the son of Menéndez,

whom Don Pedro had loved beyond any other human being.

The will of Heaven, I must tell you, had blessed the quite satisfying if unexciting marriage of Menéndez, to Doña Maria de Solís (whom, to the best of his recollection, he had not seen now for some ten years) with three not improperly prized tributes of esteem in the form of daughters and with one boy, that flesh-and-blood paragon. The will of Heaven had caused young Juan Menéndez, when he was returning out of New Spain with a small fleet of which his father, so very proudly, had put this adored son in command, to disappear. It was not even known where, if in any place, these three ships had foundered. By one account the disaster had happened off Bermuda; by another, near Cape Canaveral; whereas a third rumor had it that in the Caribbean, these ships had been captured by French corsairs, who had then disposed of their prisoners, as was customary, by feeding them to sharks. But Menéndez cherished, even nowadays, the hope that the ships had been wrecked on the mainland; that his son had escaped death, somehow; and that Juan yet lived as a slave among some wandering tribe of West Indians. At this time the Indians of America—and in particular, the people of Caloosa, for religious reasons—had collected many such white captives saved from the not infrequent wrecking of exploring parties and merchant vessels.

Now, the young Werrowance of Ajacan had very much the features, and just the proud high look, of lost Juan. This Nemattanon too was dark; and in his every movement the West Indian displayed, as did lost Juan, the quiet nimbleness of a leopard. He had, above all, the same slow way of smiling at you, with a sort of delayed half-puzzled admiration—which sprang, it is true, from the fact that both these young men had found Pedro Menéndez de Avilés to be efficient and pig-headed beyond actual belief. Since he did not know about this, however, Don Pedro regarded Nemattanon with an increasing affection; and talked, very gravely and fondly, to the amused Ajacan demigod, about the more important affairs of human existence, which, to the fixed judgment of Menéndez, were then, as always, and as must be forever, Spain and the unapproachable glory of Spain.

Nor did this half-paternal sort of instructiveness limit itself to worldly concerns; for Don Pedro now determined to preserve from hell, and from out of the dark gulfs of unending torment, the imperilled soul of Nemattanon.

As a zealous churchman, who was too devout to meddle with theological matters, Menéndez unloosed to this holy task his Jesuit Brothers; and they followed the approved methods of the clergy in dealing with the savages of the West Indies. They began, that is, to dispose Nemattanon and his listening people to accept the fundamental tenets of the True Faith by enlarging upon the ONENESS of their God's omnipresent nature; upon the DUALITY of their God's nature, as the first Begetter and the final Destroyer of all which exists in this world; and after that, upon the TRIUNITY of their God's nature, as a Father, a Son, and a Holy Ghost. This gambit, it was felt, would show at once, to the unmathematical-minded heathen, that the King of Kings was not at all like their more primitive deities.

Nemattanon stroked his smooth chin with his fingers; yet afterward he counted one, two, and three, upon these same fingers with a civil but unmistakable air of obtuseness.

The Brothers, turning toward direct personal argument, dwelled upon the facts that inasmuch as their God was the incorruptible Judge as well as the loving Creator of all life, including the life of Nemattanon, for this reason, out of filial piety, Nemattanon ought to adore his fond Father in heaven and detest his unprincipled father in the forest—that reprobate, Quetzal, who in gratifying his demoniac lusts had exposed Nemattanon to the errors of mortal life, and who had laid bare the existence of a newborn infant to the unrelenting justice of Heaven.

Nemattanon scratched his head. To the fact that, unlike other people, he had no mother, he had grown accustomed; but this notion that he possessed two fath-

ers was wholly new. You could not at once reconcile it
with your own personal observations of biology.

The Brothers explained with how great tenderness
their God at all times rewarded the virtuous, as was
shown by His ready pardon of King David for the misdemeanors of double-dealing and murder and adultery;
and with what speed their God punished any serious
kind of wrong-doing, as was proved by the death and
the eternal damnation of Ananias for withholding a
part of his church tithes.

Nemattanon said, "But, señors—" He paused. He
then said,—

"But, señors, the discrimination of your God is indeed acute; and I entreat you to continue."

So the four Jesuits passed on to speak of the rewards and penalties of the next life; of the immortality
of the soul, and of the abominable vigor of Satan, and
of the resurrection of the dead, which did not permit
Jews or Lutherans, or—they coughed here, quadruply
—even the best-meaning pagan potentates, to escape
from one tiny pang of their just torments, at long last,
no matter how vaingloriously such unbelievers might
fare in the flesh. The Jesuits spoke likewise of how the
Blessed Saviour put on mortality, and had suffered cru-
cifixion, in order to ensure the comfort of sound Catholics who did not listen to the insidious counsels of
heresy. They dwelt, with tender appreciation, upon the
loving and untiring evangelism of the Holy Inquisition

—then lately established in Cuba for the special benefit of these northern provinces of Lord Philip—through means of the thumbscrew, the boot, the rack, the question by water or by the cord, and the superb heart-lifting spectacle of an auto-da-fé, at which heretics were employed as faggots to keep warm the True Faith.

Nemattanon continued to smile politely: but he reflected that his own people had played with their prisoners in very much these fashions before Quetzal came into Ajacan to advise a more civilized sort of public diversion.

The Jesuits then employed yet other blandishments. The four Brothers began to sing. They entertained Nemattanon and his tribesmen with pious melodies as to the Creation of the World, the Fall of Man, the Voyage of Noah (to which was appended a spirited mimickry of animal- and bird-calls), the Plaguing of the Egyptians, the Fiery Furnace of King Nebuchadnezzar, the Incarnation of Christ, the Amatory Career and Repentance of Mary Magdalen, the Resurrection of Lazarus, and some two or three other events of Sacred History, all sung in a high key, to a lively tune, with an accompaniment of flutes and tambourines and kettledrums.

This program the quartet concluded by distributing to each one of their auditors an inexpensive remembrance, such as a hand-mirror or a pair of scissors or a pen-knife or a small brass bell. The holy men then

withdrew to pray privately for the success of their public religious endeavors.

Although the people of Ajacan were much interested by what seemed to them the demented conduct of
their guests, yet grace did not instantly enter into their
dark heathen hearts. Their Werrowance alone was
visited by some gossamer-like doubts as to the complete
insanity of the Jesuits.

His main trouble was, of course, that his feeling
about Christianity was the natural emotion of a piously
reared American. The perplexed young man could not
imagine how any persons who were not necessarily subjected to restraint and seclusion, for the public good,
could ever put faith in, or affect to comprehend, such
barbarian fancies as his shocked warm ears had but now
imbibed; and it troubled his sound sense of piety to hear
these wild Christians blaspheme against Quetzal: nevertheless did Nemattanon know, somehow, that these so
pathetically deluded heathen priests, like his dear dull-
witted friend Menéndez, were sincere and well-meaning
creatures. So the grandson of the White Cloud Serpent
had made up his mind to save the insane East-people
from the but too well justified anger of Quetzal, should
that outcome prove humanly possible, because of a
pleasant notion and a strong desire which had come into
Nemattanon's thinking.

★ 5 ★

Now YOUNG Nemattanon goes into the forest, to where
the small village called Burgess Store stands today, to
consult with his divine father concerning the East-
people.

The House of Quetzal, which then occupied the
present site of the Fairfields Methodist Protestant Brick
Church, did not, in spite of their shared religious signifi-
cance, resemble its latter-day successor to a confusing
degree. The House of Quetzal was bright with red and
yellow ochre; it was builded four square; and at each
corner of it, like a sentinel, stood an image about six
feet in height. These images were shaped, severally, like
an ape, a dragon, a bear, and a leopard, and each one of
them was painted with lifelike colors.

Here Quetzal lived alone except for the dark priest
called Agomek, who attended to the varied needs of
Quetzal in a rôle somewhere between that of an archbishop and a valet, with over-tones of the executioner,
inasmuch as it was the constant duty of Agomek to see
to it that all dissenters from the religion of Quetzal expired properly.

This Agomek now opened the door for Nemattanon; and at once Nemattanon frowned. In spite of the acknowledged piety and wide usefulness of this quiet clergyman, the young Werrowance had not any patience with the unnatural habits of Agomek.

Then the two officials greeted each other, with that unctuousness which seems as unavoidable as it is unmeaning between leaders of the state and of the church everywhere, before Nemattanon went in.

Quetzal sat beside the stump of an ash-tree. He was looking downward into a round mirror which covered exactly the top of the tree stump. In this magic mirror, as was well known, the God of Ajacan could see at will the future, the present, or the past, doings of humankind, whichever he elected. He lifted very bright, grave eyes, from under shaggy snow-white eyebrows, toward his son, without at all moving otherwise.

"Hail, father!" says Nemattanon; "and how do matters go with you?"

"Malodorously," replied Quetzal, sniffing with his divine nose; "for I dislike the smell of disease; and you bring with you a bad taint of dogma."

"Now, but do I indeed, sir! I must have caught it from those lying East-people who have come into Ajacan."

The God answered, slowly and consideringly, "They are not altogether liars."

"Still, sir, the stories which they tell about their own country are quite unbelievable."

"About Catalonia, and the quiet blue Mediterranean, and"—the Lord of the Ninth Wind smiled—"about dear Avilés, 'where earth bears men who are no tricksters nor babblers, but honest, truthful, faithful to their king, generous, friendly, high-hearted, daring, and exceedingly warlike.' Yes; these are quaint places."

"Ah, but, sir, how did you know about these places?"

"I have here my mirror, Nemattanon,—as you have your cane, the One Reed. Their stories, my son, are true enough."

"Then this world, father, is not at all the sort of place I had thought it!"

"Such is indeed, my child, a perturbing discovery. Yet now that you have made this discovery, the world will be at haste to re-adjust itself to your superior notions, perhaps."

"But I did not mean that, sir. I mean that it seems the world is far bigger and much more splendid than I had guessed."

Looking fondly at the handsome young Werrowance, who had never in his life been outside the Northern Neck, Quetzal said:

"Yes, Nemattanon. There are in this droll human world a dozen matters, or it may be as many as thirteen matters, about which you do not know everything quite completely."

"And the world to come, sir,—I mean, the strange

heaven and hell about which they tell me—is it at all possible that such barbarous, tasteless gaudy places can be permitted to exist?"

Quetzal answered his son: "You speak of matters with which you and I have no need to concern ourselves. Your home upon the other side of the grave has been arranged; an entire bough upon one of the more desirable trees has been duly reserved; and into the unending happiness of Tapallan you shall enter, in the form of a purple-colored bird with a golden head, in due course. Meanwhile, you would do well to make the most of this not at all unenjoyable world so long as you stay in it."

"Yet Ajacan, sir, is but a little corner of this world."

"Contentment may live in a corner, Nemattanon."

"Yes; but—" says Nemattanon.

"And by my advice, Nemattanon, you will make safe this corner while it as yet belongs to you."

"What is it that you mean, my dear father?"

"I mean, Nemattanon, that you would act with wisdom should you destroy every one of this band of Spaniards, now they are here in your power."

"Well," says Nemattanon, thoughtfully, "according to the Jesuit priests, that would be a great favor to the East-people, since after dying as martyrs to their religion, they would instantly become angels; and in that most unalluring heaven of theirs, which they seem to think well of, they would inherit, each one of them, a harp and a crown."

"Do you grant them this favor, then, my son, and permit them to get these playthings at once, for your own good no less than theirs."

"Still, sir—" said Nemattanon, uncertainly.

"Otherwise, Nemattanon, yet other Christians such as this Menéndez and his monks will be coming into Ajacan, by-and-by, now that they have discovered our country. Should you let them take back into Mexico the news of their discovery, then all the permitted years of your living will be plagued by such people. For such people are sincere and virtuous; they are controlled by a sense of duty, they are misled by a most horrible zeal for well-doing, to which they very gladly sacrifice their own comfort, and to which they will soon sacrifice yours. They are bent upon compelling every human being to honor their Christian faith; and they will end by conquering all this part of the world, not merely because they have guns and armor, but because their whole-hearted sincerity is irresistible. Yet that conquering need not happen in your time; nobody can prevent it from coming about by-and-by: but by killing these Spaniards out-of-hand, you can preserve the intelligent old happy ways of Ajacan during your own lifetime, and you can keep your kingdom untroubled until after all your troubles upon earth are done with."

"It is perhaps my duty, sir, to dispose of these strangers—"

"It is," said Quetzal.

"—And indeed my strong filial affection is now prompting me, almost irresistibly, to offer up these blasphemers against Quetzal, the son of Iztac, to the all-terrible Lord of the Ninth Wind,—my dear father,—in a civilized and becoming manner—"

"You could not possibly do anything more sensible, my son."

"—Except only for the consideration, sir, that if I did give way to self-indulgence, and if I followed my mere personal desire—perhaps a bit selfishly, sir,—why, then, I would have to remain here in Ajacan without ever seeing anything of the world at large."

"So!" said Quetzal; and he began to look unpleased.

"The consideration is perhaps overstrained, through the sieve of my dislike for all forms of selfishness," Nemattanon admitted, frankly. "To you, who are immortal, it may well seem trivial."

"It is not, by long odds; it does; and do you get on with your humbug," says Quetzal.

"Yet I am mortal, dear God of Ajacan," the young man continued; "my youth and vigor are mere loans; I have but a little while to live upon earth: and I am wholly certain that, upon reflection, your well-known kindness would not compel me to waste that time in a corner."

"What is it—you soft-speaking, fine-looking young swindler,—that you would be wheedling out of me?"

"Your permission, sir, to go south with Pedro Menéndez."

"Hah!" Quetzal said; but his look said a great deal more.

"—And then, just for convenience' sake, sir, without meaning a word of it, of course, I would have to become a Christian, as he desires me to do, because through that device alone can I travel freely about the barbarous many-colored world of these Christians; for it is my desire"—Nemattanon added adroitly—"to make plain in the more rational places of this world the fact that, even though Quetzal chooses to live in retirement, yet his race remains noteworthy, and broad-minded about freedom as to religion."

The God kept silence for some while.

"So, my son fails me," said Quetzal; "and Ajacan must be endangered before its due time because its Werrowance does not hold fast to his duty as a king by killing these Christians now. Well, but all kingdoms perish soon or late; the pastoral which, for my own diversion, I have staged here could not hope for perpetuity; and in the eyes of a god a few years are of no great account. You are yet young; there still is time for you to be convinced of my wisdom—even in Mexico, as my mirror somewhat over clearly shows me—before the Catholics and the Lutherans have made out of all the West Indies a stench, a slaughter-house and a hog-trough. You are right enough, it may be, to be quitting my service; for I am one of the old immoral kind-hearted immortals who believed that men found enough trouble upon earth without Heaven's having to add to it. So my charitable ways become out-of-date, now that the storm god of Sinai is in vogue. Very well, then, Nemattanon! for the while let us leave my House to the keeping of Agomek—"

"Ah, but is it wholly wise, my father, for you to be trusting, as you do trust everything, to that dark lover of boys?"

"Agomek has his foibles, my son; yet Agomek has intelligence also: and besides that, you must let me tell you, it is not a divine failing to trust any man whatever."

Thus speaking, Quetzal took up the birch-wood cup which sat beside him, and he drank its contents. He said then,—

"But I was about to ask, Nemattanon, that you should come with me to the chief of these Christians."

★ 6 ★

THEY FOUND by the water-side Menéndez, upon his knees, before the large cross of rough-hewn timber; and until the Captain of the West Indian Fleet had ended his praying, the Werrowance of Ajacan and the Lord of the Ninth Wind waited, with the indulgent mutual smiling of grown persons who humor a child. Then the Spaniard looked sidewise, after having concluded his appeal to Our Lady of Utrera, whose forte it was to protect seamen; and Quetzal spoke.

"See now," says Quetzal gently, "how very glorious are the ways of Jehovah! and with what loving care, even in the grinning teeth of unfaith, does Divine Providence sustain the zeal of Heaven's more murderous agents! Old pirate, you need not any longer stay perturbed by the inability of an omniscient God to direct matters with a fair show of human intelligence."

"What do you mean?" distrustfully says Menéndez, as he arose and dusted the sand from his knees.

"Why, but, my dear señor!" Quetzal purred. "I refer of course to your divinely inspired efforts to reach China by means of a water way which, through Somebody's inadvertence when He made earth, you discover to exist only in the best maps. You did not like such gross incompetence in architecture. To find Jehovah so very far out-of-date in His geography was disturbing; you faced with displeasure your resultant need to go back into Mexico defeated and empty-handed. Take comfort, Señor Pedro Menéndez! you who did not, and who will not ever, lack courage! for you shall return rejoicing, bringing with you, as the Psalmist has put it with an amiable if inaccurate rusticity, the palm of victory in addition to your sheaves. The Werrowance of Ajacan here has become convinced of the truth, or at any rate, of the usefulness, of your faith. My son desires to go back with you as a Christian convert."

"I rejoice," said Menéndez, "to my heart's core. Now indeed are my prayers answered; and instantly, my dear Nemattanon, you shall be baptized."

"By no means," said Quetzal; "inasmuch as in the minor rôle of the boy's earthly father, I insist that he become an apostate, not here upon a fine clean sand-heap, but in the Cathedral of Mexico, with the Viceroy in attendance, and before an appropriate audience, not of gulls and ospreys, but of wine-bloated Spanish thieves and their Indian whores."

"I cannot but resent your description of the Viceroy's court," returned Don Pedro sternly, "because it is both disrespectful and accurate. However! the political effect of a public baptism, in the City of Mexico, of a native prince of these northern parts would, it is certain, be beneficial." He said then,—

"What are you, Señor Quetzal, that you misguide the over-credulous West Indians into heathen practices here in Ajacan, but stay so familar with Holy Writ and with the best Christian society of New Spain?"

"I am Lord of the Ninth Wind, Señor Menéndez. I am the local God of Ajacan."

"Still, it occurs to me"—Menéndez went on, frowning meditatively—"that I have heard of a young rascal called Somebody-or-other Lerma, who served Christ under great Cortés. Cortés became angry with him; and this Lerma had to find refuge among the Indians, who received him, so some report said, as a god. Nobody ever heard what became of this Lerma."

Quetzal did not seem interested. Quetzal said only:

"With your Cortés and your Lerma I have no concern. I was a god in Mexico a long while before Cortés came into Tenochtitlan to make open the way for Christ's all-embracing love through the use of gunpowder. I quitted my people then, it appears, in some manner or another. Quite properly attested accounts declare that I cast myself upon a funeral pyre, which consumed all of me except my heart. After that, my heart ascended into the sky, and my heart became the evening star—"

"But," said Menéndez indignantly, "nobody ever heard of such nonsense!"

"Just so," Quetzal agreed. "I was going on to observe that the story displays some elements of the improbable. The main drawback to being a god, señor, is that one becomes involved rather constantly in legends of an outrageous nature. So let us leave it to the scholars of posterity to decide whether I was a god of the air or a sun myth or perhaps a culture hero. It is enough for us three to know that at this instant I am God of Ajacan."

"Yet it is just this fact, Señor Quetzal, which troubles me. By the True Faith I am compelled to regard every heathen god as a blaspheming devil in masquerade. That is awkward."

"Yet your chaplain will inform you, Señor Menéndez, that those spirits whom your Church calls devils went into rebellion even before Adam was made. One ought at all times to be indulgent with elderly persons."

"Still," said Don Pedro, shrewdly, "and in spite of the veneration due to your age, you remain a devil. Even though I be your son's guest at the moment, and for all that I cherish his friendship, yet for an officer in the service of his Catholic Majesty to have any dealings with an adversary of Heaven appears unbecoming."

"So deeply, señor, would I lament our ever having to meet as enemies," said Quetzal, "that not a half-hour ago I was urging my son to forestall any such grim possibility by killing off your entire party."

"Come now," said Menéndez, smiling thinly, "now that does put a different face on this matter."

"But he refused to have any part in your murder. He may yet live to change his mind"—says Quetzal thoughtfully. "Of that, I forewarn you. Still, for the instant, my misled, high-minded, high-thinking absurd Nemattanon has refused. For the instant there is between us all a truce; and during that instant, I submit, we ought—like, let us say, good Catholics and good Lutherans—to preserve the amenities."

"Now, by Christ's blood! but it may be that you demon gods are no whit worse than Lutherans," Menéndez admitted fair-mindedly; "and many of my better friends have turned Lutheran, even my own comrade in arms, Jean Ribaut, whom they call rightly the Invincible; for in Europe that foul heresy spreads everywhere."

"That you discourage it," said Quetzal, "I have been privileged to note, in my mirror."

"One does what one can to extend Christ's kingdom," Menéndez replied modestly; "and I have accounted for some hundreds of Moors, Turks, Jews, Anabaptists, and such-like wild heathen cattle, without grieving. But Lutherans, señor, are different. Such Lutherans as my dear Jean Ribaut are well-born and all-honorable. Many of these Lutherans I have found to be such gallant and pleasing persons that after enjoying a battle with these quite splendid fighters, I have not at all enjoyed my duty afterward to destroy the survivors painfully."

At that, Quetzal took out from the bosom of his white gown a glass bottle which was filled with a clear liquid.

"Señor Menéndez, in your kingdom as in my kingdom, no government can afford to condone heresy,—by which I mean, of course, the tenets of a minority. Such heresy is anti-social. The lone flights of heresy disturb the comfort of gregarious persons who contract every conviction more amicably, from their best-thought-of neighbors, as if it were a cold in the head. So in Ajacan we try to preserve orthodoxy at all times. We inculcate at all times a proper respect for my divine powers of being disagreeable, through this disinfectant which, as a need for it arises, staunch Agomek administers quietly. This, as it were, tonic against discord makes an end of dissent painlessly—along with, of course, the dissenter's life. And my medicine against heresy is at your service. You shall have quarts of it to flavor for your Lutherans, your Turks, your Anabaptists, your Jews and so on, their last meal upon earth."

Menéndez took the bottle; he looked at it consideringly; but he shook his small proud head.

"I cannot," he regretted, "accept this offer, Señor Quetzal. To frail human reason, I grant you, such hateful heathen methods do appear more sensible. Yet Rome has laid down her rules as to the correct manner of dealing with heretics. To dispose of them without physical agony—as I infer, do you and your wicked servant, this Agomek—that, I can but remark, señor, is a solution which the inspired mouth of the Church has not ever recommended to her secular arm. With all thanks, I return your poison."

Thus speaking, Pedro Menéndez gave back the gleaming bottle to Quetzal; and as Quetzal stood there, in the spring sunshine, holding bright death in his hands, he smiled at Menéndez half pityingly, so the tale says, because of that which the Lord of the Ninth Wind had foreseen in the charmed mirror of Quetzal.

"Either to have kept this bottle or to have destroyed this so tiny bottle," says Quetzal, "would have changed your fate; but a thing done has an end. Inasmuch as you reject my gift, Señor Menéndez, I shall put it aside for this while; yet I shall always preserve it, very carefully, against your possible needs, by-and-by."

★ 7 ★

So was it agreed that Nemattanon should go out of Ajacan with Pedro Menéndez; but the young savage man promised the dear wife of his bosom that, in no long while, he would be returning. And a great many other matters he promised to Leota, including his eternal and complete fidelity. She smiled at that, a little sadly. These two had been married for some time.

She, in brief, agreed to his going, in the same while that she kept on broiling the meat for his dinner, with a composure which a proper-minded husband could not but regard as unfeeling.

"It is not you that will come back to me, Nemattanon, but a strange man whom my eyes perhaps will not recognize. But my heart will know you. Meanwhile, it is of course right that you, his son, should do as Quetzal commands."

"If only," sighed Nemattanon, "I could have persuaded him to let me remain here, where so long as I have you, my dear soul's dearest, I can lack for nothing whatever!"

"Yes?" said Leota.

"You will believe me, I trust, that I begged for his

46

indulgence upon this point most forcibly. I knelt. I beat my breast. I looked at him with reproach in one eye and anguish in the other. I employed, in short, every known sort of eloquence to dissuade him from separating us, for no matter how brief a while."

"Yes?" said Leota.

"Yet he, alas, has remained granite; and he insists that it is needful for me to observe the world at large before I can well settle down in this special corner of the world, to rule over it with heroic competence."

"Quetzal is more wise than we are, Nemattanon; so it is right that each one of us should obey him."

Nemattanon answered: "I shall always obey Quetzal, keeping strictly his commandments; and with a complete heart I shall always love him: yet for this while, Leota, I must pretend to put faith in these Christian slanders against my divine father—inasmuch as he himself has ordered me to do this," Nemattanon continued, with a fresh flowering of the imaginative.

"Yes?" said Leota.

"It is not pleasant, I can assure you, my dear wife, for the only begotten son of the Lord of the Ninth Wind, and a grandson of the great White Cloud Serpent, to have to indulge the absurd ideas of the East-people by declaring himself a descendant of devils. Yet in that way alone can I complete my education and enjoy the advantage of foreign travel. So what must be, must, I suppose."

"Your dinner is ready," said Leota.

Part Two

The Cousin of
the King of Spain

Since the time that the wise King Solomon built the holy temple of Jerusalem, with the gold and silver which he caused to be brought from the Islands of Tarsis, Ofir, and Saba, ancient or modern history does not record such treasures to have been derived from any country as from New Spain. Let us grant thanks to God, and to His Blessed Mother Our Lady, for giving us grace and support to conquer these countries, where so much Christianity is now established.

—BERNAL DIAZ DEL CASTILLO

★ 8 ★

THIS TEMPLE of the Spaniards was pleasingly cool inside, throughout its five rigid aisles and the large stiff wooden boxes set alongside them, in which the East-people chose to worship, Nemattanon found himself thinking. Inasmuch as the place was rather obscure, so his main vague impression was that of a prevalent light brownness smelling of incense. The building was shaped like a cross; and everywhere, upon the dim saffron-hued walls, you noted small paintings of the last sufferings of Christ Our Redeemer. You knew a great deal about that pleasing folk-lore tale of Christ Our Redeemer, nowadays. Above these but partially seen paintings, a row of stained-glass windows depicted, upon a larger scale, and far more vividly, on account of the glaring sunlight outside, the quaint legend of some saint or another. It was about these things Nemattanon was thinking at an instant when he felt that, inasmuch as at this instant he was becoming a member of the Church of Rome, his mind ought to be dwelling upon other matters.

Stubbornly his mind adhered to the noting of trifles. His mind reported that the low brass railing before which he stood was in reality a closed gate through which the priests of Jehovah could approach their God's altar; to the right and left, Nemattanon saw, this barrier continued as a balustrade of green porphyry topped with gray marble. Within this balustrade, to his right, a life-sized, life-colored statue of Christ Our Redeemer bowed down its head, as if with languor, to inspect, in the same moment that, with his fore-finger, Christ Our Redeemer pointed to, the bleeding heart of Christ Our Redeemer. For some reason, Christ Our Redeemer— which name was not, as you used to think, all one single word—was supposed to have carried his heart outside his body, swung loosely about his neck, like the bulbous fat ruby pendant of a necklace. That appeared strange. No civilized deity—such as Quetzal, for instance— would have considered doing anything of the sort. At the foot of this statue some two dozen lighted candles, inside plump red glass tubes, were arranged in three tiers; and these candles gleamed waveringly.

But to the left hand side of you, beyond blue-shaded candles, another life-sized statue, of the Holy Virgin, held, half screened by her blue robes, very much as a mother would have cuddled her baby, a cross, about fifteen inches long, which had budded with green leaves and with three or four little crimson flowers. That too appeared strange. One must ask about all these droll affairs, by-and-by, with a proper air of respect and of profound interest.

It then occurred to Nemattanon that before him stood a bishop; and that the kindly-faced, gray-haired old man was speaking some sort of outlandish ritual. The nose of the bishop was shiny. Beyond the white robes and the top-heavy bright topknot—why, but yes! it was what you called a mitre—Nemattanon could see the high altar. He noticed how steadfastly it glowed with red-and-yellow flowers and with white, quite steadily burning candles, which had been arranged in the form of an upright equilateral triangle. You knew about triangles, nowadays, because since you came into Mexico you had studied the books of Euclid of Alexandria. Nemattanon recollected then, on a sudden, that instead of observing such irrelevant material matters, he at this moment ought to be listening to the high priest of the East-people with a respectful air of deep interest such as no Christian person within eyeshot could fail to observe with approval.

So he did listen, rather attentively, all during the while that the Most Reverend Bishop of Mexico administered the Sacrament of Confirmation to his Royal Highness the Prince of Ajacan—upon whom, on the preceding Sunday, had been bestowed, in Christian baptism, an appropriate Christian name as well as a surname.

The Prince reverently heard the Bishop explain for what reasons confirmation can be administered only once during its recipient's lifetime; why it must be administered by a bishop; and from what heavenly sources this rite draws a fortifying grace to make strong its receiver to practise the True Catholic Faith without swerving. The Bishop did not explain, however, why they had put a white band on your arm. His Excellency then asked a few well-selected questions on Christian doctrine; and his Highness answered these with composure and correctness, for he had memorized his responses perfectly.

The Bishop laid his hands on the candidate for eternal salvation. Upon the forehead of his Highness his Excellency made two marks, with oil, saying,—

"I sign thee with the sign of the cross; and I confirm thee with the chrism of salvation, in the name of the Father, and of the Son, and of the Holy Ghost."

The old gentleman's nose continued to be as shiny as if he had put on it some of his own oil, Nemattanon reflected in the instant that he knelt down to pray silently, to Quetzal, while above Nemattanon's bowed head, the Bishop addressed Jehovah.

In this way did Nemattanon deny the faith of his people, and become a Christian experimentally.

★ 9 ★

IN THE Viceroy's pew, Don Pedro Menéndez, fondly
observant of his godson's admirable behavior, wiped his
eyes upon his coat's sleeve without concealment, now
that the dear lad's future had been made reasonably safe
against Satan; and the Viceroy, too, regarded the ceremony with approval.

The religious convictions of Don Luis de Velasco,
Count of Santiago, and Viceroy of New Spain, were
sound if not exuberant. In the life of a politician, whom
the imaginative described as a statesman, such matters
had to keep a subordinate gravity; and as the rule, Don
Luis had found missionary expeditions to be a nuisance.
Through the best of motives, the clergy intermeddled
with the private affairs of inconveniently remote savage
persons, who, then, in their naïve way, expressed their
perhaps not wholly unjustified irritation a bit too em-
phatically, through scalping, burning, or disembowel-
ment of the clergy, to the detriment of Spain's honor.
These noble martyrs to the True Faith thus compelled
you, month after month, to be avenging them, in out-
of-the-way places, with troops which you needed else-
where to collect taxes.

But Menéndez' party had come back from their amateur efforts in evangelism wholly uninjured, bringing with them tidings of a hitherto undiscovered country not set down upon any map, as well as a quite tangible prince of this fabulous sounding kingdom, who of his own free will had chosen to inherit heaven through the proper avenues. All this was most gratifying.

Even so, as concerned the awkward matter of Prince Nemattanon's diabolic origin, perhaps the less said, the better. From the official standpoint of a viceroy, as Don Luis explained to his good friend Menéndez, the god of a heathen tribe had not any legal standing; and so might be presumed, legally, not to exist. This Quetzal, after all, might be some merely human impostor. In fact, it occurred to the Viceroy, this Quetzal might be that deplorable Lerma who had insulted, in public, the great conqueror Hernando Cortés, at the Battle of the Causeways—

"I have heard of that matter; but it was before my time," says Menéndez.

"It was an affair," says the Viceroy, "which took place when the Spaniards first besieged this very City of Mexico. They were driven back, across the lake, upon narrow causeways. The unconquerable Cortés was hurt there, and he tumbled off his horse, head-foremost, into the mud, where he stuck upside down, half suffocated and helpless. Six Indians took hold of his legs, and they had prepared to cut off his head as soon as they could haul it far enough out of the mud; but it was the will of God that God's champion should escape dying thus ignobly."

"In order," says Menéndez, "that the Marquis should die, later on, in poverty and disgrace."

"The decrees of Heaven," the Viceroy remarked mildly, "are not subject to my jurisdiction. I can tell you merely that two soldiers, named Christoval de Olea and Vasco de Lerma, came to the assistance of their general. They killed the six Indians, and Olea also was killed. Then Lerma pulled Cortés out of the mud, still upside down, like a cork coming out of a bottle. The rude fellow re-inverted, and he propped upright, like a sack of coals, the great Marquis of the Valley."

"I can well see," said Menéndez, "that no gentleman would quite relish having his life saved in a manner so undignified—not even by another gentleman, and far less by a common soldier. Still, in the heat of battle, one might make allowances—"

"Ah, but, Don Pedro, after he had looked at the mud-covered Marquis, who happened at this instant to have a disturbed crayfish hanging on to his left ear, this Lerma laughed."

Then one hidalgo regarded the other hidalgo, with the age-old wonder of the upper classes as to the outrageousness of the lower classes.

"To laugh was not pardonable," said Pedro

Menéndez. "It was an affront to the honor of the Marquis such as could not be settled pleasantly with a duel. A gentleman cannot fight with a common soldier. To laugh was not discipline."

"No," said the Viceroy; "when the head of a nation's army has become a paralytic figure of fun, one ought not to laugh. High God! but I should think not. Such doings would ruin any army. Cortés would have had the knave hanged if only Lerma had not made his escape during the continued retreat, which lasted six days. He was never caught; but a rumor got out that this sniggering scoundrel had imposed himself upon some northern tribe or another as a god."

Menéndez shook his narrow head.

"No, Don Luis; for I have seen this Quetzal who rules over Ajacan. I can assure you that he is not, and that he could not ever have been, an honest Spanish rascal. He is an incarnate pale devil, with the beard of a patriarch and the white-and-gold robes of a saint in glory, who poisons off his unfriends like rats."

Yielding this special point, the Viceroy submitted that, even so, to proclaim their princely convert the spawn of hell would have an uningratiating sound. It would savor of oddity. People would not understand it. Merely as Prince of Ajacan, therefore, should Nemattanon be received into the Church, at once, with every sort of proper ceremony, but without any mention of his dubious ancestry.

Such was the Viceroy's decision. So far as went a Christian name, he continued, the Indian Prince should have the most splendid in all Mexico; and be called henceforward Pedro Menéndez de Avilés. It was a name than which, the Viceroy remarked, clearing his throat, he would now, without detaining you unduly, make bold to declare so-and-so, *et cetera,* and so forth. It was a name concerning which, for that matter, he felt himself yet furthermore compelled to orate high observations as to the envy of defeated rivals, the drowned glory of other sea-captains (ever since Noah's time, at least), the verdict of posterity, and the scroll of fame,—all which observations the Viceroy emitted with a grave fervor, because in addition to an excellent heart, Don Luis de Velasco had also the politician's fondness for repeating with gusto any sort of nonsense which he had heard often enough.

Menéndez arose; as when one hidalgo addresses another hidalgo, so did he bow punctiliously in response to the flowering of the Viceroy's remarks; but from their implied fruitage Don Pedro dissented.

—For this christening, as Menéndez pointed out, would bedew a royal brow. To the Prince, for this reason, ought, in propriety, to be given the Viceroy's own name, inasmuch as, in Mexico, Don Luis was the supreme official representative of the King of Spain.

"Loyalty," returned the Viceroy, "forbids me to

question your logic, Señor Pedro; and my name is at the service of his Royal Highness."

So then did it come about that, in the Cathedral of Mexico, both Menéndez and the Viceroy had served as the sponsors in baptism of Nemattanon; and that, upon the Sunday before his confirmation, Nemattanon had been christened Luis de Velasco.

—Whereafter, as the Church received him, so likewise did the polite world, with open arms. It was deplored only that the Prince of Ajacan should display a temperament so staid as to devote to books, and to the humanities in general, so many quiet hours which might better have been dedicated to a more genial nature of time-killing. The Province of New Spain was now thriving; and in the sunlight of its prosperity had ripened, among the better-thought-of Spanish gentlemen and their concubines, a luxuriant harvest of well-nurtured delights in the form of drunkenness, of duelling, of nepotism, of torts, of murder, of sodomy and of Sapphic sports, of theft, of gourmandizing, of malversation in office, of gambling for high stakes, of laxity in religious observance, of unthrift, and of inaccurate tax returns, along with yet many other customary diversions of the newly enriched.

But the young Prince of Ajacan was resolute to acquire all possible accomplishments; he pursued, with the unsullied ardor of a noble savage, the clarion call of a sound education rather than the insidious timbrels

of self-indulgence; and so, through the not ever flag-
ging aid of his industry and of his high ideals, combined
with a naturally alert mind and a reasonable amount
of hypocrisy, he became cherished, by the élite of Mexico, as a prodigy of mental talents and of personal
charms.

★ 10 ★

Now AT THIS time Don Luis de Velasco (as we must
term Nemattanon henceforward) had begun to frequent, more and yet more often, the home of a fine-
looking Indian woman called Antonia. He desired, in
order to perfect his education, to conform with all the
better-thought-of Christian customs; and the esteem
cherished, by the more wealthy gentlemen of New
Spain, for this pious and accomplished lady was then
but a little less wide-spread than it was ardent. Few if
any of them had ever encountered a more delightful
companion in bed.

Yet Doña Antonia did not tax her admirers un-
scrupulously. She took from them only as much as
they, variously, could afford to give without straining
their resources; for her nature was generous, and her
moral principles remained so firm that for weeks she
would let her beauty stay unemployed in any sort of
gainful labor rather than accept a client whose appearance she did not think agreeable. Her virtue, it is
true, was the more nobly rewarded, by-and-by, on account of its remission's having thus been made a flat-
tering mark of distinction.

She was of royal birth, being a daughter of the deceased Cazique of Caloosa, and sister to Lord Carlos, the present ruler over that great Indian kingdom; and the Prince of Ajacan found her to be, for a princess, intelligent. In her appearance, moreover, she so much resembled his own dear wife Leota as to make the time spent with Antonia a sort of vicarious fidelity.

So with Doña Antonia he began to talk, with an increasing and a well-nigh marital freedom, as to his observations in Mexico; for in view of the plans of Menéndez, to extend in due course the blessings of Christianity and of a civilized Spanish government into Ajacan, Don Luis was now noticing rather carefully the effects of these same benefits on the people of Mexico.

That the native Indians had to pay for these benefits, Don Luis did not deny. He found that in the opinion of every Spaniard about the Viceroy's court, the native Mexicans were creatures more nearly animal than human whom an omniscient Deity had predestined to slavery in order that, through this kindly dispensation of Providence, the Viceroy's people might be enabled to live at ease, with a clear conscience, at the expense of the Mexicans. Through this wise beneficence upon Heaven's part, and after paying a suitable fee to the King of Spain, more than five hundred Spanish noblemen had acquired encomiendas, as they called their land grants, for thousands upon thousands of acres, along with the privilege to collect tribute and to exact labor, at discretion, from any of the Mexican Indians whose homes stood upon the allotted tract. These Indians were not permitted to remove from their birthplace; for any such unpraiseworthy act of restiveness they were killed; and they stayed thus fated to raise wheat, or sugar, or it might be cotton, for their Spanish proprietor's profit, so long as life lasted, remarked Don Luis de Velasco.

"That is unpleasant for them, no doubt," said Antonia, yawning, "but I really do not see what you and I, my dear Prince, have to do with it."

"We have this much to do with it, O most divine Antonia," he retorted, "that you and I are both native-born Americans of the old stock. As touches many modern improvements, we remain congenitally conservative. We would therefore, it is conceivable, not glow with a fine sense of progress to observe the cruelty and greed of the Spaniards making more civilized the living of our own people, either in Caloosa or in Ajacan."

She replied with astonishment, "Never, during a professional engagement, have I found any Spanish gentleman to be other than both loving and generous."

Looking pensively about, Don Luis observed his surroundings. This room was hung with brocaded tapestries which presented the edifying continence of Susanna, of Hippolytus, of Lucrece, and of St. Anthony under quite explicit onslaughts against their physical virtue. It was the explicitness rather more than the continence which had been found by Antonia's clients to be contagious. Upon the floor gleamed a green-gold silk carpet; and all the tables and chairs, as well as the night-stool, were of solid silver. The bed also was made of silver, with archangels upon each post holding up tablets which declared, "Doña Antonia sleeps here, where only the upright may enter, after due prayers to the Holy Virgin."

—From which premises the deduction was obvious, Don Luis reflected, that a considerate young woman who shared this bedroom with the leading gentry of New Spain had not any least reason to question their beneficence.

"Truly, my heart's heart," he admitted, "though your logic be out-at-elbows, yet your arguments are opulent. Your arguments are concrete. Your arguments leave me dumb."

"So there, you see!" said Antonia triumphantly; and she kissed him.

He returned her caress; and with a renewed animation he went on, now, to concede, not merely the beneficence, but the gay wisdom with which the Spaniards were innoculating Mexico.

—For to the Spanish hidalgos who had not got land grants (the Prince continued) had been given silver mines, in which were condemned to life-long labor all such Indians as, with open wickedness, had infringed the laws made for them by the superior intelligence of the Spaniards. The drawback to this maintaining of justice was that, on account of bad air and dampness and decayed food, these miners persisted in dying with the unanimity of insects which do not perish singly but in swarms. This forced a mine-owner to be replenishing his stock of miners almost every month.

Now, at first glance, that might seem a difficulty in the competent operation of your mines; it might seem regrettable; and yet how pleasantly, and with what thrift, had this check to industrial progress been disposed of by common-sense! The mine-holders had found out it was not a bit difficult to provoke an able-bodied Indian into pettishness, by robbing him, or by burning his house, or by violating his wife, or, in the unfortunate event of the poor fellow's being afflicted with an elderly and ill-favored wife, by raping one or two of his daughters. You needed only to organize an informal pleasure party of this nature, every now and then, in order to incite a villageful or so of Indians into rebellion. You put down that rebellion, as was your plain duty to Spain; you took prisoners; and you thus got an unfailing supply of new convicts, as the increment of mere recreation, said Don Luis de Velasco.

"Let us think about more important matters," said Antonia—who, as has been told you, was, for professional reasons, a most careful Catholic,—"and do you remember, my Prince, that at any rate these wretched Mexicans have been fetched back into the fond bosom of Mother Church and rescued from the gross errors of idolatry."

—For which rescue (said Don Luis) they should be content to pay a fair price. The Church, while bent upon saving the souls of these Indians, was not so improperly solicitous about mere carnal benefits as to mind very much what happened to their bodies. It was far more important, in the all-seeing eyes of the Church, that the pagan temples erected by the misled forefathers of these Indians should be replaced by Christian cathedrals. There was still a paucity of cathedrals, and in fact, as yet, but a few hundred Christian churches had been builded in Mexico, by the gratuitous labor of the more fortunate young Mexicans whom the Dominicans and the Jesuits, through a selective draft of the province, had set apart for this noble task.

Did these fate-favored Mexicans (the Prince of Ajacan continued) appreciate their good luck? or did they approach their holy labors with suitable rapture? You had merely to look at these surly savages while they sweated and grunted, or even scowled outright. It was a blow to one's faith in human nature, to observe with what grumpiness these ignoble martyrs quarried the needed stones, and passed them from hand to hand, in a living chain, toward the appointed site, before lifting upright these stones, and carving them with joyous symbols of mankind's redemption from evil. Moreover, you could not but criticize with disfavor the monotonous and shirking way in which these workmen continued to drop down, completely dead and partially broiled, under the tropic sun, without ever pausing to consider that, through such bodily indulgence, they delayed the service of Heaven.

"I believe you are joking," said Antonia, with a firm feminine disapproval of humor, as being frivolous. "You ought not to make jokes, Luis, about dying, or about Heaven, or about any other unpleasant things like that. Nobody ought to. It is not really the fault of the Mexicans. It is just the heat. The Mexicans cannot very well help dying, nor can any one of us help dying, when her turn comes."

Even so, Don Luis replied, it would be far better for everybody if in discharging this natural function the Mexicans could arrange to exhibit rather more self-restraint. The Mexicans (he submitted) were dying nowadays with a flagrant immoderation, merely because a civilized people had brought into the West Indies a fair assortment of the more civilized diseases. The Mexicans died of these unfamiliar diseases, with an inconsiderate hurry, without seeming at all to weigh the inconvenience to which they were putting their Christian proprietors. Such conduct, if not actually irreligious, was, in the most mild possible terms, over-hasty and flippant and thoughtless of others' comfort. It amounted to an indecorous indulgence in death such as nobody about the Viceroy's court could speak of without sorrow, inasmuch as to find your slaves dying off, overnight and not individually but by the dozen, of influenza or of syphilis or of smallpox, upset the plantation. It was a narrow-minded native custom which put you to the immediate expense of replacing your good-for-nothing dead laborers with the more sturdy African negroes, who were now being imported in shiploads—

"Just so," said Antonia, yawning yet again. "And the negroes are quite inexpensive if you buy them by the dozen with ten per cent. off for a cash payment, when once you have got used to the smell, of course. A negro who, what with this, that, and the other, would make a stallion envious, costs rather less than a lapdog. Not that any really well-bred and rational woman ever buys a lapdog nowadays when she can have so much more for her money. So why, my dear Luis, do you need to keep on saying the opposite of what you mean, at this hour of the night, when we both ought to have been in bed long ago."

"You mistake me, my dove," returned Don Luis, as he took off his jerkin, and began to unfasten his codpiece, resignedly, "if but because no true-born American has ever ventured to distinguish between the ironist and the idiot. For the rest, I am merely weighing, with a philosophic detachment, the many blessings which the civilization of Europe is now bringing into the two Americas, with—as Mother Church assures me—the full connivance of Europe's God. I am not certain that Ajacan merits these blessings."

★ 11 ★

THUS FAR speaks the tale, coherently enough and with a reassuring prop of the plausible. Yet some of our knowledge as to the life of Don Luis de Velasco at this period stays a little uncertain. It is said, for example, that now and then the Prince of Ajacan, taking with him his queerly carved cane, would go out into wild places where he forgathered with Quetzal's monstrous race, the old fallen gods of Mexico. In view of Don Luis' notable respect and affection for his father, this rumor, even though it be mere legend, appears probable enough.

But it is said also, with a less pungent flavor of likelihood (in spite of the tale's toleration by such careful historians as Michael Kenny and John Gilmary Shea and Woodbury Lowery) that at about this time Menéndez decided to send back Don Luis de Velasco into his native land, in company with two Dominican priests—whose names are given as Brother Pablo de San Pedro and Brother Juan de Acuna—so that the two clergymen might preach, in heathen Ajacan, the Holy Catholic Faith. By this account, Don Luis, as soon as their ship had got into the open sea, and sailed north

of the Bermudas, prayed fervently, in his native tongue,
without addressing either Jehovah or the Holy Virgin,
and without trespassing upon the attention of any
Saint; whereupon the Lord of the Ninth Wind unloosed, from his happy but unsanctified kingdom, in
the Northern Neck of Virginia, a huge storm which
conveyed the caravel, unhurt, across the Atlantic
Ocean, and up the Guadalquiver River, into the port
of Seville.

Now one cannot but, I submit, regard this part
of the story through reading-glasses of suspicion.
Menéndez, one grants, had firmly set his heart upon
the defeat, the conversion and the subsequent pillage
of Ajacan; it had become with him a fixed idea which
he was preparing to make a fact; yet by no recognized
logic can one imagine his having entrusted the first
move in this holy work to Dominican underminers.
He distrusted, and he disliked with too strong a violence, that sublime Order, as a rival to the then newly
founded Society of Jesus, whom in theological affairs
and evangelistic labors Don Pedro favored and employed always. So the considerate and faithful student
of our land's beginning will reflect it was quite prob-
ably in some other way than through the storm-sway-
ing magic of Quetzal that the son of Quetzal got to
Seville and thence, by-and-by, to the court of King
Philip the Second.

The main point is, at all events, that Don Luis did

reach the King,—who received him, near Madrid, at the Escorial, in a darkened room hung with green tapestry, and who questioned his handsome young visitor, affably but with thoroughness, as to Ajacan.

—To which royal interrogatories, Don Luis de Velasco replied with an American amount of adroitness, of eloquence, of veracity, and of explicitness. He spoke, without vainglory, as to the twenty noble cities and the seventy-two main towns of Ajacan, no one of which, as the Prince admitted, was builded wholly of gold, because after due trial his people had found a uniformly aureate architecture to become monotonous. Their buildings, for this reason, were very much varied with sardonyx and ivory and crystal and jasper; and were decorated, unostentatiously, with amethysts and emeralds and rubies, hardly any one of which gems was larger than a dinner plate.

In reply to further questions, his Highness described Ajacan as a fairly extensive kingdom, but denied its being far more than double the size of Europe, if one included Russia. He denied also the extravagant report that his native land teemed with unicorns. Unicorns had become rather rare, of late days, he protested; and while dragons still survived here and there, few of these monsters huge enough to be dangerous were encountered except only in marshy places along the upper reaches of the Potomac River. Griffins and hippogriffins stayed common enough, but were less no-

table, in the opinion of Don Luis, than were the
splinter cats or the hugags or the shagamaws of Ajacan.
He described these animals, of which the King had not
heard previously; and from the fauna of Ajacan, passed
on to its flora, which in a general way the Prince borrowed from the more highly colored accounts of Paradise.

In brief, between patriotism and politeness, the
young American was led on to develop the natural resources and the main geographical features of his native land with the aid of a lively imagination rather
than so tamely to respect truth-telling as to disappoint
his host's hunger for marvels; and Lord Philip was delighted.

He granted forthwith, to his good friend and
cousin of Ajacan, the rank of a grandee of Spain, in
addition to a suitable income, which was to be paid
to Don Luis henceforward, every quarter, by the Viceroy of Mexico. Nor was this act of profusion mere regal extravagance. Lord Philip was planning to invade
Ajacan at the first possible moment, since this aurifer-
ous huge kingdom, by all report, had not anywhere
in the known world its equal for splendor and wealth;
and so, to keep the Prince of this country attached
to him by ties of friendship, but above all, to retain
Don Luis within arm's reach of the King's executioner,
appeared a sound investment. Moreover, in his pallid
bleak way, King Philip approved of the young man's

frank ardor in religious matters; and was thinking, quite seriously, about not removing Don Luis' head, should he prove properly compliant, when Spain stripped his country.

Don Luis de Velasco, indeed, was liked no less cordially than he was admired by everybody. The gentlemen of Spain, it may be, regarded with some natural envy his pre-eminence in all noble qualities and cultural graces. Such friendly pangs are perhaps inevitable to Europeans when they observe Americans. But to the ladies, this grave and modest young paragon, coming as he did from out of the all-golden West, as the acknowledged heir to an unimaginable kingdom in that magic land, appeared like the Prince of an ancient fairy tale made flesh and blood. That he was indeed flesh and blood, they took pains to discover; for they pursued him, with bright eyes and with detaining hands, resistlessly; so that here again, for the honor of Ajacan and at the dictates of politeness, his amours became more many and more varied than he desired.

He begot therefore, at this time, so the story says, two natural sons—one of them, called Don Camarcho, being the child of Doña Catalina de Tapia. In later life this boy was Commander of the Order of Santiago, and proved a fine soldier. The other son, named Don Alonzo (who became a commander of the same order), was the child of a gentlewoman of the family of Gamboa, but neither her Christian name nor the name of her husband is known.

In Spain the Prince begot also, it is recorded, three natural daughters, of whom one died an abbess, at Medina del Campo. Their names have not been preserved.

⋆ 12 ⋆

So THEN DID the first native-born American to enjoy the now commonplace benefits of a refined education, of sound moral principles, of foreign travel, and of judicious hypocrisy, win full-handed applause from a highly critical audience; for at this time the court of Lord Philip was the most splendid in Europe.

Hardihood and bloodshed exemplified, between dawn and sunset, the virile and high-hearted spirit of Spain, whether it were through the media of pitched battles or through the handsome etiquette of the duello, upon even the most hastily organized occasions for homicide; and standards no less rigorous, if progenitive rather than death-dealing, were raised in the evening when, after indulging in a stately coranto or a pavane, and in extravagant gambling at the new game called El Clavo, and after saying one's rosary, the polite paired off for discreet fornication. No sort of open immorality was permitted at the court of Lord Philip, where, instead, the highest possible criteria of respectability reigned.

Here, to the finding of Don Luis, good taste demanded of an hidalgo that he should be no less a past

77

master in inflicting death than proficient at all times in expressing the amenities of life, alike in the salon, the council chamber, the bedroom, and in the punctilios of religious observance. The hand which could wield the rapier against an undesired acquaintance and shoot down a Jew, a Huguenot or a Turk with equal dexterity, must be no less adroit to sound the lute or to indite a lofty political assurance which had not any definite meaning, if one desired success among the well-bred.

—For perfection (the Prince continued in thought) perfection was the goal of these gracious Spaniards: and not merely perfection in all arts and sciences, and in the gallant conduct of one's earthly affairs, but perfection also in every detail of one's standing with Heaven, howsoever laboriously a clean conscience had to be acquired through a daily subduing of heresy, with fire and steel, and through a prompt performance of the penances recommended by your confessor after some fortuitous infringing of morality; and perfection, moreover, in the comeliness and in the vigor and in the haleness of your body, in all its so many daylit and nocturnal employments, so that, with a becoming piety, you might accord to yourself, as a child of God, a not unsuitable shrine throughout your epiphany upon earth. Such was the goal of the hidalgo in those times. And since the young Prince of Ajacan had, by inheritance, the clear intelligence and the nim-

ble wits of a devil, he found that all such attainments
flocked to him with more speed than they seemed to
display in coming to merely human devotees of culture.

It was written indeed as to Don Luis, at this time,
by the judicious Suárez, "the Indian Prince is a being
such as we may imagine in Paradise before the Fall;
a precious, unique and ever to be remembered embodi-
ment of man's former nobleness. He improves day by
day in beauty, wisdom, and worth. His quiet even tem-
per is like a calm lake on a moonlit night. He is so accomplished in all things polite and virtuous that the
like of him is not to be seen anywhere in Spain."

Such was his well-deserved high place in public
esteem when, after this bright flaunt at court, Don Luis
was honored yet further by being sent back into Mexico, as the King's personal envoy, bearing letters addressed to the Viceroy, so the story narrates.

And the story tells, also, about how the King of
Spain's ambassador was received by the Viceroy of Mexico, in the open space before a gray palace, from which
red and yellow banners flowed and fluttered and flapped
flatulently. The streets of the city had been hung, in
preparation for the Prince of Ajacan's arrival, with
tapestries, with garlands, and with cloth of gold. Hi-
biscus and poinsettia blossoms strewed the roadways as
if with blood. The bells of the city pealed; drums

rolled; trumpets and clarions sounded, half joyously, and yet too as if in high-minded indignation; while arquebuses were being fired, hurtlessly, toward heaven, every instant or so.

The air had turned misty, and it smelled strongly of gunpowder, for some while before the Viceroy had come forward, under the palm-trees, attended by Don Pedro Menéndez de Avilés, as well as by the Archbishop of Mexico, by the Corregidor, by five magistrates, by three canons of law, and by four aldermen, each one of them in his robe of office.

Toward this noble assembly rode the Prince of Ajacan, upon a white stallion. His Highness was today resplendent, in a breast plate, a shoulder piece, and a gorget of burnished steel, and a flowing, brilliant red sash. A bit lower showed his wide breeches of cloth of silver and gold, worked with green silk and with strings of seed pearls. His stockings were crimson colored; he wore very high, soft boots of white leather with gold spurs. In his left hand, as the Prince bowed graciously toward the applauding multitudes, he carried a peaked hat of red cut velvet adorned with a band of emeralds and with a tuft of green feathers.

In so great splendor did the former Werrowance of Ajacan come back into New Spain as the ambassador—so the heralds now proclaimed—of his right royal friend and loving cousin, Lord Philip, King of Aragon, King of Castile, King of Sicily, King of Naples, and

King of the Indies, both East and West; the Dominator of Asia and America; the Duke of Milan and of Burgundy; and the right heir to the thrones of France, of England, and of Jerusalem.

The Viceroy bowed seven times, with due ceremony, to the ambassador before making bold to embrace the godson; the Viceroy gave vent to an oration; and then withdrew to read, in private, the King's letters.

★ 13 ★

DON LUIS DE VELASCO went away from these proud
ceremonials, with his other godfather, to the lodgings
of Menéndez. The Prince had found Don Pedro in
that rigid quiet state of religious fervor with which,
no matter with what smiling tenderness the young man
had come to admire this lank soldierly evangelist, Don
Luis was not ever able entirely to sympathize.

"—Because everything now is prepared," Menéndez explained, "for the complete conquest, both spiritual and corporal, of Ajacan. You are in train to
return to your native land, my son, as the representative
of the Holy Father as well as of his Catholic Majesty."

"Along with misery," the Prince said, "and with
bloodshed, and with a vast deal of pious humbug, as
my attendants."

"No," says Menéndez; "for I myself will serve as
your escort. Nor shall we face any difficulty in spreading God's Word, inasmuch as I will be taking with
me five pieces of artillery as well as five missionaries—"

A polite gesture of protest interrupted his speaking; and to Menéndez the Prince of Ajacan addressed, reflectively, the following observations:

"My dear Pedro, that I am, nowadays, a sturdy Catholic and a loyal vassal to my good cousin the King of Spain, nobody, I hope, will question. A question of that nature might prove unwholesome. How then should I regard your scheme, for robbing all my people, for murdering such of them as do not out-of-hand become Christians, and for making slaves of those who do become Christians? As between friends, I regard this notion with an amount of enthusiasm which I can best describe as deficient. Nor is that the sum of my disquiet. You are planning a direct attack upon the power of Quetzal, through the aid of I do not know how numerous a regiment of priestly persons and prayers, what masses and exorcisms, or how many gallons of holy water. Hospitable as is the nature of my infernal father, he cannot be expected to welcome any such sacred policing. His resentment may become extreme; his powers in the two Americas are not inconsiderable. So, my dear friend, I forewarn you that his disapproval of being meddled with by our Mother Church—which you, I am certain, do not respect any less than I do—may, it is quite possible, assume the form of personal injury."

"Against the True Faith," returned Menéndez, "the malevolence of demons is without weapons; all now is ready for the planting of the Gospel in Ajacan; and I defy the dark power of Quetzal."

Even while he was speaking, the Viceroy entered the room, followed by a dozen guardsmen, who had come to execute the orders which Don Luis had brought into Mexico, to place Menéndez under arrest.

"You may now perceive," says the Prince of Ajacan, shrugging, "what it means to defy the Lord of the Ninth Wind."

"Alas," the Viceroy dissented, "but our friend here, the magnificent Captain, has defied a force far more terrible. He had made light of the power of money."

"So! then my present enemy," said Menéndez, as he unbuckled his sword and handed it over to the leader of the guardsmen, "must be the Casa de Contratación. With what have they charged me?"

"Why, but indeed," replied the Viceroy, "I abhor the verbose. I dislike the obscene, also, far too deeply for me at this time to annoy you, and to evoke my own blushes, by reciting the enormities with which you have been accredited by the Casa. We will let it suffice that I have here the King's orders to send you back to Spain instantly. And in Spain, my poor friend, you will have to stand trial for pretty much every misdemeanor, and for all the major offences, which our more inventive criminals have as yet thought about."

Don Pedro said: "You bring bad hearing; and

yet, in the long run, the Casa was sure to get the better of me. One has to pay at all times, and sometimes one has to pay rather dearly, for being honest."

The Viceroy quite agreed.

"It is a luxury, Don Pedro, in which no public official ought ever to indulge beyond the limits of decorum. Over and yet over again, my dear friend, I have warned you everybody expected a Captain of the West Indian Fleet to see to it that the proper persons were favored with a proper deficiency in rectitude, and with, as it were, a polite obtuseness as to arithmetic. Your refusal to commit, or even to connive at, these logical immoralities has become no whit short of a public scandal. Your private and peculiar integrity has upset the general integrity of our naval service ever since the first moment you took office."

"My dislike of a thief has made of every well-to-do merchant in the shipping trade my firm enemy," Menéndez assented, "because I would not accept bribes to wink at his thieving."

"Such honesty does you vast honor. Still—!" said the Viceroy, to whom bribes were as commonplace as breakfast.

"I have preferred to keep my eyes open, my faith clean, and my purse empty," said Menéndez. "So the Imperial Board of Trade has worked lavishly to buy the King's permission to make an end of me; to-day, at long last—so I infer—he has listened to them."

"The clink of gold, Don Pedro, is an all-penetrating sound. It ascends into high places. It is wiser"— and the Viceroy shrugged—"to accept in due time these phenomena of nature."

"Very well, then!" said Menéndez. "Where money speaks, merit stays dumb; and I can face trouble without crying over it."

"Alas, señor," says the more logical Viceroy, "but you do not face trouble. You face ruin."

★ 14 ★

Now THE Casa de Contratación, I must tell you, was
the Imperial Board of Trade for Spain and all Spain's
colonies; so its West Indian ships were subject to
Menéndez. The members of the Board had found this
special Captain of the Fleet to be unendurable. He
meddled daily with their immemorial custom of smug-
gling; he objected to their healthy commerce in forged
passports; he would not even sell to the ship captains
of the more wealthy merchants a profitable advantage
by permitting their ships to leave port in advance of
their rivals; whereas time and again Menéndez had in-
terfered with the philanthropic importation of a cargo
of kind-hearted girls, blessed with pleasing persons and
imperceptible morals, into Mexico—where the favors
of a white woman commanded almost any price which
one chose to ask. In brief, Menéndez allowed to the
great merchants, who were members of the Board of
Trade, no privileges such as before his time they had
been accustomed to purchase, at a fair price, from his
predecessors; so that their ships came to be treated
like any other ships, by this moonstruck Don Pedro,

who expected even the best-thought-of people to be bothered about keeping the laws of the kingdom.

In such straits, the chief merchants of León, Valencia, Catalonia, Aragon and Castile had been forced to organize, unostentatiously, so as to revive the health and volume, and the normal conditions, of their West Indian trade. They took counsel, one with another, as to what crimes it was needful to prove their oppressor had committed; and if they fixed upon just those in which Don Pedro had prevented their own indulgence, that was merely because these special offences were the worst they could think of in such hurried circumstances. They hired five competent forgers, and some fifty witnesses (with a pair of bishops to lend dignity), and they bribed the proper judges. With the proofs of Don Pedro Menéndez de Avilés' infamy thus firmly established, the Imperial Board of Trade tendered, as a token of its humble esteem, five purses of gold to Antonio Pérez, the King's secretary; and sleek Pérez conferred with King Philip.

Now, upon hearing the proposals of the Casa, the King became properly indignant.

"No," said the King. "No, Pérez, I cannot consider deposing my good Menéndez from an office to which he was appointed by my own revered father, the great Emperor, now that Menéndez is going to get for me the twenty noble cities and the seventy-two main towns of Ajacan."

"Majesty," said Pérez, "the treasures of Ajacan are speculative, in addition to being, if they indeed exist anywhere, upon the other side of this rather large world."

"Fair play," says the King, "is a jewel. I am not denying that inconvenience may be a facet of it."

"—Whereas the gold pieces of the Casa de Contratación, Sire, are tangible; they are in Madrid; and tomorrow morning, should you so elect, they will be in this room."

"That is true," the King answered; "yet my honor would be involved, and my good name more or less damaged, should I consent to the ruin of an all-faithful servant."

"You are wholly right, Sire; and I think that in view of the circumstances, they ought to pay you double as much."

"No, Pérez," replied Lord Philip very nobly; "for me to suggest that would be unworthy of a Hapsburg. I cannot take any hand in this vile business, nor will I stoop to accept the blood-money which these scoundrel merchants have offered me for the ruin of an honest gentleman, until after they have trebled the amount."

This was agreed to: and Lord Philip relented. He assured the Board of Trade, over his own special signature "I the King," that the conviction and the severe punishment of Menéndez should be attended to, after the unavoidable formality of a fair trial, which would give every one of the hired witnesses an equal chance to excel in mendacity. His Majesty, who had his own quiet sense of humor, then thriftily got rid of the Prince of Ajacan, for whom Spain had not any further need, by sending the young savage upstart back into Mexico, as the bearer of sealed orders for the arrest of Menéndez and for a discontinuing of the Prince of Ajacan's pension.

★ 15 ★

"MY POOR FRIEND,"—said Don Luis, to Menéndez, after all these circumstances had been made plain, and the Viceroy had left them—"here is devil's work. I cannot but suspect that Quetzal has some part in this infamy, which, at one stroke, restores me to dependence upon his hellish abilities, and prevents you from introducing the Christian Faith into Ajacan."

"Take shame to yourself," said Menéndez, "that you should be imputing to the most gentlemanlike devil who begot you an excursion into the everyday infamy of a respectable merchant! Do you at once entreat of Heaven a pardon for your lack of filial respect toward hell! and after that"—his voice sank—"do you also at once be getting out of New Spain; for my downfall involves you."

"For what reason, Pedro?"

"For the reason, my son, that you will henceforward be made a prisoner, inasmuch as the Viceroy will not know what else to do with your person."

"In fact," says Don Luis affably, "the Prince of Ajacan was of large value but a half-hour since, when everything had been made ready to use him as the figure-head of a crusade to convert and to annex and to rob his native country. In, as it were, the twinkling of a bed post, his importance dwindles."

"Put it so if you like," says Menéndez,—"you silky smiling young devil's son, whom I love somewhat in spite of myself."

"—For with Don Pedro Menéndez de Avilés thrust out of office and imprisoned, there is not any commander at hand who is eager, or who, for that matter, is bold enough, to conduct any such holy expedition to rob Quetzal of his power, and his people of their freedom, in the name of the storm god of Sinai," says Don Luis.

Menéndez answered: "Just so. The sleek lecherous time-servers about the Viceroy are not interested in religious affairs, or in any noble conquests for Spain, but only in getting gold from out of the great mines of Mexico into their own pockets. For that reason the ship which carries me oversea, to my dungeon, will carry also a letter in which the Viceroy will ask the King for instructions as to just what to do with you. You will be kept meanwhile in prison. Should you die in prison, Luis,—a trifle hastily, perhaps—it would further everybody's comfort."

"Except only, now that one thinks of it, my comfort," says Luis de Velasco. "I doubt if I would like dying in prison immediately." He said then, in a changed voice,—

"You are at bottom a good friend to me, Pedro."

"Yes, my dear son," returned Menéndez; "for I love you nowadays both for your own sake and because of your likeness to a boy whom, it may be, I shall not ever see again. However! the occasion is urgent. We lack time to display emotion. You may hope at best to become a vagabond; but for me there is no hope. I must now be convicted of all sorts of infamy on account of my old-fashioned dislike for iniquity. I must be degraded from office. I must be fined so very heavily that by no chance can I ever pay my fine. And so, unless Heaven orders it otherwise, I must be imprisoned for the rest of my lifetime because"—he moistened his lips—"because all these happenings are the desire of my good lord the King, whom may Heaven preserve always!"

The Prince says fleeringly: "My gouty cousin of Spain has well profited by his study of Holy Writ. It has taught him how to sell both you and me to our unfriends, dear Pedro, for some thirty pieces of silver."

"Let us avoid blasphemy, my son. If the King wills to convert my body into money, all my body and all my will too are at the King's command."

With that, Don Pedro embraced his godson; and the lean hidalgo went away, with composure, to face the perjurers and the hired judges and the all-powerful King who were predetermined upon his destruction.

⋆ 16 ⋆

I WILL NOW tell you how Don Luis de Velasco came into an apartment which was furnished, a bit prodigally, with religious paintings and with Venetian glass and with massive teak-wood furniture that had been inlaid, to the full extent of its maker's ingenuity, with embossed silver. The walls were covered with a gold and silver hanging representing the story of St. Mary the Egyptian; the ceiling displayed a canopy of tawny velvet adorned with plates of crystal and of hammered silver. About this large quiet room had been stationed, by the hand of profusion, tall golden scent-burners, which exhaled, as if in reluctant weariness, vague vapors smelling of sandal-wood.

Here, upon a couch covered with crimson satin, lay Doña Antonia—who, for her own part, in view of the warm weather, was not covered with anything, should the observer happen to overlook a light apple-green scarf which lay disposed about her middle.

"O all-incomparable Antonia!" says Don Luis, with that well-bred gallantry which he had acquired from and among the élite of Spain . . .

"And now," he resumed, by-and-by, "do you permit me to deal less fondly with affairs far less pleasant."

"Indeed, my Prince, but at the instant you appear dejected."

"It was as a prince, Antonia,"—he amended—"that I dined to-day. But my supper is the bitter bread of exile."

He then told her the story of his sudden downfall through the double-dealing of his regal cousin, Lord Philip. And Antonia, now that the scarf had been rearranged about her, with proper modestness, followed his story calmly. Her conclusion was,—

"We had best go to Caloosa, I think, because any woman breathing can get around Carlos; all his wives do; and so, besides being respectable, we will not have to worry about going to jail."

"Truly, my heart's sole idol,"—the Prince admitted—"but I have not the happiness to understand one word you are saying."

"I mean only, my dear love," Antonia replied, "that my conscience has begun to be an annoyance. My conscience says that it is not proper for a young woman of royal birth to be living here without a duenna, and along with I forget how many gentlemen, because you know how people do talk. They are only too glad to say the most outrageous possible things."

"Even the fair name of innocence—" the Prince began.

"Just so; and I quite agree with you," said Antonia. "Still, that will keep; you can tell me about that later; but a sacrament ought to be looked after without dilly-dallying."

"Forgive, my pet, my obtuseness. Were we indeed speaking of sacraments?"

"Very certainly we were, Luis. For as I was saying, when you interrupted me, since you are a prince, and now that you have become an exile, and will have to go away at any rate, I believe the time is at hand for just the two of us to go away together, into Caloosa, of course; so that we can get married there, by the Shaman. And marriage is a sacrament. Everybody knows marriage is a sacrament."

The eyebrows of the Prince of Ajacan had ascended, gently but appreciably.

"You must pardon my bucolic display of emotion," he protested. "But I am touched by the hot sense of unworthiness, no less than by the insensate spur to escape, which, in every honest male creature, is awakened, always, by the announcement of a determined woman that she intends to make out of him her husband. I can but answer you, Antonia, *Non dignus sum.*"

"And in saying that, Luis, you are quite, quite, quite wrong. I never heard of such nonsense. I disagree with it entirely. What does it mean?"

"The remark is Latin. Its import is a marked feeling of inadequacy. For as I take it, Antonia, because of your affection for me, who am now a vagabond, you are planning to destroy a virtually wife-like connection with some thirty Spanish hidalgos and their plump pocketbooks."

"Well, more or less, my dear, although I really cannot think of but twenty-eight off-hand; and for the present, anyhow."

"All such solid social ties you are about to burst as lightly as though they were shoe-laces—"

"It is unfeeling of you, Luis, to be talking in that heartless manner, as if I had ever any least need in the world, with my feet, to be wearing tight shoes—"

"You propose, Antonia, that all the bright, hard-earned luxury about us—the noble paintings, the highly valuable tapestries, the massive furniture, and so on—should, as it were, be burned up by the ardor of disinterested affection. You intend that all this fine Venetian glass should be splintered—or perhaps melted would be the more just expression—in the glow of your devotion to me. Alas, Antonia, but to an offer so magnanimous and so unworldly, I can but reply, *Non dignus sum*—which means, by the way, 'I am not worthy.' In brief, I become appalled by your generosity, which exceeds even the sum total of your twenty-eight lovers' generosity; and I would prefer not to have you as my wife."

"Very luckily, Luis, your preferences need not

make the least difference. I have decided to overlook them from now on. An intelligent married woman simply has to do it, in dealing with her husband—"

"And besides that,"—the Prince pursued—"it occurs to me that I already have a wife, to whom I have promised my eternal and complete fidelity."

"Why, but of course. A man promises anything. That is expected of him. So nobody pays any special attention to it. And anywhere in the two Americas a cazique—or as you so quaintly call it, a werrowance—is entitled to as many wives as he likes. Not," said Antonia darkly, "that for one instant I would ever permit it."

"Your objection, so far as it concerns our native marriage laws," the Prince of Ajacan granted, "is streaked with validity. Yet both of us have put by such generous heathen customs, in order to become Christians. You must surely perceive that when it comes to polygamy, no Christian gentleman of good standing is allowed to profess what he practises. Our Church, Antonia, does not grant to its communicants more than one duly licensed companion in his bed."

"When you became a Christian, Luis,"—she reminded him, with gentle dignity—"you became also a bachelor. You were not ever really married, you see, by a real priest, to that poor, deluded, immoral heathen woman in Ajacan."

He answered, overcome about equally by the devotion, the beauty, and the persistence of this princess:

"That is true. As a Catholic, I am not married at all; and as a werrowance, I remain free to marry, indefinitely, at my own indiscretion. You have, O my adored Antonia, the mind of a canary and the moral code of a cat. Your logic, like the logic of all other women, is an unanswerable and sound reason for doing whatever you may prefer to do. Your logic, in brief, is superbly convenient. So let us now seek shelter at your brother's court; and inasmuch as you consider it a point of some importance, we will ask his consent to our living together with the frank impropriety of married people, for a while at any rate."

Pleased by this chance of soothing her troubled conscience with the anodyne of a wedding, Antonia arose from the crimson-covered couch; and with gravity she put on underwear.

"—For somebody might come in at any moment; and a betrothed young girl," Antonia explained, "ought always to be extremely careful about appearances."

⋆ 17 ⋆

THE AFFIANCED pair set out that night, with the combined aid of moonlight and of a suitable bribe to the guardsmen in charge of the city gates. Yet, here again, the tale wears a cloak of obscurity. Nobody knows, with any exactness, just what befell Doña Antonia and Don Luis immediately after they escaped from the City of Mexico and went northward into interminable forests.

It is certain only that the two of them did reach, in due course, the kingdom of Antonia's brother, Lord Carlos of Caloosa; and that they found the tall Cazique, at this special instant, engaged in prayer to Toya of the Palms.

I must here tell you that, every evening, at sunset, it was the Cazique's duty to offer to this same god, Toya, the heart of a newly killed animal, because otherwise, as was well known in Caloosa, Toya would not ever bring back the declining sun; nor unless the heart were human, would the god contrive for you, upon the following morning, the sort of weather you needed. So did it happen that, for agricultural reasons, the Caloosans had become famous everywhere as the most kindly of American tribes, because in battle they were at large pains not to kill their enemies, but instead to take prisoners, whom they maintained handsomely until the time came to use them at sunset.

Returning to Lord Carlos, I must tell you how, with the day's devotion attended to, and with his mind at ease now that a warm clear sunrise had been ensured by a rather superb specimen of the Seminole Indian, the Cazique of Caloosa averted to family matters; and he received his sister with frank affection but with conditional tolerance.

"—For whatever have you been doing, Antonia, since you gave up your position as a social problem in Mexico?"

"I have been travelling, Carlos, because travelling broadens the mind; and my betrothed husband, the Prince of Ajacan, has been travelling with me, so that he might compromise me enough to get your consent to our marriage."

"Prince of Ajacan," says Carlos, a shade sternly, "what have you been doing, all this while, with my sister, and with her confiding nature, and with her yet other possessions?"

"One hardly noticed," replied Don Luis.

"Whatever are you talking about?" says Carlos.

"—Inasmuch as the whole country was densely wooded," Don Luis explained.

"Was it?" says Carlos, with a hint of surprise.

"Your question," Don Luis deplored, "betrays an ungracious spirit. Your demeanor curdles the milk of human kindness. Yet I can assure you, Carlos, that in the mountains which we first entered, chestnut and oak, as well as beech and hickory, in addition to both short- and long-leaved pines, clothed the declivities."

"Oh!" said Carlos; and he passed, from being surprised, into being puzzled.

"—Beyond which," said Antonia, "rhododendron blossomed in many valleys, and upon small hills flamed the azaleas."

Carlos said: "But what, in the name of Toya, can azaleas and oak-trees have to do with whatever at this instant the three of us may be talking about?"

"We came then," Don Luis continued, "to vast grassy savannahs, which were brilliant with yellow and crimson flowers; and afterward to still other forests composed of ash and maple and gum-trees—including," he added, with the particularity of a scholar, "the red-gum, the sweet-gum and the black-gum."

"Above us," said Antonia, "the magnolia reared its towering and sedate, sweet-scented dome; the palm-tree tossed its noble plumes—though to me, Carlos, they really do look rather like fish-bones; and the live-oak spread out its ever-green branches protectively."

"Among such picturesque surroundings," Don Luis said, "nobody would ever pause to notice what your sister and I might be doing. No person of any

least sensibility could have turned away either his or her
mind from so many ingratiating aspects of nature to
pry into the drab antics of human behavior."

Carlos said, "Nevertheless—"

"Your sister and I are persons of extreme sensibility. Our sensibility is notorious. It follows, naturally,
that we did not for an instant notice what we were
doing."

"But—" said Carlos.

"—And besides that, Carlos, any such selfish concern with our own private affairs was rendered impossible by an ever-changing throng of graceful and
engaging companions. In the hills, for example, we
found panthers; through the forest ranged the white-
tailed deer; but about the lowlands wandered black
bears, feeding upon orange-colored oranges, and dig-
ging up from out of the sand the gray eggs of the
green turtle."

"Wolves, catamounts and wildcats," remarked
Antonia, "were at their hunting everywhere. I shall
never forget them."

"No, Carlos, they were not everywhere," Don
Luis amended; "for they avoided the swamps, which
were alive, instead, with alligators, as well as with
herons and rattlesnakes and frogs and water-mocca-
sins."

"About the streams and ponds were wild turkeys
and ducks and doves," said Antonia reminiscently.

"Upon them, by a quaintly human touch," said Don Luis, "preyed all their stronger fellows, such as the eagle, the hawk, the vulture, and the buzzard. It was quite gratifying to find every known rule of civilization observed overhead."

"Fish also were abundant," Antonia stated—"although I do not mean overhead, exactly. They were in the water."

Lord Carlos said: "I can deduce, from out of this information as to fish and wildcats and declivities and rhododendrons and buzzards, nothing whatever except a lack of candor. Should the pair of you continue to lie to each other only one half as confusingly as you are both now lying to me, then your marriage ought to be happy. Nevertheless, we will have to consult with the Shaman, inasmuch as it is he who decides for the royal family of Caloosa—as you should well know, Antonia,—all such affairs."

⋆ 18 ⋆

I WILL NOW tell you how very slightly the room into
which Carlos led his sister and Don Luis de Velasco
resembled the superb, if sin-stained and too luxurious,
bedchamber in the City of Mexico wherein philanthropy had installed, and from out of which true love
had evicted, Doña Antonia.

This room, for the sake of coolness, was sunk half-
way in the ground. It contained seven seats and three
couches woven out of reed-work; all were supported
by round pillars which had been painted, with blue or
black or yellow or red, so that, as if at random, these
pillars differed from one another in color. Overhead
had been hung the white bones of very large animals,
of a species with which Don Luis was unfamiliar: to
disturb these bones, he was told, would bring about
bad luck. A pair of eaglets, which glared at him, mo-
rosely, with unblinking, circular, bright yellow eyes,
sat perched among these bones; and upon the floor,
which was strewn with blue mats and red mats, a pair
of gray shaggy dogs drowsed, with their ears partly
erect. Such was the shrine of the Shaman Hirrigua, as
people called the high priest of Toya of the Palms.

This holy man was reputed to be a hundred and twenty-four years old. Rumor added that he was a foreigner, saved out of a shipwreck by the great-great-grand-uncle of Carlos, but the Shaman had been in this country so long that nobody remembered his coming.

Hirrigua did not speak, after Carlos had told him the occasion's demand. Instead, this small gray wisp of a man nodded thoughtfully. From the wall he took down a war-shield woven in many-colored basketwork. He placed this shield upside down upon the floor; around this shield he drew, with some sort of green chalk, a circle; and within this circle, between its circumference and the rim of the shield, the Shaman inscribed figures. That these figures were Utic, and all dated from a late period of the Second, or Tiger, Dynasty, Don Luis noted with some natural interest. The Shaman knelt on the shield, so that no part of his body touched the ground.

When Hirrigua was thus free of earth, he spoke, in a low and imploring voice, words which had not any meaning to Carlos and Antonia. It is said, with I do not know how much truth, that Don Luis de Velasco understood parts of this invocation. The Shaman began to move convulsively. He twisted his arms and legs so that the bones could be heard to snap out of place. Froth bubbled at each corner of his toothless, wide gray mouth, which was like the mouth of a frog.

Instead of speaking, he moaned, and he uttered small yelping noises. All at once, he was quiet; arising stiffly, he came out of the green circle, and he began to tell the Cazique of Caloosa about Heaven's verdict.

"Between these two there must be no marriage," said the Shaman. "The Gods have appointed for Don Luis and for Doña Antonia a noble future; yet hardly any more hereafter shall their fortunes touch. My princess, you must cry farewell to your tall handsome lover. It is the fixed will of Heaven that you should become the wife of one whose decreed work is more great than is the permitted work of your lover."

Antonia answered.

She answered by pointing out that she had always tried to think just as pleasantly about Heaven as circumstances permitted. She felt it her duty to add that if Heaven had ever encouraged this attempt, she had not noticed it. However, one did not complain; and perhaps, after all, the less you referred to things like that, the better, because, for one, Antonia did not believe in scepticism. People needed religion. At the same time, Antonia intended to retain her own private opinion as to the fairness, and the mere simple decency, of clergymen who preached to an inexperienced, credulous girl, and kept on preaching to you, over and yet over again, that the way for a person to stay free of sin, with the men what they were, all day and all night, and to prevent your conscience from bothering you,

was for a person to get married. Not just to anybody,
she meant, of course, but to a prince or a king of some
sort. For you to do that, Antonia added, was simply
reasonable.

"Whatever in the name of Toya," said Carlos,
with fraternal impatience, "can you imagine you are
talking about?"

He found out in this way that Antonia was not
talking at all, but merely exercising a great deal of
reticence such as the circumstances did not, perhaps,
justify.

Because if after that (Antonia continued), and
without giving any least explanation, another clergyman had prevented you from getting married—except
to a complete stranger, and goodness only knew when,
—then a person ought to be allowed to say a number of
things. It would be only human nature to say these
things. Nobody anywhere, especially Toya of the
Palms, whose wisdom was unlimited, could blame you
for thinking these things at any rate. Antonia was not
going to talk about these things, not just now, or to
say one single word more as to the subject, not here
in a temple, so nobody need worry about thunderbolts.
She had the greatest possible respect for Toya of the
Palms, she stated; and she did not intend to have his
divine wrath turning her into a cinder with those dogs
and those dreadful looking birds watching her.

Thus far spoke Antonia with animation; whereafter she began to weep quietly.

"Such," said Don Luis, "are the frenzies of foiled love; and my personal anguish, O my life's one idol," —he added politely—"is equally unmitigated. My heart is, in fact, shattered. Even so, we cannot well fight against the will of Heaven. We two must accept our decreed fate."

Hirrigua the Shaman took out of his bosom a small silver crucifix; and Don Luis, for all the extreme composure with which he had allowed his heart to be shattered, read the engraving upon the back of this crucifix with a start of surprise.

"Don Luis de Velasco," says the Shaman, "it is needful that you leave Caloosa, going northward and taking with you this. The right owner of it, as well as does your decreed fate, awaits you northward."

"But in what place?"

"Beside the River of Dolphins."

"How shall I find this River of Dolphins, about which I am now hearing for the first time?"

"You have your cane," says the Shaman—"the One Reed. And for the rest, you have your fate. Yours is a notable fate. It is not unworthy of you who have made merry in remote countries such as none of our people has visited, or even imagined, and who have fared as a prince among the pale-colored tribes that live handsomely oversea. All that gay part of your living is past, Nemattanon—"

"Why are you calling me by any such quaint name?"

"So that you may know I speak the truth, Nemattanon, now I prophesy. It is laid upon you to give away, as a free gift, the country into which you are now going, and to keep for yourself no part in it."

"My nature is generous," Don Luis conceded. "Still, that seems rather prodigal,—for me to be giving away, with the levity of a Pope, lands which do not belong to me."

"It is laid upon you," said the Shaman, "to bid time stand still; and for a large wonder, time will obey you so long as you keep any voice with which to give orders. You will raise up your war-cry against gods; and your war-cry will prevail against both Sinai and Bethlehem until, at long last, death leaves you silent."

With so great solemnness spoke the Shaman of Toya of the Palms; and by his prophesying Doña Antonia was impressed, and to any appreciable extent intimidated, not the least bit.

"—For if you are talking good sense, O Shaman," says Antonia, "however can this horrid husband that I am going to get by-and-by be a greater person than my broken-hearted, poor handsome Luis is going to be by-and-by?"

"Your husband," said the Shaman, "will bid time

quicken. He will bid time bring forth; and him too time will obey. He will establish the beginnings of a new order and of new peoples; he will make fertile all this land with blood; from out of his cold zeal will come a new world. In my dreams I have seen it; and this world terrifies me."

★ 19 ★

Now Don Luis said farewell to Doña Antonia for this while, and he left with her a promise of his eternal and complete fidelity. She gave him, in exchange, with which to remember her, a fine diamond ring earned in Mexico, as the main part of her loot from out of an ageing major-general's imperfect conquest of the desires of the flesh.

—Which trinket was, it may be, superfluous. In any case, with that well-bred gallantry which he had acquired from and among the élite of Spain, the Prince of Ajacan protested to Antonia that her ring could not be needed to make him think about her, upon any conceivable occasion, because the dear memory of his life's one love could not, by any magic, be put out of his heart, or be from his dreams evicted. He declared also a vast number of polite despairs, such as appeared suited to this moment of anguish; and if he got rather more comfort out of his eloquence than did his hearer, that, after all, is a reward common to most fine talkers.

Afterward the Prince travelled alone. It is said that his queer cane guided him. However this may have been, he came to a river, where a fort had been builded;

and upon the bank of this river, the Prince of Ajacan noted, to begin with, a stone column. It was engraved with a king's crown, but the arms underneath the crown did not display castles and lions, nor did the man who sat upon the other side of this column, and partly hidden by it, have the look of a Spaniard. He was a person approaching middle-age, with a short chestnut-colored beard and curled moustachios; he seemed to be in poor health.

"Why, pray, do you sit beside this stone column as if you were guarding it?" asked Don Luis.

"I sit here of necessity," the stranger answered. "I sit here because of a deplorable fever from which I am but half recovered; and but for which fever I would now be serving my God and my King very gloriously, at sea yonder, instead of dawdling about, upon this hot, bad-smelling mud bank, like an infirm and toothless watch dog."

"In fact," Don Luis said, experimentally, "I can perceive that the Spaniards have builded a fort to defend this river—which is, I have not any doubt, the River of Dolphins."

"No, my friend," said the other; "you mistake matters completely. Here is the River of May; and it was the valiant people of beautiful France who builded the fort you are looking at, when they took over this part of the country."

"Yet how can that be, when the Pope has given all the West Indies to Spain?"

"The Pope has not any power over Lutherans. And so, not very long ago, Monseignieur Gaspard de Coligny, Lord of Chatillon-sur-Loing, and an Admiral of France—who, in addition to being a brave soldier and a staunch patriot, is, above all, an earnest Huguenot—made up his mind to unite with his assured happiness by-and-by in heaven a fair amount of prosperity upon earth. He reflected that by depriving Spain of her ill-got possessions here in the lands called Florida, he would be advancing, in matters of religious conviction, the freedom of such persons as agree with him in their religious convictions, as well as increasing his income. For the good Admiral hates Spain, I must tell you, both as a loyal Frenchman with whose country Spain is continually at war, and as an ardent Protestant in spite of whose noble efforts to destroy all superstitious adherents to the false religion of Rome, the depravity of Spain continues, with a regrettable narrow-mindedness, to destroy Protestants. Because of such grave considerations did Monseignieur de Coligny make up his mind to found a French colony here in the west."

"You appear," said Don Luis, as he sat down beside this friendly stranger, "to be no less informed in high affairs of state than in the low motives which support them. For this reason, monsieur, I shall now make bold to implore of your loquaciousness an account of the grand deeds which French patriotism has been achieving in this part of Florida through the avenues of grand larceny."

"I reply willingly," said the Frenchman.

And having uttered these words, he set about proving their truth.

I must tell you (the Frenchman began) that the great Admiral de Coligny selected as his commander a not incompetent sailor called René de Laudonnière. From Havre de Grace, of which Coligny is governor, set out three ships containing three hundred communicants of the Reformed Religion. Of these evangelists, one hundred and twenty were soldiers of fortune, and a hundred and seventy-six were gentlemen adventurers accredited with various crimes by an illiberal-minded constabulary. Along with these brave colonists came four very, very much more brave young women, to whom nature had granted a pleasing amount of good looks in combination with unusual gifts in the way of industry and endurance.

The party reached Florida without mishap; and their ships entered the River of May. The Timuquan Indians received them with friendship. The gallant French found here a delightful place in which to begin life anew, among palm-trees and cedars red as blood, upon a knoll overlooking the south bank of the river, a place so gracious that in it melancholy could not survive as the acquaintance of a fair-minded person. From any sort of attack by land this place was secure, because of the interlaced streams and marshes surrounding it.

Here they sounded trumpets; they sang one of the less virulent psalms; with the aid of the Indians they builded a fort, out of stone, mud, and sand; and in honor of the French King Charles, they named it Fort Caroline. They mounted artillery so as to command both banks of the river. The Indians showed them how to construct pleasant homes, which were thatched with palm-leaves; and these savage people brought to the French many gifts, in the shape of game and fruit and blankets and basket-work, as a token of good will. Thus affably did Divine kindness smile upon the Reformed Religion.

The favor of Heaven continued. Henceforward these intrepid seekers after virgin lands wherein to practise a simplified form of worship, cleansed of Romish corruption, lived in prosperity, inasmuch as hereabouts the genial earth yielded up every nature of her fruits, at the proper season, without asking to be scratched by the plough even never so slightly. Here the heat of the sun was tempered to an agreeable ardor; here frost and hail were unknown; and here no Protestant was subjected to the inconvenience of manual labor. Whenever clothing or a woman or food was needed, the French had but to take these necessaries of life away from the Indians, without in very many instances having to destroy the first owner.

But above all, since the regular route of the Spanish vessels returning from Mexico ran conveniently near, the Frenchmen put their armed ships to a remunerative employment, by setting up as pirates. They captured one richly laden Spanish merchant vessel after another; they outfitted five more galleons, so beaming were the smiles of fortune upon their success as buccaneers; nor in the manner of harsh Spain, did they ever murder the crew of a ship that had been surrendered. Instead, the more chivalrous French made it a rule to cast overboard all survivors, unhurt, to the sharks. So responsive was the kindness of Heaven toward the tact of the French that everything prospered with the Reformed Religion in its new citadel.

The Lutherans, it is true, did have a continuing trouble with the Indians. These avaricious pagans refused to guide their white friends toward the near-by gold mines, upon the flimsy pretence that there were not any such gold mines. Even after the Indians had been confronted with the most modern maps made in Europe, by the chief scientists and by scholars of international repute,—upon which maps these gold mines were marked unmistakably—still, the hard-headed savages held fast to this subterfuge. Nor did any sort of argument allure them into truth-telling.

It was to no effect, for instance, that shortly after the French landed, Captain Laudonnière had surprised a large settlement of Seloy Indians, to the south of the fort, near the River of Dolphins, and had captured their Cazique. With an irrational obstinacy, the Cazique pretended to know nothing about any gold mines; and in the end his stingy prevaricating chilled even the proverbial good-fellowship of the French.

So, having set up a gallows, they fastened him there, by a chain about his middle, and with a great fire they consumed this cazique, gallows and all, to be an example to his fellow liars. Heaven, it was noticeable, so far continued Its favoritism of Heaven's sturdy champions that on this same afternoon the Lutherans were permitted to capture and to kill eighteen other bloodthirsty Seloy warriors, in eleven ways which combined amusement with an enlarged knowledge of anatomy. Having in mind, however, the merciful disposition of Christ and the knightly notions of Coligny, the French did not think it would be pleasing to their patrons, either in heaven or at Havre de Grace, should they dispose of the sulky Seloy women and of the smaller children in any of these eleven ways. For this reason, after having destroyed the provisions and the canoes of the Indians, the Lutherans were at pains to avoid a charge of bloodshed by transporting all these women and every one of the children to a near-by island, to starve there unmolested.

"And yet," remarked Don Luis, shaking his handsome head, "yet all this charity toward the blind errors of heathendom was, no doubt, wasted. The West Indians do not appreciate the large benefits which they are deriving daily from a more intimate contact with the civilization of Europe. They object to being tortured or shot down, and they even grumble about being starved to death upon snug quiet islands, in order to enjoy these large benefits. They behave, in fine, like curmudgeons."

"Ah, but, my dear friend," says the Frenchman, "you hear the tale of our troubles hereabouts with the quick sympathy of a whore in the same instant that you epitomize them with the omniscience of Heaven! That stubborn avarice of the Indians and their repulsive lack of faith in human nature, both these harsh vices have led to imperfect political relations ever since the moment we landed."

—Because, even in the face of such irrefutable arguments as burning and castrating and dismembering these pagans, with the most patient sort of butchery, still the Indians declined to be friendly. They stayed wholly unreasonable about pointing out the gold mines of Florida. The pagan women were especially ungracious, even after seeing their husbands killed and the brains of their brats smashed into a pale pulp, nor did the yet more laborious persuasive of boring small holes, with a white-hot gimlet, through the tongues of these women induce them to become more pleasant-spoken and candid.

Here, yet again, Don Luis shook his head.

"We inhabit an unsatisfying world," says he, "in which even for the casual pleasures of amour we stay dependent upon creatures so unreasonable."

"Yet women make good nurses," declared the Frenchman, tolerantly, "as one of the four girls who came with us has well proved during the wakeful nights of my late illness."

The eyebrows of Don Luis ascended.

"It is a privilege," his Highness remarked, "to hear of this fair euphemism who acts as a night nurse among buccaneers. I desire her acquaintance. But, if you please, monsieur, do you continue."

Very well, then! said the Frenchman. The hard-headedness of the Indians remained discouraging; but at piracy the Huguenots prospered. So pleasing was the report which came to Havre de Grace, every quarter, as to the profits of the Reformed Religion from the Spanish merchant trade, that Coligny procured yet more colonists; and in fact he had but lately enlarged his enterprise by sending oversea three hundred brave pirates of strict Protestant principles, in seven galleons, under the command of the very celebrated French seaman, Jean Ribaut. By young King Charles, Ribaut the Invincible had been duly commissioned to be Governor of Florida; and Ribaut's fleet came unhurt to Fort Caroline.

Yet, of the seven ships of Ribaut, four were so large that they could not easily pass through the sandbars at the mouth of the River of May. When Ribaut entered the fort, these galleons—the *Trinity*, the *Union*, the *Trout*, and the *Shoulder of Mutton*—all lay at anchor over night. In the dusk of evening they observed that another galleon, attended by four caravels, was approaching; and as these ships advanced, from their decks came a sounding of trumpets. The French answered, with their own trumpets, courteously.

Then a voice demanded of the French: "What fleet is this? You have good trumpeters."

The reply was: "Because of their politeness the French excel every other people in each polite art. We are galleons that come from France to bring supplies for a fort which our King owns in Florida, and for yet other forts which he plans to build, and to put in command of them his Captain General."

"Are you Catholics or Lutherans? What thief heads you?"

"We are of the Reformed Religion; and our leader is Jean Ribaut, called rightly the Invincible."

"You are more fortunate in your leader, and in

your trumpeters, than in your faith. I admire most heartily your trumpeters; and in no place between Madrid and Mecca is there alive, as yet, a better seaman than Jean Ribaut."

"All we, who are his friends, agree with you," said the French; "and if his rather numerous enemies do not argue the matter, that is because Jean Ribaut does not leave any enemies with their throats uncut."

"And it is a great pity," the polite cold voice continued, "that before this week is out, the Devil will be getting a pirate so skilled and courteous. Yet this, O noble señors, is the armada of the King of Spain. We have come into these upper parts of his Ocean Sea to destroy each one of you heretics. We defer our duty —with your permission, señors,—merely until we have landed our women and infants and our food supplies in safety."

—After which display of insane insolence the five ships turned southward; and Ribaut was notified, at the fort. He laughed, he stroked his huge bushy beard, and he made ready his fleet of fifteen proud galleons.

He held a feast that night, at Fort Caroline, and his captains consumed, it is said, two barrels of wine in drinking toasts to the doomed Spaniards.

"By our faith as gentlemen," the gay French swore, upon their sword-hilts, "we will punish rightly these Spanish swine. We will kill them one and all; but their commander we shall hang at the yardarm of his own ship, so that no bragging Papist will ever come again to trouble us in our own land of Florida."

Then the fifteen French ships went merrily to make an end of the five Spanish ships. Good Lutherans were so eager to have a part in this praiseworthy task that at Fort Caroline no able-bodied man stayed behind willingly. At Fort Caroline remained only a small garrison to protect the place, under the captaincy of René de Laudonnière, who at this special moment had the bad luck to be ill in bed with a fever.

"Yet inasmuch as I secured, from among the indefatigable four girls who came over with us, an invigorating nurse," the Frenchman continued, "Margot has seen to it that I am now upon the way to recovery."

"Then you, monsieur, I infer to be Captain Laudonnière in person," remarked Don Luis de Velasco, with his customary quickness in logic.

—Whereafter, with a no less habitual deference toward candor, he introduced himself as Prince of Ajacan, and therefore as the heir of a none too important kingdom, which howsoever superior in the matter of mere crude, rather indiscriminate opulence it might be to Europe and Asia combined, yet in size remained inferior. And the Prince added:

"These Spanish swaggerers will be destroyed, of necessity, inasmuch as the French patriots are fighting them three to one. That fact, my dear captain, delights me. I do not desire any good anywhere for my double-dealing cousin, the King of Spain, or for his triple-dealing servants either, now that among them they have brought about the destruction of my most virtuous and valiant godfather and best-loved friend."

Laudonnière, at that, smiled, saying, "Do you then honor me, Monsieur the Prince, by attending, in the rôle of my guest, the execution of this braggart don, this Pedro Menéndez de Avilés."

"Why, but who, pray"—Don Luis asked, with polite interest—"who may be this same Pedro Menéndez de Avilés."

"He is the insane Spaniard who boasted that he came hither to destroy every one of us," said Laudonnière. "He is the Captain General in command of the five Spanish ships. And so, should you who detest all Spaniards, consent to visit me for a day or two, then I can promise you the acquaintance of Margot, in addition to some tolerable wine. For dessert you will have the pleasing spectacle of this infernal Menéndez hanged at the yardarm of his own flagship when Jean Ribaut the Invincible comes back in triumph."

"Now, but very certainly," returned Don Luis, "you Frenchmen do not grudge to your guests any sort of pleasure."

Thus speaking, he went into Fort Caroline side by side with Captain René de Laudonnière.

Part Three

The Godson of
Pedro Menéndez

I expect, with God's aid, to travel so like a good corsair that the enemies will fear me. They will not be safe from me; I shall give them their fate with the help of Our Blessed Mother in heaven: for I mean to serve your Majesty with all care in this New World according to the confidence placed in me. May the Lord favor the Catholic Royal Person of your Majesty, with an increase of yet further realms and lordships, such as Christianity lacks, and as I intend to get.

—PEDRO MENÉNDEZ, TO KING PHILIP

★ 20 ★

I WILL NOW tell you how, when the King of Spain heard that the French Huguenots had impiously taken possession of his Florida, and reflected that the naval commander most to his purpose was in jail, his Majesty at once became a pattern of every sort of loving-kindness and of broad-minded mercy. He paused only to release, under the heavy hand of misfortune, the human side of a king's nature by driving out of the room the courier who brought this bad news; by deposing two grandees from the Royal Council; and by ordering off a half-dozen Moors to be baptized and hanged. After that, Lord Philip remitted half of Menéndez' fine; and he himself paid the other half of it, with the generosity of a Hapsburg, from out of the treasury of the Casa de Contratación.

The merchant traders who had purchased the imprisonment of Menéndez, and who now had to buy his freedom, at the stiff rate of a thousand ducats, did not complain. The fixed route of their ships, in coming from Mexico or South America, on their way past the Bahamas, ran too near Florida for Spanish commerce to permit the rascality of any other nation's nabobs to con-

trol this peninsula. Already the French held it; already
the French, as you have heard, were robbing the Spanish
ships. Pedro Menéndez, no matter what might be his
weakness for introducing rather too much honesty into
a business transaction, remained the sole living Spanish
seaman who might yet, it was possible, get back Spain's
lost lands from these uniformly dishonest French
pirates.

So Menéndez, after being bathed and shaved and
more or less cleaned of vermin, was robed in crimson
and appointed Adelantado, or as we would say, the Governor and Captain General of the Province of Florida.
He set sail from Cadiz with one galleon and fourteen
light caravels, some 2,600 men, and a Papal blessing.
Two-thirds of his fleet were sunk or dispersed, under the
onslaughts of especially outrageous tempests, so that
when Don Pedro sighted the low Florida coast, on the
feast day of St. Augustine, he had left only his galleon
and four of the caravels. It was a scantiness which did
not at all trouble the Adelantado, inasmuch as he still
kept the Pope's blessing, through which an official re-
quirement had been put upon God Almighty to look
out for the success of Pedro Menéndez de Avilés.

So, to begin with, the Spanish Governor of Florida
warned the French intruders in general, and the French
Governor of Florida in particular, as has been recorded.
Don Pedro went south to the River of Dolphins (or, as
we now call this ocean inlet, in defiance of geography,

the Matanzas River), and he entered it. He disembarked
his people, with all the supplies. Two out of his five
ships—the *Salvador* and his one galleon, the *San Pelayo*
—then set sail for Cuba. Upon the following day, the
Spanish Governor was fetched ashore, in a rowboat,
with suitable pomp, amid a waving of red and yellow
flags, a sounding of trumpets, and the salutes of artillery. His chaplain, who at the moment was Father
Francisco Lopez de Mendoza Grajales, advanced
chaunting the *Te Deum Laudamus* and carrying a cross,
which Menéndez and the officers who attended him,
after falling upon their knees, were allowed to kiss
reverently.

The Adelantado evicted the Seloy Indians from
their near-by council house, and he mounted cannon
within the palisade of this building, which henceforward became the Fort of San Juan de Pinos. Menéndez
took possession of the entire continent in his King's
name; and in honor of the great Bishop of Hippo, upon
whose feast day the Spanish Governor of Florida had
first sighted his Province—over which, it is true, the
French Governor still had control—Menéndez called his
landing place St. Augustine.

The Mass of Our Lady was then celebrated, so the
tale says—upon Ocean Street, but a little distance to
the east of where San Marco Avenue develops into
Dixie Highway and enters a gaunt grove of billboards
commemorative, for interminable miles, of competitive

dealers in pecans. Upon this same plot of ground just south of Ocean Street was erected, later, and still stands, the Chapel of Neustra Señora de la Léche y Buen Parto. Such was the beginning of our civilization, with the founding of the first Christian city in the United States of America.

⋆ 21 ⋆

IT WAS at this moment—which tact, under the raised glance of patriotism, makes bold to describe as one of the most important clock-ticks time has yet hiccoughed out—that a tall young man came down, from near-by the present location of the stables of the St. Augustine Riding Academy, in the Garnett Orange Grove, toward North River. He thus approached the kneeling Spaniards, who, in their best holiday gear, diversified at this moment the future sites of the Cemetery of Nombre de Dios and of quiet Ocean Street. The new-comer was unarmed; he carried a queer cane; and he asked Menéndez, with a meditative, friendly slow smile—very much as he had asked Menéndez in Ajacan—what was their need in this place?

A disturbance followed, and a commotion such as shattered any further religious rites. The Adelantado embraced Don Luis with astounded joy; the Adelantado wept, so great was his joy; and he called for his row-boat, since the tide was still out. He then went with his dear godson through the broad, dry sunlit sandbars—where the sedate gulls were at luncheon, and tiny sand-pipers ran about eagerly in their search of remnants. The two gentlemen went aboard Menéndez' ship, where the *San Andrés* lay at anchor, just outside the harbor, so that, over their wine, the two might talk privately. This they began to do, at once, under a red and white canopy, upon the rear deck of the *San Andrés*.

"Wherever do you come from, you spruce devil's son?" Menéndez asked fondly.

Don Luis answered: "How dare I tell you? I come to you, in the manner of my Satanic race, from after having walked up and down the earth. I have been in many places since we last parted, Pedro. Concerning some of these places I had best not speak, because for you to believe in their existence would not be healthful for a sincere worshipper of the storm god of Sinai."

"That, my dear son, is nonsense," said the calm champion of the True Faith.

"Perhaps," says Don Luis: "but it is not nonsense that I have been in Caloosa, where the Cazique Carlos had, when I left him, a large number of white captives."

"They shall be liberated, let us trust, with God's help," returned Menéndez. "Otherwise, I will attend to it myself."

"Yet, Pedro, some few of these, your brothers in Christ, were Lutherans."

"Them too I must liberate from this wicked Carlos; and after that, I shall turn them over to the Holy Inquisition in Cuba, to be destroyed properly on account of their own wickedness."

"In Caloosa, Pedro, I got bad news—especially bad news," the Prince added, "for you."

"And whom"—but the Adelantado foreknew the answer—"whom does this news concern?"

Don Luis took out of his bosom the crucifix which the Shaman had given to him. He said abruptly, so as to get through his unhappy task at a spurt,—

"During the Hunger Moon, last year, the owner of this crucifix was sacrificed to Toya of the Palms, in order to ensure for Caloosa a more plentiful crop this spring."

"Yes: why, but to be sure," said Menéndez. "I myself gave this crucifix to him when the boy was confirmed."

He spoke calmly; he looked older, that was all. He kissed the crucifix. He laid it down after having cleared a place for it, reflectively, among the wine glasses. He said,—

"How did my son die?"

"Dear Pedro! but the ritual of their sunset offering to Toya—Well, but let us say, it is so complicated, and so leisurely, that nothing whatever of a pleasant nature could be gained by discussing it."

"I understand," said Don Pedro. He was silent. He said by-and-by:

"Henceforward it is you alone, Luis, that are my son. Let us not speak further"—the lean Adelantado gulped, just once—"of anyone else. I shall go into Ca-

loosa. Very certainly I shall go into Caloosa as soon as
the King's business has been discharged in his Province
of Florida. It is my first need, you comprehend, to destroy the French pirates and to take possession of their
fort."

Don Luis looked at Menéndez for some while, consideringly, with a sort of derisive and half-puzzled
affection. He placed his hand upon the tense hand of
Menéndez.

"You are not human. You are absurd," said Don
Luis. "And still, I love you, Pedro Menéndez de Avilés,
almost as much as I distrust you, because of all persons
living I believe you to be the most brave and the most
stubborn of Christian gentlemen. Eh, well!"—and the
son of Quetzal shrugged—"but precisely as you declared to me in Mexico, we lack at this instant an oppor-
tunity to display emotion. Time presses. I must make
haste to evince my affection by violating the sacred laws
of hospitality. I must betray my late host, Captain
René de Laudonnière, so far as to tell you that at this
moment fifteen very large French galleons are upon
their way to destroy you and your colony. I know,
Pedro; for I come straight from Fort Caroline."

"What, pray, were you doing among the foul
Lutherans?"

"Pedro, your question partakes of the embarrassing.
I can but tell you—with it hardly matters how many
blushes—that to attend him during his illness Laudon-

nière secured an exceedingly well-spoken and a very
lovely blonde nurse. So where I went to dine, I remained to adore. My hopes flourished, for all that my
desires, on account of Laudonnière's ubiquity, stayed
unsatiated; and in this way, love kept me at Fort Caroline a deal longer than I intended."

"Such matters do not interest me, you young rip."

The Adelantado spoke half absent-mindedly. You
would have said he had quite put out of thought his
son's murder. Or rather, to serve Spain and that strange
brutal God of Spain (Don Luis continued his reflec-
tions) came first with Menéndez. Menéndez was now
about that service; and as set against it, his own human
affections did not matter one straw's worth. Of me too
he is fond, the younger man thought; but if ever I once
stood in the way of Spain's welfare, or if I hindered
Rome's power, as these French Lutherans are now doing, then how irrelevant would my lean Christian godfather find his affection for me! I believe that, at
bottom, I dislike Pedro Menéndez, under all my love for
him, under all my admiration . . .

Don Luis did not voice this thought. He was none
the less fated to remember it.

Now Menéndez had taken up from beside him,
and he was pensively looking at, the jineta which was
the symbol of his rank as Governor of Florida. This
jineta was a short, brightly gilded spear adorned with a
red tassel.

"So there are now two Governors of Florida," he said, "and my rival for the possession of this little lance is Jean Ribaut. These heretics have fifteen ships, you tell me. Above all, they have that superb scoundrel, Jean Ribaut, to command their ships. That he is a better seaman than I am, nobody ever questioned. I confess I had not looked for such heavy odds."

Says Don Luis, "They are odds which, in the terms of a convenient cliché, one needs to describe as overwhelming."

"No, Luis: for as against the Pope's blessing, here in my pocket, I do not value Ribaut and his fifteen ships as worth fifteen jackstraws. The Lutheran fleet does not matter. It is far more important that you, my dear son, should have been misled by carnal lust into defiling yourself for so considerable a while in this nest of French pirates. Your depravity was beyond any doubt prompted by Heaven: for you can now tell me what their fort is like; how it is situated; but above all, how their fort is surrounded."

"Fort Caroline," replied Don Luis, "stands upon the south bank of the River of May. It faces westward, just at the head of the sand bars which obstruct the river's entrance."

"Such sand bars seem to clog up the mouth of every river in these parts," Menéndez answered. "That is not always convenient. Only this morning I had to be rowed ashore for the ceremonials, without any more dignity than we were rowed back here, because until the tide rises, no ship can get into the harbor yonder on account of the shallows."

Don Luis said: "And just such shallows protect Fort Caroline. Moreover, to the east of it, rises a tall bluff, upon which is kept a sentinel, to observe the sea, a good five miles distant. No fleet could ever hope to take the place by surprise."

"One can but infer it is the intention of Heaven," said Menéndez, "that when I go to Fort Caroline I must travel by land."

"Pedro, but now it is you who speak nonsense: for upon the land side, the fort is surrounded with streams and marshes through which no human army could march. I know; for it was my misfortune to have to struggle through these bogs only yesterday. Fort Caroline, as the French may well rest assured, is impregnable."

Menéndez answered: "Jericho was impregnable until Joshua took it. Can a Spaniard not perform as much with a Pope's blessing as a Jew has done with the horns of a ram? And besides that, Luis, you got through those marshes—with the aid of your cane, the One Reed," Don Pedro amended. For the instant his eyes glinted. They were like bits of ice. He said then,—

"Do you tell me how this strong lair of Satan is builded."

So Don Luis explained that Fort Caroline was

shaped like a triangle, of which the river side was a palisade of tall pine and palmetto posts. The two other sides were builded of faggots and sand and turf (the Prince continued), with a moat surrounding them. Outside the fort were a bake-oven, a storehouse, and a number of palmetto-thatched houses—

"They do not matter. Get on!" Menéndez rapped out, shaking the jineta restively. "What lies to the south of these French heretics, between them and me?"

Well, an open meadow stretched southward, to the edge of a pine forest, where there was a spring of excellent water, though it both smelled and tasted, slightly, of sulphur. There the marshes began. Don Luis told also how the soldiers were quartered, inside the fort, toward the south; how their commander Laudonnière had established his lodgings, on the river side, with a private door opening upon the wharf; and in brief, the Prince described Fort Caroline with extreme thoroughness.

Don Pedro listened in silence; he smiled bleakly; and you saw that in the while he was listening he meditatively drew, upon the deck before him, with the gilt point of his jineta, a plan of Fort Caroline.

"I shall make use of all your wickedly acquired knowledge, my son," he declared, "so soon as the French fleet has been disposed of."

At that, Don Luis shook his head; and he spoke indulgently, saying,—

"With the frankness of a thunder-stricken person who addresses an insane person, you must let me ask you—O my quite incredible, grave godfather!—how do you propose to deal with the French fleet when their ships outnumber you three to one?"

"Their fleet outnumbers me five to one," Menéndez said—without large interest and merely, as you saw, in the cause of strict accuracy. "I thought it best to send two of my ships into Cuba."

He explained, then, that his people needed supplies in the way of food and of clothing, for which he had sent into Cuba the *Salvador;* and that, among his people, he had found twenty-two persons whom he suspected of inclining, in some degree, toward the abominations of Lutheranism. For that reason, he had likewise forwarded, upon his one galleon, the *San Pelayo,* all these persons into Cuba, to be dealt with there, properly, by the Inquisition. This tribute to the Catholic Faith, upon the eve of a sea battle, had weakened his already inadequate forces, no doubt, should you judge the affair by mere human standards—as Menéndez went on to grant, with that insane rationality which distinguished the man, always, when he talked about religious matters. Don Pedro did not pretend that as a rule three small ships could do battle with fifteen large ships. He remarked only that the problem set for the French was not arithmetical.

"Their problem is how to deflect the will of

Heaven; and they will fail in solving that problem. For I have the Pope's blessing; so that God, in His own way, will destroy these heretics."

It was at this instant that Don Luis, who sat facing the north and the fogs which had gathered there, began to laugh.

"Dear Pedro," says he, "then it is high time that the Father and the Son and the Paraclete, as well as the Blessed Mother and all the more belligerent archangels, should be buckling down to the job set for them by Giovanni dei Medici, The French are at hand."

★ 22 ★

WHAT FOLLOWED was highly touch-and-go work. As I have told you, the flagship of Menéndez—which, since he sent away the *Pelayo* with its cargo of human fuel for the Inquisition, had been the *San Andrés*—now lay at anchor, outside the shallows of the River of Dolphins, when the French fleet approached, coming up suddenly out of a fog. Menéndez' other ships, *The Holy Ghost* and *Our Lady of the Rosary*, were inside the harbor, which, with dry white sand bars streaking the harbor's mouth everywhere, they could not leave, nor any ship enter, until the tide rose. The Adelantado was cut off from his own people at St. Augustine utterly when, without warning, the *San Andrés* was, not confronted but surrounded, by an armada of French vessels. To attempt either an escape or a battle would have been equally futile. There was not, for the Adelantado of the Province of Florida or for his flagship, any hope conceivable.

In these straits Don Pedro demanded aid of the inconceivable. He knelt, and he prayed to Our Lady of Consolation, who was called otherwise Our Lady of Utrera, and whose forte it was to defend seamen.

It is granted that, with the Pope's blessing in his pocket, Don Pedro's manner lacked unction. He spoke with haste. He was almost peremptory. He, in brief, had less the air of asking a favor of Heaven than of pointing out to Heaven, respectfully but with firmness, the immediate need of proper supernal action. It is granted, also, that nothing in particular happened except that the French fleet drew nearer, encircling the *San Andrés.* They did not open fire: that was not needed. They had trapped Pedro Menéndez, whom the French officers had sworn not to kill honorably but to hang at the yardarm of his own ship.

Then Don Luis de Velasco faced northward and, spreading out both his arms, he began to speak in his native tongue. None understood him, completely, but among his hearers none doubted that the Prince of Ajacan uttered a prayer; and by the pious rapscallions serving under Pedro Menéndez this supplication, in the nature of things, was granted to be addressed to Our Lady of Utrera.

The sequel was for this reason approved of, in an equal degree, by devout Catholics and by the courteous who put faith in politeness, because, to the more fervent and the more gracious praying of Don Luis de Velasco, Our Lady of Utrera responded at once. She responded with a miracle. No sooner had the son of the Lord of the Ninth Wind invoked Heaven, in his own tongue, than a sudden, very vigorous flaw of wind struck the *San Andrés*. The anchor-chain snapped under the force of this wind; and by this wind the ship was lifted, upon a quiet upheaving, like a restrained belch, of the Atlantic,—very daintily and with exact precision,—straight over the sand bars, and among an effusive white squawking scatter of seagulls, into the River of Dolphins.

Our Lady of Utrera, it became evident to the happy Spaniards, had covered all, at one stroke, through this adroit miracle. There was left, now, not any chance of a French ship's pursuing the *San Andrés*, without being wrecked, until after the tide had risen high enough, a good two hours later.

Yet, now that her hand was in, this proved only a beginning to the friendly intervention of Our Lady of Utrera and to her industry in looking after a Pope's protégé. Until but a moment before this puff of wind struck the *San Andrés*, the sky had been clear; the sun shone brilliantly; and a blue and serene and half-asleep ocean had been distributing, upon blindingly bright sands, an equable series of long, level, low, very lazily lifted waves into feathery white fallings. The fog came then, from out of the north, with a thief's unobtrusiveness; and under cover of the fog, the French.

All changed, now that after this brisk puff of wind, burst out of the north a howling darkness and a demolishment. The same wind which had been the saving of the Spaniards became for the Frenchmen ruin, inasmuch as this wind increased instantly from vigor to fury. It was now a hurricane. And rain battered every-where—rain which was not falling downward, but moved sidewise, with a crushing violence, in mile-wide sheets and in writhing heaven-high solid columns of water, as the storm raged southward across an insane ocean.

For a moment the French ships struggled among waves tall as the mainmast. Yet the Spaniards saw that, quite incredibly, no one of these ships had been dashed to pieces upon the shallow coasts of what is now Anastasia Island. Instead, with an even more incredible swiftness, the French fleet had passed southward, tossed lightly about, with a horrid jauntiness, under a flickering of continuous brisk lightnings, and pursued by admonishing bellows of thunder.

The storm swallowed all. The siege of St. Augustine was at an end.

"The value of a properly directed prayer," remarked Don Luis de Velasco, "is attested."

Menéndez, for an instant, stood glaring at the younger man with small furious eyes, which were like the eyes of an enraged pig; and Don Luis wondered. He saw then that his godfather had put on a sudden air of cold and aloof composure.

"Most graciously," says Menéndez, "has the might of Our Lady of Utrera come to protect us."

"Why, but yes! to be sure!" returned Don Luis;

"and Our Lady of Consolation,—even though she appears a bit hard of hearing—is now proved to be in demolishment rather gratifyingly whole-hearted."

"That she has always been," said Menéndez—"to the relapsed heretic."

He looked fixedly at his godson before the Adelantado declared,—

"We must show ourselves to be not unworthy of her high favor."

—Whereafter, among the raging downpour of the storm, the glitter of continued lightnings, and a noise of thunders which were like the smashing up of continents, the Adelantado caused to be celebrated the Mass of the Holy Ghost. He got together his men. He ordered to remain at St. Augustine, in the Fort of San Juan de Pinos, a hundred persons. These included the women, the sick, the very young, and in fine, only such weaklings as were not able to abet him in dealing with heresy.

These persons, as well as the fort and the new town, would be at the mercy of the French Lutherans, to whom mercy was unknown, if the French came back; but Menéndez had made up his mind that Heaven would not allow the French to come back—if ever these most hateful rebels against the True Faith were permitted to return at all—with an inconvenient quickness. So he marched northward, at once, in the miraculous storm provided by Our Lady of Utrera, having with him every able-bodied man under his command. He marched toward Fort Caroline.

It is not required of you to regard this special part of the story as credible, because I well know it is not possible for anyone to believe a sane commander would entrust to the keeping of bedridden persons and to women a besieged fortress, so that he might quit it to attack a fortress belonging to his besiegers, some forty miles distant. Yet Menéndez, you must let me remind you,—with the apologetic cough, of course, and with the superior face-making necessitated by a mention of the out-of-date,—Pedro Menéndez put faith in Heaven.

Heaven had lifted his ship over the sand bar when his escape had become beyond reason, by any human standards of reason. Heaven, when the French held St. Augustine blockaded, had sent forth the winds of Heaven to annihilate the French. In addition, Heaven had delivered to Pedro Menéndez a complete and accurate account of Fort Caroline, as well as a guide through the marshes surrounding it. With the French fleet blown southward, and perhaps wrecked, Fort Caroline, at this happy instant, stayed as weakly protected as a true Christian could hope ever to find this wicked stronghold of theft and of sectarianism.

It was not possible, in the face of three successive miracles, to doubt that Heaven meant to protect the Holy Catholic Faith with efficacy. It would be impious to conceive that Heaven intended Don Pedro

Menéndez de Avilés to carry on his special and, it might
be, his somewhat essential part in Heaven's work, at his
own selfish convenience.

So Menéndez went north at once. He did not wait
for the storm to end; he left his fort undefended; and
he did not trouble, for that while, to inquire what
might have become of the navy and the armed forces
of Jean Ribaut, with whom he was conducting a war
upon which the ownership of half this world depended.
His faith was in the next world.

★ 23 ★

I WILL NOW tell you how the Prince of Ajacan guided the Spaniards through what seemed an unendurable nightmare. The wind and the blinding rain buffeted and tore at them, without ever ceasing. They beat their way through palmetto thickets; they struggled breast deep in mud; and they continually tumbled headlong into unseen rivulets, because in this dark jungle they could not perceive anything at all clearly except when very horrible fierce flashes of lightning showed to the Spaniards Don Luis de Velasco treading ahead of them, among the giant boles of palms and live-oaks, and flourishing about, like the staff of a drum major, his queer reed cane.

"This Indian is a devil," the men said. "He has brought us into hell. He leads us toward Satan's self. It is not wholesome to be following after this Indian."

"My godson does God's work," replied Menéndez; and drove them on.

In this fashion they got, somehow, to the rear of Fort Caroline. Don Luis laid down his cane; and of a sudden the storm lulled. The storm ceased. All knelt and prayed for the Blessed Mother's favor during the im-

pendent battle while the Spaniards waited for daylight.
Birds twittered tentatively. From the pine-trees rain
drops fell, at irregular intervals, with a sharp tapping
noise when they struck against armor.

As soon as the east became gray, the Spaniards
attacked. They burst open the unguarded south gate,
and thus surprised the fort while most of the garrison
were yet in bed. Since the powder of the Spaniards was
wet, and the cords of their arquebuses had become
water-soaked, they could use only their swords and
pikes to kill the French, some few of whom expired
with decorum in their nightshirts where the majority,
who had slept naked, perished nakedly. Yet of the
French garrison not all were put out of living, because
forty-odd of them escaped in the darkness. Nor, inasmuch as Menéndez had given orders to spare the women
as well as all the boys who were under fifteen, were very
many of these killed during the tumult intentionally.
Moreover, the Adelantado was at immediate pains to
rescue and to preserve the French drummers, and the
trumpeters whose music he had admired, so that these
gifted artists might be added to his own military band.

His first friendly care, after the last throat had
been slit, the few prisoners hanged, and the resultant
corpses added up to a gratifying total of one hundred
and thirty-two dead Lutherans, was to ask for Don
Luis de Velasco—to whose gallant conduct in betraying
the French fort, the Adelantado remarked, all Spain

stood indebted. It was answered the Prince could nowhere be found.

Menéndez, who at this instant was washing his hands reasonably clean in a tin basin, looked thoughtful; later, he smiled.

"Nor, I imagine, can the young nurse of Laudonnière be found. Very well, then! My hell-born godson is quite able to look after himself."

—Whereafter Menéndez returned briskly to public affairs. He gave orders to remove the French arms from over the main entrance to the fort, and to replace these abhorrent symbols of theft and heresy with the golden castles and the blood-colored lions of Spain, surmounted by a cross and two angels. Fort Caroline he re-christened Fort San Mateo, inasmuch as it had been captured upon the feast day of that saint. With his own hands the Adelantado burned nineteen packs of playing cards, which were found in the fort. He, whose life had been one continuous chance-taking, most deeply disapproved of the vice of gambling. He burned also at this time six large boxes of religious books, so called, exceedingly well bound and handsomely gilded, but pertaining to the abominations of the Protestants' wicked faith.

With these moral duties discharged, Menéndez burst open the fort's arsenal, and he discovered it to be well filled with dry powder and new arquebuses. He then collected his soldiers, and addressed to them the ensuing exhortation:

"My dear and very valiant brothers in Christ, it is not we but Our Great God Himself Who has performed these wonders, miraculously, in behalf of Spain and of His Own holy cause. He has revealed to us of late His exceeding tenderness, which in this arsenal He perpetuates. I consider that without delay we ought to make plain our gratitude to the sublime Father of all mankind, inasmuch as, in this moment of need, His everloving care has provided us with firearms."

Having uttered these inspiring words, the Adelantado knelt, and he entreated a continuance of Heaven's charity, before leading his men into the woods south of the fort. His prayers were there answered, at once, with a benignant generosity, since in these woods they found thirty-eight naked Frenchmen, whom the Spaniards shot down, laughingly and at leisure, with the French guns. It was excellent, said the Spaniards, to wind up a hard day's work with this half-hour of sportsmanship.

Menéndez then gave way to the frailties of human flesh so far as to rest for the first time in four days. He slept, they record, for almost four hours, so extreme was his exhaustion. He appointed Gonzalo de Villarroel to take charge of Fort San Mateo. The Adelantado left with his Lieutenant Governor all the Spaniards except thirty-five soldiers, with whom Menéndez returned, down the sea coast, toward St. Augustine. He learned there that the French fleet had been wrecked with such handsome thoroughness that all but two ships were lost.

He learned also that a large number of the ship-wrecked Lutherans, after having been cast ashore upon an island some few leagues distant, still lived there, besieged by Seloy Indians, who had already killed and scalped about fifty of the French. He marched thither, still attended by his thirty-five men; he drove off the Indians; and through a polite feint of having come to make prisoners of these beleaguered and half-starved Lutherans, he induced them to surrender and lay down such weapons as they possessed.

With the French at his disposal, it was thus granted him to kill a hundred and forty heretics upon this island without their being able to make any resistance. Having thus happily satiated the needs of patriotism and the dictates of the True Faith, Menéndez went back to his civic duties at St. Augustine.

⋆ 24 ⋆

WHEN THE SPANIARDS made ready to attack Fort Caroline, then in the first gray half-light of dawn, Don Luis left them. He went to the river bank; he paused beside the dark lapping waters; and with a key which happened to occupy the pocket of the Prince of Ajacan, his Highness unlocked an inconspicuous private door that led to the quarters of René de Laudonnière. When the Prince returned to the wharf, he brought with him a young and exceedingly beautiful blonde girl.

The tale declares that her name was Margot; and the story says also that, to an accompaniment of loud Spanish shoutings and the wails of Frenchmen who were being murdered under protest, the two young people turned, with quickness and wisdom, into the forest east of the noisy shambles. To Don Luis de Velasco— as he remarked with that well-bred gallantry which he had acquired from and among the élite of Spain—Fort Caroline appeared at that instant to be an undesirable residence for the most lovely of her sex.

"Indeed, your Highness," replied the fair-tressed nurse, "but I was not ever so heartily frightened in my life since a depraved marquis, upon whom I was then attendant in Dauphiné, advanced ignoble suggestions as to the surrender of my virtue. I was sound asleep, inasmuch as during my present employment I have learned to disregard the unpleasant habit of snoring to which M. de Laudonnière is a victim. I was awakened only when my dear poor René kicked me with extreme violence as he climbed over me out of bed, and clothed merely in his nightshirt, rushed forth to encounter the invaders with his sword and target."

"An experience so blood-curdling, O most divine Margot, the tongue of sympathy may well make haste to describe as annoying."

"It was a spectacle before which, my dear Prince, sharp tremors seized my limbs. My senses well-nigh failed me. My brow was bedewed with cold perspiration."

"Nor do I at all doubt," Don Luis remarked, in ingratiating tones of compassion, "that your hair stood upon end."

"I can assure your Highness that not one strand of it remained supine. I feared that some harm might befall my distraught and reckless ward, for these Spaniards, even in the most private relations, are libertines devoid of principle. How well do I recall the Aragonese abbot who abandoned me, in Amsterdam, in circumstances such as the memory of a modest gentlewoman declines to revive! The police of Amsterdam are not sympathetic to misled innocence. There was also the merchant of Madrid; yet his requirements, even when in bed, were so unnatural that I shall not allude to him. So let us now"—the fair girl continued—"avert our eyes from these more unpleasant aspects of human nature; and do you permit me, my Prince, to render you my heart-felt thanks for having saved my chastity from the attacks which might, before this moment, have been made upon it by platoons, if not indeed by regiments."

The Prince answered: "In the name of Heaven, mademoiselle, do you compose your disordered spirits! Dismiss from thought the scenes of blood and horror from which we have lately escaped; and comprehend that, under my protection, your lovely person is safe from annoyance! I esteem it a happy privilege to repay, in some degree, that hospitality which your hands displayed upon Captain Laudonnière's sofa, when I last came to Fort Caroline; when the denials of your ruby lips were, in turn, denied by the warmth of your sapphire eyes; and when at my first glimpse of you, I found my heart had been transfigured into a magazine of combustibles."

"You speak with a noble directness, my Prince, which merits a return in kind. I confess that from the instant I saw you, my heart was yours, in fee simple, even in the teeth of a maid's modesty; and I regret only that through force of circumstances, I should have dressed with such haste, before leaving today's carnage, that I must now seem to you a frump."

Upon that point Don Luis reassured her in suitable terms; and for a while neither one of them spoke.

Then a palmetto clump groaned, it rustled, and it delivered up a dapper tiny person, who carried in his hand a large pair of shears.

"I have fled from the unwholesome neighborhood of murder," declared the young tailor—for such indeed was his profession—"only to be brought in contact with this sort of behavior. The north parts of Florida are exceedingly full of evil."

"Now, my dear Pierre," cried out Margot—as she upraised her person from the ground and addressed this unmannerly intruder in tones of gentle reproof—"but however do you happen to be hiding in these bushes, and embarrassing people, instead of waiting down yonder to have your throat cut like any other intrepid Lutheran?"

The tailor answered: "As good luck would have it, I arose very early this morning, to resume work on a suit of clothes which I was making for M. d'Ottigny. I had but entered the courtyard, with these shears in my hand, when two Spaniards set upon me with a pike and a partisan."

"There," said Margot, with indignation, "there, just at hand, was your chance to win the bright crown of martyrdom. Yet you let it slip, I infer."

"Truly, mademoiselle," the tailor admitted, "but I

was not thinking about religious matters, in the while I jumped over the rampart—for all that it is nine feet high—and came, without any delay, into the forest bringing with me, as you may perceive, my shears; for at the instant I did not weigh the teeth of wild beasts, or the great jaws of alligators, against the malice of Spaniards."

"My dear poor friend," replied Margot, "your sentiments, although unadorned with heroism, may at first glance appear natural. Yet you speak, precisely as you have acted, with an excess of unpremeditation."

"Now but do I indeed, mademoiselle?"

"Yes, my deluded Pierre: for these gallant Spaniards, who spring of the same race as the brave Cid, fight against soldiers alone. One of your gentle and indispensable calling would be wholly safe, in any circumstances, among the gentry of Castile and Aragon. No matter what, alas, may be their religious errors, the Spaniards remain famous all over the world for their high standards of benevolence and for the purity of their personal conduct."

"Still, mademoiselle, it seems to me that but a minute ago your opinion was otherwise."

"I spoke then in girlish petulance," Margot deplored. "I can now see that at this special moment a tailor would find himself in frantic request among these distressed gentlemen. After so many miles of struggling through these dense Florida woodlands, and after shar-

ing in the mêlée of mortal combat, the clothing of the
Spaniards must be in tatters."

Inspired by this unlooked-for intrusion of the sar-
torial, the tailor brightened with a professional interest;
and he remarked,—

"Now but that, mademoiselle, that is conceivable."

"It is incontestable, my good Pierre. Nor is there
anybody among them able to repair, or even so much
as to patch up, the tatters of these great-hearted and
free-handed hidalgos."

Pierre stroked his chin, saying,—

"You are perhaps right, Mademoiselle Margot."

"Conceive then, my dear friend, of the joy, the
acclamation, and even the modest opulence, which, at
Fort Caroline, would attend the arrival of the only civilized tailor in North America."

"That is quite certainly true," replied Pierre; "and
I shall feel justified in demanding from these ragged
Romanists a double price for my labors."

Thus speaking, he ran down into the open
meadow; and as he approached the fort, he swaggered
with a fine sense of his unique distinction in a large
continent, even until he had got to the rear gate of the
fort and a party of eleven Spaniards came out of it.
They ran with shouts of joy toward Pierre the tailor;
they cut him into quite small pieces; and they laughingly carried back into the fort the dismembered frag-

ments of his body, upon the points of their spears and their pikes.

"Thus easily," remarked Don Luis, with a resigned shrug, "does abstract reason bog down among the crude jostle of mortal doings; and with such expedition does the common-sense of women obliterate the undesirable."

You saw that Margot was troubled by the obtuseness of all male creatures.

"Ah, but, my Prince, I advised him quite frankly for his own good; and I was really"—she pointed out—"right. The Spaniards did stand in deep need of a tailor. No rational person anywhere upon earth could have foreseen that they would reduce the one tailor at hand, not merely into incompetence, but horrible raw morsels. And yet"—she added, with a revival of her customary good nature—"it is pleasant to feel that, after all, he has won the crown of martyrdom; and I grant you that to be rid of dear poor Pierre is a convenience."

"For you to be making out of this imbecile an angel," Don Luis protested, "was not wholly kindly toward Heaven. Yet love has very little to do with ethics. I also am not sorry that we two are alone."

And he laughed.

But she did not laugh. She struggled, instead, never so slightly, in the fond embrace of Don Luis, looking up at him with an air of mixed meekness and reproach.

"I have become," she lamented, "as pliant to your

will as is the tender twig to the hand of the gardener. That is not as it should be; for I feel that your intentions threaten the inestimable gem of maidenhood. Your Highness, have my welling tears no eloquence to disarm your improper purpose?"

"Mademoiselle, their gentle sprinkling does but invigorate the buds of my adoration."

"Why, then, my Prince, I have not any choice except to entrust my imperilled virtue to the will of Heaven and"—she added, sighing resignedly—"to you."

With that, the blonde head of Margot went backward to rest and nestle upon his stalwart shoulder; her eyes closed; but her lips parted, and her lips seemed to grope upward, somewhat in the fashion of a hungry fish, as his mind noted in the same instant that his senses glowed, and his body appeared to melt into the girl's soft body, fusingly, and his mind ceased to notice anything whatever with its customary acuteness. They went into the dusky, all-hiding woods without speaking.

★ 25 ★

INASMUCH as the Prince of Ajacan came out of the forest, upon its eastern outskirts, without Margot, it followed that his Highness approached the Atlantic, near Ponte Vedra Beach, with the fluent proud loneliness of a leopard. Nor was his fair-haired French companion ever again seen alive in that part of Florida, or for that matter—as the Spaniards remarked afterward, with an unkindly pointedness—anywhere else.

"I regret, in some respects, the abrupt departure of Margot from out of my life," Don Luis spoke, with reflection, as he paused to wash clean his hands, and after that, his face, at the first creek he found.

"Yet," answered Reflection—for so very great and lively were the powers of fancy which the Prince possessed that by them Reflection appears to have been personified—"yet the emotion which you entertained toward this nimble and loquacious gentlewoman was a passing infatuation rather than love."

"Infatuation is a fine stimulant; and in youth it is a delectable playfellow," says Don Luis.

"Even so," returned Reflection, "infatuation is a

fierce and reckless fire, which consumes itself, if only you grant it enough time."

"Perhaps, like a great many other dull truisms, that is true," said Don Luis.

"The love which lasts," Reflection continued—as this praiseworthy attribute turned away from effete grieving to the irrational, fine altitudes of moralizing— "must display in its nature something more clearly uncorrupted than is mere physical attraction, no matter how ardent may be that attraction. Love needs to beget reverence, and faith, and congeniality."

"And in brief, just such noble sentiments as I trust always to entertain, at a respectful distance, toward my own dear wife Leota," Don Luis said, impressed by the coincidence.

"You perceive, my Prince, that you can remember your wife's exact name quite clearly, even when she is far away. Such nominal fidelity is striking," Reflection pointed out. "It attests the unbreakable strength of marriage ties among properly reared persons. Now, one does not like to speak ill of the departed," Reflection resumed. "Yet this Margot had aroused in you, after all, not any one of the high-minded emotions which we have but lately enumerated. Her appeal was made upon lower planes; and while your body responded to her enticements, your mind stayed deaf to the admonitions which were being shouted by your prudence, applauded by your intelligence, and re-echoed—how very unavail-ingly!—by your conscience."

"Still—" said the Prince, a little resentfully, be-cause he had been led by Christian instructors to enter-tain respect for his conscience.

"Margot," said Reflection, with unrelenting stern-ness, "was not in touch with the more lofty side of your nature. Margot had spent far too many nights with miscellaneous males for her to be restrained, content-edly, by the more rigid moral code to which you have been accustomed by your divine dear father in Ajacan."

The Prince said, more and yet more impressed by the wisdom of Reflection:

"Her standards, in short, were not my standards. Her standards were"—he uttered with reluctance the condemning word— "un-American."

"That is it, precisely," said Reflection. "The dis-crepancy between your fine sturdy ideals and the com-paratively lax tenets of the more frivolous French would have led to misunderstandings, perhaps even to squabbles. You, my poor Prince, do not like squabbles; and so, by-and-by, when you found you were living in open iniquity with a woman of whom you had grown tired, your conscience would have begun to trouble you remorselessly. The iron would perhaps have entered into your soul. You might well have come to curse the mo-ment when you permitted the susceptibility of an inex-perienced young werrowance to allure you downward into the shallow pleasures, the too shrill recriminations, and the considerable household expenses, of an immoral alliance."

"I would then," said the Prince intrepidly, "have felt it my duty, in behalf of my better nature, to end that alliance. Nor would the son of Quetzal—you must let me assure you, O too prudent Reflection,—have hesitated in performing his duty."

Reflection replied shruggingly: "Yet, in modern conditions, an impetuous and candid murder, even in the cause of continence, is but too apt to evoke legal attention. You have most happily escaped, it may be, from a great many forensic sophistries now that here, in these quiet woods, you and this glib French girl have parted—forever and with thoroughness—without implicating the police. And time, for the rest, time is the one cure for your transient sense of regret over a transaction which, in this clear-cut manner, logic has compelled us to acclaim as being all for the best."

"Very well, then!" says Don Luis de Velasco. "You are no doubt right; and I shall grant to time a fair chance of completing its healthful work."

Thus reasonably consoled by Reflection, the Prince of Ajacan continued to stroll southward, twirling his queer cane, as he approached St. Augustine. He was, you see, an American.

★ 26 ★

I PAUSE merely to remark that—so incessant are the malignancies which follow after every person of distinction, like ink-colored curs yelping about heroic heels as the buskined great progress with stateliness adown the highway of fame—reports were spread afterward, rather widely, by Spanish scandal-mongers and by historians so-called, that Don Luis de Velasco had murdered Margot. The scene of his supposed *crime passionnel* is still designated, in Duval County, Florida, about three and a half miles southwest of Mayport.

Yet in point of fact—as one tells the tale in Don Luis' native home, which is now the Northern Neck of Virginia—the Prince had quitted Margot in the forest because in the forest they encountered René de Laudonnière.

The unfortunate French captain—who by this time retained not even his nightshirt—was hiding in this forest, breast-deep in a creek, along with three other Protestants whose apparel was no less absentaneous. His companions in unease and nakedness (so very exact is the Virginian version) were: Élie des Planques, a native of Belgium; a man named François la Crête, from Rouen; and an Englishman, called George Smith, whom Captain John Hawkins had left at Fort Caroline, to die there, in relative comfort, of the scurvy. Young Smith had so far cheated the expectations of his physicians as to survive alike their care, his physical disorder, and a massacre; and these four Protestants only, so the tale says, had managed thus far to evade the patriotic destructiveness of Menéndez.

Very well, then! with an obliging promptness such as befitted a person of honor, the Prince of Ajacan restored to Laudonnière, who appeared in sad want of nursing, his nurse. The Prince himself had not any personal need of her service, now that his gallant fancies had been gratified. And that was all, so far as the affair involved Don Luis.

Yet that was not quite all as concerns Margot, it is said in the Northern Neck, because, no great while later, one of the two French galleons which had not been wrecked by Our Lady of Utrera came into sight of the five lost Lutherans. They signalled with Margot's last bit of underwear; and were taken aboard. Laudonnière ordered the captain (who was called Maillard, though the tale does not mention his Christian name) to return at once toward France; and this ship, the *Grayhound*, set sail. Foul weather drove the galleon into Swansea Bay, in South Wales, whence Laudonnière went with his nurse to London, and there got help from M. de Foix, the French ambassador.

Laudonnière was in Paris some while before January, explaining as he best might, to Coligny, how the Reformed Religion had been robbed of a continent by a hurricane. Laudonnière, in fact, gave over the rest of his mortal life, as well as a rather long book, to this awkward task. But Margot stayed on, in England, in Lincolnshire, because she found that Don Luis had left with her a souvenir of their stay in the Floridian forest so remarkably crescent that in order to keep safe her virtue she had need to marry George Smith. This perfidious young Englishman had been so unprincipled as to take advantage of the girl's innocence upon several occasions. Inasmuch as their first son was not born, however, until a good nine, or as some say, ten days after their wedding, everything passed off without any shock to the proprieties.

The child was christened John. It is reported that he inherited the imaginative faculties of Don Luis. It is said also that, after reaching manhood, he adventured among the Turks and, still later, came into Virginia. Many go to the extent of believing that Smith Island, just off the tip of the Northern Neck, where the lighthouse now stands, was so called in honor of this same Captain Smith.

All this account, you will notice, is painstakingly circumstantial. Its complete accuracy as to the names of everybody concerned (except only, to be sure, the first name of Captain Maillard) ought, in itself—for any open-minded student of American history—to dispel the unpleasing odium of murder such as vague, biassed, unauthentic Spanish gossip has imputed to Don Luis de Velasco, upon this special occasion.

★ 27 ★

AT ST. AUGUSTINE, Menéndez was embracing his god-son with affection.

"You arrive in good time, my dear Luis, from I shall not ask you what sylvan iniquities. I say to you instead that Our Lady of Utrera, so great is the bounty of her continuing favor—"

—Whereupon Don Luis de Velasco cleared his throat; and the Adelantado asked,—

"What was it that you said, Luis, as to the unquestioned kindness of our Heavenly advocate?"

"I observed 'Ahem!' Pedro; and my reasons were bronchial."

"No doubt," the Adelantado agreed. "At all events, our revered Lady of Consolation, by the miraculous great storm which she sent forth to protect Spain—"

He paused here, as if to await comment. Don Luis, still affably attendant, said nothing.

"Our Lady of Utrera has seen to it," Menéndez continued—with the alert cold smile which reminded you of a brisk day in December—"that Jean Ribaut himself, along with some two hundred of his men, has been washed ashore upon an island to the south of the

River of Dolphins. They are no more able to cross this river than they are able to reach the mainland. So they live there, as yet, upon a parched naked sand bank. They have saved from shipwreck their money and their arms, but no more."

"What more than a sufficiency of murderous weapons and a well-filled purse, Pedro, could a fair-minded Christian be asking of Heaven?"

"Food, my dear son: for they begin to find ducats and gunpowder indigestible; nor can they very well float across to the mainland upon their war banners. So these Lutherans remain stranded there, in constant dread of the Indians—and it may be with some apprehensions as to Pedro Menéndez," the Adelantado conceded with that wintry and rigid smile to which Don Luis had not ever become accustomed. "They feed by ordinary upon roots and grasses; the two hundred of them feast now and then upon a half-dozen oysters; for the French heretics cannot get any other food."

"It would be a pity, by the crude code of my demon father—whom the more delicate refinements of civilization have left untouched," says Don Luis, apologetically— "to let helpless persons starve. Yet these same Frenchmen thought otherwise, about the women and children of Seloy; nor as to your Spanish standards, in such dietary matters, am I a judge."

"No honest Catholic would ever permit a misfortune of this long-drawn sort to disfigure the death of a

heretic," Menéndez assured his adopted son,— "even
if that dear Jean and I had not squandered together, in
and about the waters and the worse jails of the Mediterranean, so many happy hours of our boyhood, when
both of us were merry young pirates."

Taking with him two small boats well laden with
provisions, and with about fifty or, as some say, three-
score soldiers, the Adelantado went down that inlet of
the ocean which we now call the Matanzas River, to
where it enters the main body of the Atlantic. He disembarked there, upon Anastasia Island, to the north
side of the inlet. On the south bank the French, because
of their need either to reach the mainland or to die, were
attempting to build a raft out of scrub palmettos, since
they had not any timber more sturdy. When they perceived the Spaniards, then this shipwrecked army
sounded an alarm, and they unfurled the royal standard
of France. They played their fifes. They beat their
drums in Gallic gay defiance.

To this, Menéndez replied unanswerably. He
ordered that dinner should be served to his followers.
The quiet Spaniards sat down upon the beach. They ate
and drank, very heartily, in full view of the starving
French.

—Whereupon, since human nature and hunger incline now and then to deviate from the heroic, the

French raised a white flag. A canoe was sent across to them. Through its agency, Captain General Jean Ribaut, with eight of his officers, was fetched over to Anastasia Island. Ribaut (whom report called the Invincible) brought with him his two royal standards, his two field banners, and the great seal given to him by the King of France with which to stamp edicts and titles as the Governor of Florida; all which derisive, shining superfluities the French Governor now laid down at the feet of the Spanish Governor.

"My people accept our defeat," says Ribaut, "and I come to discuss the terms of surrender."

"The sight of you is always welcome, my dear Jean," replied Menéndez, embracing the friend of his boyhood. "I rejoice doubly that today you should arrive in good time for dinner."

"So do I," said starved Ribaut.

The Adelantado entertained his French visitors, somewhat handsomely, with food and sound wine and sweetmeats. The French officers and the Spanish officers chatted, and they drank to one another's health, amicably, and in noble phrases, since, for the well-bred, the possible need of a guest and his host to be killing each other a bit later in the day was not thought to be a check to politeness. Only after everybody had finished with the dessert did a replete and amiably tipsy Ribaut recur to the hard estate of the French. Stroking his great bushy beard, he belched comfortably; and explained that as a ransom for his party the invincible Ribaut could offer 100,000 ducats.

"High God! but the amount is huge!" says Menéndez with blunt candor, "and never in my life had I hoped to get so much money. Yet, no!" he concluded, after an instant of reflection. "No: it would not be right of me, my good Jean, to accept so very much money for the glad privilege of helping you to escape from destruction."

"For the honor of France, I must rate at its proper value the person of a French general," returned monumental Ribaut. "So, if but to humor my pride, you will have to accept an amount not by one half-sou less; and now, as I take it, the affair is concluded, my dear friend."

"Not utterly, my dear friend," said Menéndez; "for the affair is intricate. Why, but surely, Jean, you perceive my awkward position! I have with me only a few soldiers. Should I assist your fine sturdy fighting-men—who are well armed, and who outnumber my poor knaves at least four to one—should I help your people, I repeat, to cross over the inlet, why, then you can easily kill us all without trouble."

Inasmuch as this had been Ribaut's exact plan, he seemed properly shocked at the notion of any such infamy; and became still more dignified.

"We will yield up our arms," said Ribaut, in hurt

cold tones of reproach, "since you cannot trust to my word of honor."

"My good Jean!"—Menéndez was horrified—"but what sort of gross idiot anywhere would distrust your word of honor! The sole trouble is that before today you have passed your word of honor to kill every one of us Spanish swine and to hang me at the yardarm of my own ship."

"We were drinking, Pedro—"

"*In vino veritas*," returned Menéndez; "and your conscience is famous for its integrity. Your conscience, I am certain, would point out to you, when once my poor Spanish swine and your splendid Frenchmen were standing here, one to four, that your first oath remained binding. You perceive, Jean, that I appreciate the unequalled delicacy of your conscience, in common with all your many other superb traits."

"I perceive only, Pedro, that it is not well for you to mock me."

"How do I mock you, Jean, when I recall the fact that St. Augustine is five leagues to the north of us? I do not see how my fifty Spanish swine"—Menéndez held to the phrase caressingly—"could dare to march that distance with two hundred high-tempered, so splendid, and so valiant French prisoners. The attempt is out of reason. It follows, my friend, that I have to face very sadly the conclusion it would be more wise for me to leave here your gallant party, either to starve or to be massacred by the Seloy Indians—who are still irritated, I regret to inform you, by the loss of their wives and children. Yes; it is better for me not to intermeddle. It is the plain part of piety for me to let all this affair be settled, between you and the Indians and hunger, just as Heaven may see fit to direct."

But against this sort of piety, Ribaut protested by becoming rather more pious, and far more lively, than Menéndez. One should remember, Ribaut pointed out, that Heaven had already in hand a vast deal of business. One should be considerate about infringing upon Heaven's time or attention unnecessarily. There was no call to be troubling Heaven about a matter so simple. Let his men be fettered, after giving up all their arms; then you Spaniards will have no great cause to be afraid of us, the Invincible remarked curtly; and his men could march to St. Augustine well enough with their hands tied behind them.

Menéndez said, in unconcealed admiration: "Very certainly, but you French are quick-witted. Yes, Jean: you have found out-of-hand a solution for my difficulty. You may now surrender, upon these conditions, which I was too stupid to contrive."

With that settled, the French officers were restored to their men upon the other side of the swift deep inlet. The Spaniards who went over with them brought back the boat laden with arquebuses and bags of powder and pistols, with swords and pikes and targets, with helmets and with breast pieces. The Spaniards returned for yet another boat-load of weapons.

Now the French were disarmed utterly.

—Whereupon twenty Spaniards crossed in the boat and fetched back with them ten Frenchmen. This was repeated until all the French had been brought over.

As each party landed, the ten Frenchmen in this party were fed liberally. Their hands were then tied behind their backs, with the cords of their arquebuses, and the cords were knotted together so that the ten men could march, with five in the front rank and five in the second, with fair comfort.

Ribaut came over the inlet in the last boatload. He held out his hands to be tied.

And yet again, Menéndez was cheerfully horrified.

"But, you absurd fellow! one does not truss up, like a chicken made ready for the oven, a general of France. You represent here King Charles, just as I represent King Philip: since the two are brothers-in-law, let us regard this little imbroglio as a friendly family squabble. No, my dear Jean; I request only that you rest here, and make yourself comfortable, while I complete our arrangements."

Thus speaking, Don Pedro walked up the beach followed by a dozen of his soldiers, and he so passed beyond a large sand dune. In his right hand he carried his jineta—which, as has been said, was the symbol of his office as Governor, in the form of a gilded lance with a red tassel attached to it.

With the point of this lance he drew, in the white fine sand of Florida, an unwavering, very long line across the beach. He returned alone to his troops, and he gave the order to advance. All obeyed him, and the march northward, toward St. Augustine, was begun in this way.

For most of the party this marching proved not to be tiresome, inasmuch as no sooner did the first company of ten fettered Frenchmen walk beyond the sand dune, and arrive at the line in the sand, than the soldiers whom the Adelantado had stationed there killed the ten Frenchmen. They then killed the next ten Frenchmen as soon as these came around the sand dune and so got within arm's reach. These twelve loyal Spaniards continued to do this until, under the hot sun of Florida, they were well-nigh exhausted, and the knowledge that through this so tedious labor they were serving Heaven acceptably, and obeying the declared will of Heaven's Vicar upon earth, remained their sole sustenance.

The entire affair was managed with such neatness that hardly any one of the Lutherans was made aware of his danger before he became a corpse; nor did the sound of their brief gurgling protestations at all annoy Menéndez and Ribaut, where the two old friends sat, in half-drowsy sun-steeped ease, beside the bright languid ocean, talking lazily over the high doings, and the happy pranks, and the dear comrades, of their shared youth.

This was not, of course, an impressive massacre, as go our modern standards, which incline to esteem the more forthright exercises of patriotism in a strict ratio to the number of dead bodies produced. Yet in its tact and restraint and ease, and in its polite consideration for the persons who were being murdered—and in brief, for its complete if slender adroitness—this massacre, to the attentive judgment of Don Luis de Velasco, appeared to excel.

His Highness misliked crude cruelty. In enormity the Prince preferred, as set against mere enormousness, the neat handiwork of finesse. So he watched all with admiring approval, while the French went to their death without having their emotions in any way harrowed; and he applauded the kindness with which from Jean Ribaut was being kept the distasteful knowledge that, in addition to having lost for France one half of this world, the Invincible was now losing all his soldiers, ten at each trucidation.

Then by-and-by, when the last fettered troop of Frenchmen had trudged sturdily out of Menéndez' sight and out of human living, Don Pedro said,—

"The time has come, Jean, for your departure also."

"And do you believe me," Ribaut answered comfortably, as he arose from the sand, "that I delight in the prospect of sleeping under cover tonight, my dear Pedro, even though it must be in one of your dungeons at St. Augustine."

"No, Jean. You will sleep soundly tonight; you will sleep under as good covering as most emperors get in the end; but you will not sleep at St. Augustine, nor will you ever reach St. Augustine."

"So," says Ribaut, without any emotion. "What have you done, you quiet lean liar, what have you done with my soldiers?"

Menéndez told him.

Ribaut said: "It was well planned. You have outwitted me handsomely. I do not complain. I demand that, as a general of France, I may die at the head of my troops."

"That is granted you freely, my brave Jean. Indeed, I would that it were permitted me to let you continue living, as the main glory of France and of your wicked religion; but you are too skilled a mariner and too fine a fighter for me to consider any such risky self-indulgence."

"So that, in brief, I must die because of my so numerous virtues," Ribaut said. "The tribute is gratifying."

The two men shook hands; and the Spanish Governor gave to the doomed French Governor that jineta which was the symbol of Menéndez' office.

"I name you my lieutenant," he explained, "inasmuch as this small toy will empower you to give orders in my stead."

"The gesture is magnificent. It is worthy of us, Pedro. You will not complain," said the Frenchman, "as to my orders."

Ribaut went on alone. He passed behind the sand dune, to where all his soldiers lay murdered. When he had seen them, he removed his red felt hat, and he bowed ceremoniously. Then came to him Solís de Merás and San Vincente, to whom he displayed the jineta.

"It is the will of your general and of my exceedingly good friend," said Ribaut, "that you do not kill me until I have advanced beyond the furthermost of these betrayed brave dead."

Vincente said: "It is right that captains should obey their generals. That is a fine hat you have there."

"It was made in Lyons," said Ribaut, smiling. "Our French felts are famous. Observe the light weight of it. And since I have no more need of it, monsieur, I would be honored should you consent to retain this hat as a souvenir of our meeting."

"I accept it with all gratitude," said Vincente, "for you are a generous enemy."

They went forward a little way, along the seashore, treading over and among the dead Frenchmen. Then Ribaut paused.

He looked seaward; and he looked, therefore, it so happened, at a small seagull, which, at this instant, came out of the north. The bird, in its leisured progress, flew near the water; and the gull wheeled about, daintily, under the west wind's pressure. The gull's feet hung beneath it, very pink. It dropped weightlessly upon the surface of the water. It stretched, and it put backward, and it raised again, and it yet later refolded, painstakingly, its dark gray wings, as if the task of adjusting these wings about its body involved a close and exact fitting. It wrenched its head, quite as if the creature were sneezing.

Ribaut wondered if it were indeed possible for a seagull to take cold . . .

Now the wind caught the bird's tip-tilted tail; and so whisked the gull sidewise. The gray gull bobbed up and down on the blue water, tranquilly, with a sort of reflective nonchalance, and with a restrained air of finding itself, if not cordially yet to a fair degree, interested in what these quaint human beings, within but a few yards of a rational seabird, might be doing next?

What, indeed? thought Ribaut. At any rate, this disengaged cool scrutiny would have to be the last memory of the first French Governor of Florida. And it was, perhaps, not tactful, in a representative of the polite French nation, to be keeping his assassins waiting so long, in this hot sun . . .

"The Invincible dies here," said Ribaut.

Vincente, upon hearing this, whipped out his dagger, and he gave Jean Ribaut a blow in the belly, with a twisting motion which ripped out the intestines. At the same instant Solís de Merás struck the Invincible, through the breast, with a pike. After that, they cut off his head.

It was Vincente, the story says, who carried back, to be salted and stuck up over the main gate of the fort at St. Augustine, this trophy,—holding it by Jean Ribaut's thick beard, and wearing upon his own head Ribaut's fine hat. By good luck, it fitted to perfection.

★ 28 ★

IN THIS MANNER, so the tale says, did the illustrious
Señor Pedro Menéndez de Avilés put an end to any
French doings, either for good or wickedness, in his
King's Province of Florida, by leaving in this province
not any Frenchman alive. It was thus that the great
Adelantado made safe the dominion of the King of
Spain throughout all that country which now consti-
tutes the United States of America; that Pedro Menéndez established the city of St. Augustine to be the main
glory, in our Western Hemisphere, of the tourist trade;
and that through a stern, bland murderous service of
despotism, he raised up the first enduring stronghold
of democracy. He founded, in short, beside the Matanzas River, our civilization.

Here is rich epic matter. It is matter such as might
well justify the high and unhumorous manner of most
epics, even at a risk of that dullness which is admired
only by the awarders of Pulitzer Prizes. Do you tell,
O Muse,—one is tempted to hortate,—do you tell of
the low-lying, green-and-gray city which, a great long
while before the intrepid colonists of Jamestown had
begun their heroic hopeless struggle against mosquitoes

and malaria, and when the inhuman virtues of our Pilgrim Fathers remained a myth as yet uninvented, Pedro Menéndez brought into being. Of that city's very many glories, do you speak, O bright-haired honey-tongued Calliope, with a lively eloquence.

Speak of St. Augustine's half-score of industrial plants; of its two banks, which afford to depositors every sort of modern facility; of its ten office buildings; and of its fine pair of hospitals, both the East Coast and the Flagler, each having sixty-five beds, and each duly approved by the Medical College of Surgery. Tell next of this same city's eight public parks; of its wholly up-to-date yacht pier; of its million dollar drawbridge; and do you make mention of the city's nine schools and colleges. Relate yet furthermore that in the commodious and convenient Civic Center Building of St. Augustine assemble, upon the Mondays, the Tuesdays, and the Wednesdays of each week (respectively) the Rotary Club, the Kiwanis, and the Business & Professional Club, to deliberate high civic matters. The offices of the St. Augustine and St. Johns County Chamber of Commerce are located in the same building.

Let us then speak of the fine hotels and lodging houses (some eighty-five in number), of the two newspapers, of the four cemeteries, of the health-giving annual mean temperature (reliably estimated at 69.7), and of the three golf-courses, which grace St. Augustine; and of its leading industries, which (in addition to the General Executive Offices and the Main Repair Shops of the Florida East Coast Railway) include many varieties of label, publication and commercial printing, as well as vegetable and shrimp canneries, two cigar manufactories, ten Beauty Parlors, seven handsome Funeral Homes, one very small book shop, and an uncalculated number of both privately owned and incorporated fisheries that now operate in coastal waters more than three hundred trawlers: for in all these matters may mankind behold the ripe harvesting of Menéndez' labors.

Yet not at St. Augustine alone is the great commander's work made plain thus impressively, but in hundreds upon hundreds of junior cities, all which display the afore-mentioned, or at least similar splendors. And Menéndez evoked these splendors. Through the loving-kindness of a hurricane, it was Pedro Menéndez —instead of, as calm weather would have decreed it, Jean Ribaut the Invincible—who implanted, lastingly, in the north parts of America, the civilization of Europe, from out of which, under the unwonted stimulus of an occidental climate, have sprouted a number of unexpected offshoots.

Their value, in this special place, one may not debate with profit; yet nobody, one is certain, could regard the results of Menéndez' life-work with a more lively disfavor than would Menéndez. Charity compels our hope that for the illustrious Señor, in Purgatory,

the surrounding discomforts were not ever made in-
tolerable by any knowledge of his earthly errors' dé-
nouement, when, upon a far-away planet, he founded
a republic's culture, to exemplify everything he most
hated.

It here occurs to me that my remarks digress. I
had meant merely to remind you it was at St. Augustine
that, in our own land, Europeans first assumed, for all
time, the white man's racial duty of teaching, to the
inhabitants of a backward country such as one might
plunder with profit, how to lie and to steal and to
murder with the abettance of better principles, such
as yet keep their vogue,—when beside the Matanzas
River, bigotry begot upon greed that amiable, if somewhat standardized, way of living which has become, for
all mankind, the sole hope of mankind's final freedom
from too much greed and bigotry. Here was our civilization founded, in just the manner about which I have
told you, by Don Pedro Menéndez de Avilés, in order
that the Hapsburgs might continue to rule over both
hemispheres forever, and that Spanish cut-throats
might make plain the divine infallibility of a Spanish
Borgia's bull.

⋆ 29 ⋆

I NOW TELL you that when the French were got rid of, then Menéndez went into Caloosa. Though it was too late to save his son, he yet meant to rescue the white captives about whom Don Luis had brought tidings. Menéndez went with I do not know just how many ships. I do know that he left behind him one ship only; and we know that Don Luis stayed at St. Augustine, because the tale tells about what the Prince of Ajacan did there.

You must understand that for the while Don Pedro was away, he had placed a Lieutenant-Governor (who, some say, was his own brother, Bartolomé Menéndez) in command of the new city; that food ran short in St. Augustine; and that one day the colonists broke out into a mutiny. Led by a captain named Francisco de Recalde and by two priests, the Licentiate Pedro de Rueda and Father Anton de Campos, they seized and confined with ropes the Lieutenant-Governor, the camp master, the magistrates, the municipal councillors, the keeper of supplies, along with yet other officers; and left them, thus tied up, in the fort of San Juan de Pinos. The rebels seized also the only ship in the Matanzas River, and they made ready to leave Florida, so that they might become pirates.

Inasmuch as the ship was too small to convey more than a hundred and thirty of them toward waters better suited for buccaneering, Father Rueda said they would have to draw lots to decide which of them could have the bright rewards of a malefactor and which were the uncriminal persons that were going to stay behind at St. Augustine and starve patriotically. After their lottery had begun, in the Plaza, Don Luis de Velasco untied the camp master and eight other officers, arming each of them with an arquebus. He himself got an axe; and coming up from behind, he struck down first Father Rueda, and then Captain Recalde, stunning both of them. Father Campos surrendered unhurt.

The Prince of Ajacan then addressed the mutineers with a brief oration which appealed to the better side of their nature, and after soaring with a few well-chosen words into the patriotic, so far descended as to give pause to the most ruthless through a précis of the evil-doer's rewards, both on the gallows and before the throne of Eternal Justice. Without a dissenting voice, the repentant rebels decided to abandon their wicked project, now that they had only case knives with which to defend themselves against the levelled arquebuses of the nine officers, so very moving was the eloquence of the Prince of Ajacan.

I must here record that this important address

was delivered in the Plaza of St. Augustine, about half way between the present sites of the Matanzas Moving Picture Theatre and the main offices of the Florida Power & Light Company, with Don Luis de Velasco standing not far from where the monument to the Confederate Soldiers now stands. The mutineers the Prince forced to conduct a new lottery, to decide which three of them should be hanged, upon the superb live-oak tree which yet thrives just in front of the Cathedral. This tree thus entered history a good while prior to making its début in art, inasmuch as the foliage of this tree, since it first served as a gallows, has been rearranged by artist after artist—so as to give you an unobstructed view of the Cathedral—in order that the result might serve as an exhibit, before the St. Augustine Arts Club, or in Aviles Street. Recalde and the two priests the Prince caused to be imprisoned, and in the cell of Campos he put a boy, to look after the needs of Campos, until Menéndez came back.

Don Pedro, upon his return, said all this was done handsomely. He embraced his godson, over and yet over again, now that in addition to getting Florida for Spain, Don Luis de Velasco had likewise attended to the preservation of St. Augustine. Nevertheless—Menéndez deplored—it was not proper to annoy a clergyman with an axe, even though the Licentiate Rueda had been planning to embark, uncanonically, upon the high seas, as a pirate.

"It may well bring you bad luck, my dear son," said the Adelantado; "still, Father Rueda has consented to forgive you—"

"That is most kind of the good Father, Pedro, after I have prevented him and his followers from destroying all your colony."

"—Upon condition," Menéndez continued, simply, "that I have him appointed as the town priest in Santo Domingo; and which one of us," Don Pedro added, "can escape bad luck nowadays?"

The question had its own special point. Menéndez had come back from Caloosa with a fine supply of maize and honey and hemp sandals, of chickens and meat and cattle, of wine and cassava and oil, so that there was now food for all and comfort for everybody except Menéndez. Menéndez had brought back, in addition to these necessaries, a wife.

★ *30* ★

Don Pedro had not intended to get married; nor, indeed, had any earlier event in a career not deficient in the perturbing ever quite so much horrified him. I must here recall to you that his first wife was still alive in Spain, so that this second marriage, being bigamous, was a mortal sin which might very well involve him, after death, in much punishment.

It was a most awkward business, he told Don Luis. This marriage—as the involuntary participant therein granted, with a frankness such as among more tactful husbands is rare—had been achieved against every one of the Adelantado's desires.

How, then, had it come about? Well, he found that all the Christian captives except only twelve, no one of these being Lutherans, had been sacrificed to Toya of the Palms. The Cazique Carlos had received Don Pedro with all possible honor and many demonstrations of friendship; and after failing in five plots to kill him by treachery, inferred that this lean Spanish warrior must enjoy the peculiar favor of an especially efficient deity. So Carlos had offered, not merely to release his twelve Christian captives, but to turn Chris-

tian himself, along with all his tribe. Carlos required
only that the Adelantado should marry the Cazique's
sister Antonia; and in this way become the elder
brother of Carlos, so that Carlos might be as well protected as, through trial and error, he had found Don
Pedro to be protected, against the unscrupulous wiles
of assassins.

Yet it was Doña Antonia who suggested this common-sense solution, because her conscience remained
so profoundly bothered over her prolonged spinsterhood
as to induce sleepless nights even when she did not have
in bed a brisk companion. An Adelantado of Florida
—she had reasoned philosophically—was not, after all,
very much inferior to a king or a prince of some sort
when regarded as an hypnotic.

So she began to talk to Carlos. She continued to
talk to Carlos. And afterward, Antonia resumed talking to Carlos.

The result was that the Cazique, after four days
of being advised, quite frankly, for his own personal
good, by the untiring tongue of sisterly affection, took
refuge, as well as counsel, with the Shaman Hirrigua;
and after that, made to Menéndez the before-men-
tioned offer.

And this horrible offer seemed too good to be refused, Menéndez told Don Luis. At the price of a
mortal sin, it was a most profitable barter, as went
the proper service of Heaven. For anybody to have

declined to treat the Decalogue with irreverence, upon
this special occasion, would have cut off every hope
of delivering to Caloosa the glad message of the Gospel. A sound Catholic, Don Pedro estimated, ought to
be well willing to imperil his own salvation if before
the start of his flamy torments he could first rescue
twelve other Catholics from heathen bondage and impress into immediate practice of the True Faith every
one of their pagan jailers.

It followed that Don Pedro Menéndez de Avilés,
in defiance of civilized law and to the grim detriment
of his hopes as a Christian, did marry Doña Antonia;
and all the Caloosans were baptized.

Hundreds upon hundreds of these red rogues, including also his own son's murderer—the Adelantado
continued, with a flavor of fretfulness—he had thus
hauled up toward unmerited bliss, in the same instant
that, perhaps, he was locking tight the bright gates of
heaven against his own entrance. The notion—at first,
anyhow, Don Pedro amended—of having to live in
bigamy with a young woman whose virtue had not
even the lean merit of being doubtful, was far from
pleasant; at his age, such conduct seemed frivolous;
and moreover, it partook of insult to his first wife,
whom he continued to regard with sincere affection,
so nearly as he could remember Maria. He would have
to write, to Maria, in apology . . .

To all this, Don Luis de Velasco answered, "I observe, Pedro, that you describe your late excursion into bigamy as having been unpleasant 'at first, anyhow.' "

"And I," said Menéndez stiffly, "I have not the honor to understand you."

Yet the tale says that Doña Antonia had very well understood her husband. The first night after they were married she came with frightened meekness into the Adelantado's bedroom, wearing almost exactly the expression of a woman who is blushing. He then tried to get rid of her by saying that a knight of the Order of Santiago was forbidden to sleep with his wife until eight days after the wedding; and Don Pedro added, with as much gallantry as he could improvise, that he wished the eight days had gone by, because her person appeared very beautiful. She at once, without any false modesty, prepared to convert his theories as to her person into assured knowledge.

He replied by saying goodnight and opening the door into the hallway.

—Whereupon, so intense was Antonia's wonder that she searched the room everywhere, and she even looked under the bed, so the story says, to see what other woman this so unresponsive husband could be preferring to her. She was not used to this sort of cold continence in her bedroom, as she told him with friendly good humor.

"At all events," she added, "you will have to let me sleep over here somewhere, in a corner of our bridal bed; and I promise not to come near you. Comprehend, O most magnificent Señor, that if I do not spend at any rate this one night with you, my people will think we are not really married. My people will become angry. They will turn heathen again; all their souls will be damned; and for every one of these lost souls you will be responsible. I intend to avert from your conscience, my dear lord and husband, any such dreadful burden."

Thus speaking, she got into his bed; and for once in his life, Don Pedro became frightened. The young woman was entirely too logical; and besides that, she was perturbingly good-looking.

He rang for a servant, so prodigious became the rigid increase of his body's trouble and so unpraiseworthy became his desires. He caused this boy to bring into the bedchamber three beautiful embroidered silk chemises and a pair of silver-mounted mirrors and two necklaces, of pearls and of rubies. With such gifts did the appalled gray sea-dog try to redeem his imperilled virtue, and to keep safe his soul, by bribing Antonia to get out of his bed.

"But I stayed," she told Don Luis.

She smiled; and he too smiled, reminiscently, saying:

"I do not doubt your permanent attitude, Antonia. Nor do I question that some while before breakfast our good Pedro had forgotten the more stringent obligations of the most noble Order of Santiago."

"A loving wife does not ever discuss any intimate secrets of the nuptial chamber, my Prince," she replied, with a praiseworthy facsimile of embarrassment; "and even if my husband's conscience did begin to trouble him the next morning, that was just because no person of his age could well have expected to find the discharge of his duty toward the Holy Catholic Faith so highly agreeable. Yet Pedro"—the complacent wife of Don Pedro added—"has continued ever since then to be quite reasonable in the performing of his religious obligations."

"Yes, Antonia; for Pedro has believed it was his duty toward Heaven to risk winning for himself eternal torments, as an offset to having rid twelve strangers of discomfort. I cannot understand such nonsense," the Prince of Ajacan said half-frettedly. "I resent any such nonsense. My godfather's inhuman and over-holy simplicity arouses, in the same instant, a feeling of compassion, of doubt, and of inferiority. In brief"—Don Luis continued, with a shrug of aerial disconcern—"this zealot husband of yours, my dear Antonia, is that awe-inspiring oddity which one can but describe as an earnest-minded person. We are not at all earnest-minded persons, you and I; and because of his absurd intense convictions about everything upon earth, and in heaven also, neither you nor I will ever quite understand our Pedro Menéndez."

Thus lightly did Don Luis voice a fact which at this special moment seemed to him of no large importance. He changed his mind that same afternoon.

⋆ 31 ⋆

THIS AFTERNOON being clear and warm, the Adelantado was with his new wife, and with his godson, upon the river-bank east of the fort. They had dined there, all three together; afterward they sat over their wine, at long leisure, as Don Pedro preferred to do, because he disliked tippling or swigging. He did not, indeed, so much seem to drink his wine as to inhale the aroma of it; only now and then did he take a sip, which he swallowed, thoughtfully, with an air of reserved judgment as to the vintage.

Meanwhile, his speaking also had become thoughtful, for Don Pedro was telling Luis de Velasco that, now Caloosa had been converted to the True Faith, it appeared his next duty to provide for Ajacan a similar re-birth in religion.

"I plan, Luis, that you should go first with a few missionaries. The good Fathers, under God's protection and your protection, will subdue the fierce hearts of your people to the mild tenets of Christianity. I will come then, with enough soldiers and firearms to take care of their bodies; and after it may be a couple of battles, to fetch back Lord Philip's tribute from the twenty cities of Ajacan."

Concerning this enterprise Don Luis displayed no great enthusiasm, in the while that he said,—

"My people are well content under the rule of Quetzal."

"What has their contentment to do with our duty?" says Menéndez, in frank wonder. "The French Lutherans were well enough content here in Florida until Our Lady of Consolation, and you and I, Luis, had put an end to their impudent invasion of Lord Philip's property."

"In addition," said the Prince of Ajacan, "to rebuking—in, as I need not mention, a mild Christian spirit—the perverse religious notions with which these Huguenots, our misled brethren, were beginning to contaminate the West Indies."

"Yes," said Menéndez, levelly.

"—Even after the Holy Father himself had made a free gift of all America to my good cousin of Spain," Don Luis continued.

"That is true, Luis; yet it does not seem to me any reason for grinning."

"My dear friend, you mistake matters. I smile merely with derision, when I reflect how many unthinking people would say the King of Spain may have been dishonest beyond the flagrancy of most monarchs when he thus asked for what did not belong to him;

and the Holy Father tipsy, even beyond ordinary, when he gave away, out-of-hand, two continents which did not belong to him either."

You saw that Menéndez was troubled. He spoke now with the smiling indulgence which he did not ever deny to Don Luis, but the Adelantado spoke in reproof.

"These are ugly expressions, my son. No Christian gentleman, you must let me remind you, ought to speak about sacred matters with levity—"

"And for an excellent reason, Pedro, inasmuch as levity is an acid which can, and which does at once, tarnish everything except common-sense."

"—Nor can I hear these expressions," Menéndez went on, with a rather resolute continuance in quiet, "without recalling an occurrence which, because of my love for you, I have kept out of mind until to-day."

"Until to-day," Don Luis assented, "when I make bold to cross your desires. Until to-day, when yet again you become inspired by the more ennobling influences of patriotism and of a religion no less truculent."

"You are not speaking with your customary good sense, Luis. And yet—"

"There is some force, Pedro, in that 'and yet.' "

"To me, my son, the phrase appears simple."

"Still, Pedro, here are two monosyllables which begin to inflate you with moral indignation. I can see this superb virtue distilling out of you everywhither, like a spiritual sweat, now that you regard your son in the spirit after so very much the same manner that, upon Anastasia Island, you looked at the French pirates in their fetters."

"They were heretics, my son."

And Don Luis agreed to this, with a spurt of impatience, saying:

"Not at all inconveniently for the needs of Spanish patriotism, your prisoners did happen to be what Spain terms heretics; and upon such moral uplands you of course murdered them with a clear conscience. That is understandable; that was praiseworthy. Yet why, my lean grave godfather, even while your lips smile at me, do your eyes regard me just as freezingly as they did those lost Frenchmen?"

Menéndez did not answer at once. He sipped his wine without any hurry. He said:

"I do not like killing defenceless persons. When it is possible, I avoid it. Do you keep that in mind, Luis."

"It has always been with me a fixed rule," the Prince stated, "to treasure up your every utterance like a guiding star."

"I put Jean Ribaut and all the rest of them to the knife with unwillingness. I judged that outcome to be necessary."

"It was most highly necessary, Pedro, to the proper

service of the storm god of Sinai and of his Majesty the
King of Spain."

"Still, if you ask me, it was just his conscience,"
said Antonia, with the all-covering charity of a married
woman who discourses as to some special unreason in
her husband's behavior by which she herself is not in-
convenienced. "Pedro is rather wonderful about his
conscience. His conscience prevents him from getting
any real enjoyment out of his pleasures, so that I have
noticed he always puts out the light first, although I
do not mean what you think I mean. No such thought
had ever crossed my mind; and I quite wonder at you,
Luis. I meant only that his conscience always backs
him up, and it keeps him satisfied, when he is doing anything especially disagreeable. —Which is not at all what
you had in mind."

"And I still think it an excellent thing," Menéndez continued, "that Jean Ribaut is dead."

"Why, but of course, my darling,"—Antonia
prompted her husband, indulgently—"because this Ribaut and his people were Lutherans. They believed in
justification by faith, and in eating meat on Fridays,
and in letting everybody, even if he happened to be a
clergyman, marry the woman he was sleeping with usually, and in all sorts of wicked notions."

Said Menéndez: "For the heretic there can be but
one reward. It is death, Luis."

"And in bestowing that reward," Don Luis returned, "you were altogether generous to the French Huguenots, when you merely cut their throats, upon a broad, clean, comfortable sand beach, smooth as a ball-room floor. Even up to the last instant of their death agonies they could enjoy a superb view of the ocean, in the most invigorating and pleasant sort of weather—when it was really your business to have sent them into Cuba to be tortured, in a damp and insanitary cellar, by the Inquisition."

Menéndez said: "To deliver them to the Holy Office was not permitted me. My men were too few to escort so many prisoners."

"Still, Pedro, any captain less tender-hearted than you are would have burned them alive, at the very least."

"It would, perhaps, have been more strictly correct to have disposed of the French heretics at the stake," Menéndez agreed, fair-mindedly. "But at Matanzas, I must ask you to remember, I lacked fuel."

"Brute nature," the Prince lamented, "is not always considerate of the spiritual needs of mankind. I perceive your difficulty. You could not express your more intense religious convictions with the aid of mere sage-bushes and of small palmettos. In an emergency of this sort, a sound Christian requires sound timber."

Menéndez answered, "To-day, at St. Augustine, there is sound timber in plenty."

"Yes, Pedro; and you have not one heretic, you

have not even a Jew such as your Christ once was, to be made a burnt offering in the name of Christ. It seems ironic."

But the Adelantado appeared rather more optimistic than was his godson.

"Perhaps, even at St. Augustine, one might find a heretic," says the Adelantado. "I must remind you, Luis, that in Ajacan I learned something of your native language. My knowledge of it stays slight. Yet when I knelt upon the rear deck of the *San Andrés,* and you, standing beside me, prayed, it seemed to me that I understood your prayer."

The dark eyes of Don Luis had narrowed; in all other respects he remained care-free and genial beyond ordinary.

"Why, then, Pedro, you understood that I prayed for your escape from being hanged by the Frenchmen and for the salvation of your people."

"Yes," said Menéndez.

"You saw that my praying stirred up a quite useful hurricane, because of which, and because of which alone, you are yet living and now rule here in Florida."

"But no, Luis: for it was Our Lady of Utrera who preserved Spain in that moment of danger. Our escape, my dear son, was not due to any patron less wholesome —whom you, I begin to fear uneasily, may have evoked. Help came to us from Our Lady of Consolation. She endorsed, as was wholly proper for anyone in her paradisiac position, the Pope's blessing with a supernatural tempest. My own chaplain has assured me as to the fact. For this reason I am now weighing quite other facts."

"And what"—Don Luis refilled his glass, at infinite leisure—"what, my good friend, may these facts be?"

"The fact, my son, that you are the one person under whose protection a mission chapel could be established in your native Ajacan with hopefulness. The fact that you refuse to aid Mother Church in the conversion of Ajacan. The fact that you hold back in aid to my master, and to your own over-lord, the King of Spain, in the recovery of a province which belongs to him."

"Just so," said Don Luis, selecting an almond, and munching at it. "You have not any choice, as a true Spaniard, except to interpret this brace of refusals in the sulphurous light of my having prayed for you— as you now consider, with frost-nipped gratitude—injudiciously."

"I have not said that," returned Menéndez—"as yet. I prefer to remember that my knowledge of your native tongue is limited. I prefer to remember that my fondness for you"—his voice changed—"is very nearly unlimited. And so I did not understand your praying—perhaps. I hope I did not."

The Prince said, in a brisk small flare of irritation: "Put it that I have preserved you from being hanged by the Frenchmen, Pedro Menéndez, through a tempest brought about with wild heathen arts; that I have made you a present of Fort Caroline by indulging in betrayal; that I have saved your town of St. Augustine through an act of sacrilege in splitting open the head of a priest; and that, in brief, it is I, the devil's son, who in such unholy ways—rather than you, God's most immaculate champion, through your pious massacres—who have got Florida for Spain. Very well, then! your staunch patriotism, I take it, would accept Florida even though it were Satan, in his own lame fiery person, who made the gift?"

"If a good patriot found the Devil to be serving his country," says Menéndez, "he would not quarrel with his fellow laborer at that special moment. He would wait for some later occasion."

"Yes: just as you have waited, Pedro Menéndez! Florida does not content the vast tapeworm hunger of your people. So if I do not now get Ajacan also for you, why, then, that so busy conscience of yours will force you to relinquish me to the improving tutelage of Mother Church, in Cuba yonder, by way of the Inquisition. Is that your meaning, Pedro Menéndez?"

"My meaning," Don Pedro returned equably, "is merely that this matter is delicate. It is a matter in which my judgment has become confused by my love for you. It is a matter in which the Church alone is infallible, where I cannot pretend to be unbiased. Hah, but surely, you perceive my awkward position."

"It occurs to me, Pedro, that is just what you said to Jean Ribaut immediately before you had his head struck off."

"Yes," Menéndez agreed; "why, but yes! so it was."

With that, the Adelantado took yet another very small sip of wine; and he sat waiting. His face was grave; it in some degree was troubled; but his lean features stayed friendly.

So then! it has reached me at last, the Prince of Ajacan reflected—that moment which I foresaw upon the deck of the *San Andrés*. To serve Spain and that strange brutal God of Spain, comes first with Pedro. He is now about that service, here over our shared wine, at this quiet instant; and whatever tools he employs are made honorable by the aim in view, so that he can threaten me with torture and death, thus affably, with a conscience like crystal. Such is our Pedro's holy simplicity . . .

But aloud the Prince said, in tones of warm and gracious condolence:

"Your position wrings my heart, Pedro, now that I completely see your position. Not for worlds, not for a half-dozen solar systems, would I permit a continuance of your awkward position. No, my dear friend! for it is not proper, it would not be friendly, that I should put you to the discomfort of having me dissected and questioned and fricasseed by the Inquisition."

Don Luis was now talking about affairs so unpleasant that Antonia bestirred herself. She responded to the insistent and vivid need which is felt by all tactful women, when men have begun to prattle about their male ideas of the important, to speak with a commensurate but a more cheerful lack of coherence.

"That notion of having you turned over to the Inquisition," Antonia confided, to her princely guest, "is just his conscience."

Her fine eyes stayed cool and considerate.

"Not for one single moment," Antonia discoursed at large, "would I allow it. Still, Pedro's conscience really does keep on suggesting the most extraordinary doings. These figs are quite excellent. It made him marry me, for instance. Why, but, Luis, I thought you liked figs; they are good for the stomach; and at any rate, Pedro does not seem to have any such proper control over his higher emotions as keeps you and me so much more dependable people to have about the house. He suffers, just as you said this morning, from having too many convictions; and they upset him every now and then into being high-minded, all over the place, in a way which very few other women, I am certain"— Antonia concluded, with a blending of resignation, of reproach, and of modesty—"could ever put up with."

Yet her inconsequence was not the least bit inconsequential, the Prince saw. Instead, this cool-headed, kindly, and babbling Antonia was intent merely to assist a couple of male hobbledehoys to pass courteously over an ugly moment.

Don Luis de Velasco continued equably, "So I will go into Ajacan with your priests, and I will take proper care of them."

Menéndez said only, with contentment, "My son, I knew that you would not fail me."

"No, Pedro," the Prince responded; "for you have taught me that a well-bred person will do, at all times, and at no matter what costs in the way of double-dealing, that which aids the welfare of his own land. I accept your teaching."

"And for the rest"—the Adelantado cleared his throat—"you must comprehend, Luis, that I have never advanced any claims to be called a linguist. So let us now dismiss my unfortunate error, in not understanding your supplication to Our Lady of Utrera; and refill our glasses."

Don Luis said: "There spoke the humble-minded Christian, who does not ever hesitate to confess an unfortunate error when once he has got out of it his fair profit. I am not quite a Christian of your kidney, my lean godfather; yet your example inspires me; your efficiency defies comment; and I drink to you with deep admiration. As an observer, in my own lower degree, of the best Christian practices, I stand ready—I can but repeat—to introduce these same practices among my own doomed people."

Part Four

The Werrowance
of Ajacan

Your lordship is much indebted to Our Lord for having shown you gentle ways. Where you could have wielded a sword of steel, you choose, rather, to unsheathe the sword of God's Word, which cuts so easily that, according to the Apostle, it reaches to the innermost depths of the heart. These are the weapons by which Heaven bends and subdues these Indian chiefs and their dominions, and will bring them to the feet of the Gospel heralds.

—St. Francis Borgia, to Pedro Menéndez

★ 32 ★

I WILL NOW tell you how plans for the mission to convert Ajacan were arranged by Father Juan Baptista de
Segura, who at this period was the Vice-Provincial (or,
as we would say today, the Superior) of the Jesuits in
America. The tale declares that Segura had felt an un-
paralleled field for his Order to lie open in the Earthly
Paradise which was Ajacan—in the huge, golden and
bejewelled cities of Ajacan, and in the unimaginably
opulent and fertile provinces of Ajacan—after the good
prelate had heard, upon some thirty occasions, about
the marvels of Ajacan as these phenomena gleamed
through the not utterly opaque veiling of American
reticence whensoever Don Luis de Velasco became de-
scriptive as to his native land.

Segura, for this reason, decided that the Jesuits
ought to be represented in Ajacan by Segura himself.
He took with him Father Luis de Quirós, the former Superior of Albaicín near Granada. Their companions in
the enterprise of extending northward the True Faith,
and of exploding heathen errors, were three Brothers
and three Novices of the Society of Jesus, in addition to
four boys, of whom three were Indians, to be their at-

tendants, their catechists and their aids. With a cortège thus Catholic, did Don Luis de Velasco return into the Northern Neck of Virginia, as a patron of the Church of Rome, and as the declared adversary of his own diabolical father, Quetzal.

But with Quetzal the Prince of Ajacan avoided any immediate conflict, inasmuch as, after the ship had entered Chesapeake Bay, then by the advice of Don Luis, the Spaniards sailed on up the Potomac a little distance beyond Hack Neck, where stood the House of Quetzal and the former home of Don Luis. The tale says that, entering the Coan River, they landed at the head of it. This was in September; and the surprise of everybody was considerable to find—at or about where Heathsville now thrives trimly by virtue of many WPA projects—in place of the genial and all-golden province of fairy land for which the Spaniards were questing, what seemed, to them in dismayed silence, and to Don Luis among never so many shocked protestations, an exceedingly uncultured forest through which at that instant the north wind moaned, and petulant rains dribbled viciously.

Quetzal was angry, said the Ajacans. Quetzal no longer attended to the weather with his former amiability. Quetzal had loosed among them a pestilence only this summer; and the Lord of the Ninth Wind had permitted well-nigh their entire crops to perish in drought. For this reason, the Ajacans hailed the return of their Werrowance, Nemattanon, with a special delight, because they counted on his wheedling ways to restore the good humor of his divine father; and their welcome to his barbarian East-people friends, now that these outlanders had fetched back Nemattanon, at long last, to his home, was cordial.

—Which was all very well; but surly Vincente González regarded the hospitality of the Ajacans with a pessimism which stayed untacit. González, I must tell you, was captain of the vessel which had brought the Jesuits into this place; and he now urged the priests to return with him toward Mexico at once. Here, in these horrible tall dripping forests, he predicted, they would suffer beyond reason from cold and hunger, inasmuch as the native savages, no matter how friendly might be their minds, appeared to have little food for their bodies, and they most certainly did not have anywhere near enough clothing.

Don Luis agreed.

"You had best go, my friends. Disastrous magics have been sent abroad by the deplorable God of this country; and under them the land has changed."

—For, as he went on to explain to the Jesuits, it was not merely the climate of Ajacan which had altered incredibly. You could see for yourself that the twenty noble cities and the seventy-two main towns of Ajacan, about which Don Luis had told everybody, did not exist. There was left, of such indescribable and of such, in fact, well-nigh fabulous splendor, not so much as one modest villa builded out of gold and encrusted with jewels, so very devastating had been the anger of Quetzal. Not even the hippogriffins or the hugags, the huge shagamaws or the far larger splinter cats, appeared to have survived this ruthless and insidious attempt, by Quetzal, to belittle Don Luis' veracity.

There had been far too many changes, in short, no one of which worked for improvement; and Don Luis feared—with a display of grave sympathy and a couple of Scriptural citations—lest the strong magic of Quetzal might now turn away from obliterating cities, and from exterminating the more impressive genera of monsters, to contrive further evils.

"—Even against you, my revered friends. Arts which destroy the hugag may well do as much for human beings. Here, in brief, your lives are not safe; and so, you had far, far better return with Captain González."

Said Father Segura: "If God wishes to preserve us against the force of hell's magic, why, then God will do so; if He wishes otherwise, it will be none the less our privilege to obey His wish. Such matters are beyond any man's control. Meanwhile, señor, your people have many of them expressed their desire to embrace the True Faith."

"In fact," said Quirós—who, in the drizzling rain, was resting, upon a fallen pine-tree, with the placid smiling of a scholar who sits alone and at ease in his library—"they so much delight in your new appearance, my Prince, that they hope the God who has changed their Cazique into an all-accomplished gentleman may favor them in the same manner. A large number of these kindly heathen say they wish to become like Don Luis; they formally desire salvation; and so for us to remain here appears desirable."

"You are right in theory, my dear brother," said Segura, "but inadequate in expression. In view of the prospect before us, of converting all this land to the proper service of Our Lord, and of his Majesty the King of Spain, for us to remain here is not, as you phrase it, desirable. For us to remain is inevitable. If we die here, to die in God's service is not merely the duty of all our Order; it is a matter of unarguable large gain, desired reverently by each one of us."

"My friends," Don Luis returned, "you must permit me to admire the extent of your devotion rather more deeply than I do that of your common-sense. You are risking, it is certain, many discomforts; you are risking, as you both admit, your lives—"

His voice changed.

"For the love of your own Christ, you high-hearted idiots, do you go while there is yet time!"

"It is because of the great love of Christ for all humankind," replied Segura, "that we must remain here to proclaim this love to your people. To do that is our duty, señor; and it is right that every man should perform his duty as he sees it."

—For this pair of quiet-spoken prattling fanatics, Don Luis reflected, they also were complete Spaniards. And so they likewise—in Segura's phrase—must help in converting Ajacan "to the proper service of Our Lord, and of his Majesty the King of Spain."

I am facing yet once more (Don Luis' thoughts went on) that which, from the start, has been the firm-set barrier between me and all these Christians: they are whole-hearted in their obedience to notions I cannot understand. In Mexico the kindly Viceroy and his pleasant dissolute people believed, quite sincerely, that it was proper for them to treat the Mexicans like half-tamed animals; in Florida, the Catholics murdered the Huguenots (precisely as, but for a hurricane, the Huguenots would have murdered the Catholics) not out of cold cruelty, but through a glad high sense of duty: for all these Spaniards are honest in their faith that both the Americas belong to them rightfully. Just as they drove out the French, so now they intend to dispossess my people, as trespassers upon the God-granted lands of Spain. They wish, in passing, to save our souls; but not even these dear priests care about what happens to our bodies—any more than they care about their own bodies. It seems to them a mere matter of course that their patriotism should demolish both them and us. The worshippers of Jehovah are maniacs;

they are ruthless: and yet, for the life of me, I cannot hate them.

I am troubled by their patriotism, in chief, because I cannot despise it; for this notion which these pig-headed Spaniards call their patriotism is terrible, and insane, and blind; and yet it is noble. These Spaniards die gladly and very proudly on account of this notion; they dread nothing whatever in defence of this notion: why, then, should they be sparing other persons when once this notion has become involved? Nobody could expect it of them in logic.

I can but infer that by nature I am not logical, inasmuch as the fact does, beyond any doubt, annoy me that the Spaniards now prepare to destroy my people, and me too, in due course. They intend to deal with us just as they have dealt with the Mexicans—not merely without any least sense of wrong-doing, but rather with the elation of right-thinking persons who perform a sacred duty. . . .

"Very well, then!" said Don Luis, aloud. "Let each one of us, my good Segura, attend to his duty just as he sees it."

With that settled, the two Fathers wrote letters to Menéndez asking that, in view of the discrepancies between the Ajacan for which they had embarked and the Ajacan in which they had landed, the Adelantado should afford them food and furnishings and warm clothing, as speedily as might be; the ship sailed; and the eight Jesuits were left in Ajacan.

Of a sudden, everything changed. The wind ceased to lament; the sun appeared; and the calm glory of autumn suffused Ajacan with beauty that was woven out of very deep, bright colors, and with a contentment which wistfulness tinged, somehow. The tall woods were all fire and gems; the green of cedars and of pines became in these woods more vivid; and schools of fish, which were like cloud shadows upon the dimpling waters, began to pass down the Potomac, erratically, in a journey toward the ocean; but the wild ducks and geese, on their way southward, lingered when they reached the Potomac, and all day long they trooped about the great river, with a sort of impatient devotion, as if they were not able to find any rest among, or to be leaving, its quiet giant beauty.

"See now," said the Jesuits, "but how visibly does Heaven smile, now that we have entrusted all to Heaven."

"Quetzal is not angry any longer," said the Ajacans, "now that his son has come home."

Don Luis alone did not say anything. He established the Jesuits in comfort. Then he went to his wife.

★ *33* ★

"My dear wife and my heart's one love," says Don Luis, "I have travelled a long way; I have seen the bright bustling world of which Ajacan is but a tiny corner; and with what joy do I return, from the enthusiastic if perhaps hollow applause of its pre-eminent persons, to you!"

Thus speaking, he embraced Leota; who replied only,—

"I was right."

"That you are always right, Leota, is an axiom which no long while after our marriage you had taught me not ever to dispute."

"I said you would not come back to me, Nemattanon."

"Ah, but even if, in that one particular, you did miscalculate, my dear wife, it was just because your great modesty had led you to undervalue the force of your beauty, of your gentle ways, and of your personal charms in general."

Still, the woman held back from any meeting upon the leisured and courteous and airy plane which the criteria of elegant demeanor had indicated. She displayed not even the tact to be quite overawed by that well-bred gallantry which Don Luis had acquired from and among the élite of Spain. She instead spoke, plungingly, with a sort of desperation.

"Nemattanon, but you must understand! You have seen much; you have learned much, it may be; and you have been taught to play with words. That does not matter, not between us."

"Yet I can play with words rather nicely, Leota; and it ought to be to you a fine treat to listen to a husband so accomplished. Even so,"—as a slight shrug granted condoningly—"you continue to be right. Words do not matter between us two, not very much, because of your uncivil custom of distinguishing between my most handsomely chosen words and the amount of truth which, if but now and then, may happen to vitiate them. Oh, but I do not question," the Prince said generously, "that within judicious limits, truth-telling may be a virtue. The sole trouble is that experience has been teaching me of late, with the aid of such harsh tutors as arquebuses and intolerance and Bibles, to distrust most human virtues."

"Yes?" said Leota.

He nodded, with an appropriate but restrained tinge of the desperate.

"For it so happens that since I went away from you, Leota, I have been much thrown with a superb throng of heroic and brave persons, and with a fair number of virtuous persons, as they went about noble labors, intrepidly, in obedience to the trumpet call of conscience, or of patriotism, or of religion, or of some yet other highly esteemed abstraction. They were all serving—so it seemed to me—the strong black serpent called Maskanako, whom my father put out of these parts for having incited magnanimity; and because of this high-minded reptile's advice, the Spaniards and the French, the Protestants and the Catholics, were embroiled continually, hating one another with an exalted heroism. Each one of these untiring champions was bringing the very best qualities of his nature to the service of mankind's most lofty ideals."

"Yes?" said Leota.

"And the results," said Don Luis, "were oppression and misery. The results were no less brutal than witless. The results, in fine, have taught me to distrust the better-thought-of virtues and ideals as being rather too exuberant masters. In theory, one may admire these virtues; yet they work out hatefully in practice, when once you let any such noble notion get control of a crowd of human beings; and so, that this earth without these virtues and ideals would be a more happy place, my judgment urges me to accept as an axiom. Do you not agree with my judgment, Leota?"

"No," said Leota.

His face lighted, at once, with a smile of approval.

"Neither do I," said Don Luis. "So I do not plan to

abandon all these superb despots on account of mankind's inability to give way to them without results such as my judgment deplores. On the contrary! I reserve for my judgment the contempt which it no doubt deserves; and I intend to remain just as magnanimous, and just as heroic, and just as virtuous as I have always been. I shall obey, in short, every call of my own conscience, of my own patriotism, of my own piety, and of all other human high endowments, quite as if I did not suspect that, so far as goes the outcome, I shall be indulging in crime and unreason."

She looked up at him half sadly. She smiled then. She did not speak.

He said: "Why, but yes! I declaim thus foolishly because I know that all which we have trusted, and have believed in, now crumbles. I boast because I am frightened. I babble because I foresee the future. I cannot ever come back to you, Leota."

"My husband," she said, "but we have not ever been parted. There is not anything so strong that it can part us."

He said: "Through my desire to regard the wide many-colored world I have lost all faith. I have lost all certainty. And you, my dear, you have quite lost the vainglorious young fellow who adored you—even if he did, perhaps, worship a bit condescendingly. We two have lost much, Leota."

"There remain," she said, "a man and a woman who belong to each other."

He put his hand upon her shoulder, without any tenderness, almost roughly.

"Yes, my wife,—and who belong to each other more utterly than they can ever belong to any god or to any wisdom or to any toplofty human-made notion about good or evil."

She regarded him now with a not unfriendly if somewhat stolid air of reserved judgment.

"Can it be you are telling me, Nemattanon, that we still love each other?"

"Why, but really—why, but, my life's lodestone! I incline to distinguish. No: I do not mean love. I do not even mean fidelity, I think; in any case, I shall not give way to the imaginative by telling you the correct taradiddles about my unbroken chaste abhorrence of all other women. I mean our marriage, that actual marriage which has so very little to do with coition. I mean that unbreakable union because of which we two shall not ever need to meet life lonelily, not ever any more, my dearest, so long as we both live. I mean, in brief, that after all, you are my wife; and that after all, throughout every moment of our parting, I have remained your husband—it may be, even in spite of myself."

"Yes?" said Leota; yet she understood.

You saw that she understood, thoroughly.

He said then: "We two need not admire or love, we may even somewhat dislike, each other. Yet our alliance is eternal. It endures against all the world, against every possible happening, and against evil as well as against good, with the same firmness. Leota,"— the man cried out—"but I cannot tell you what I am trying to tell you. I cannot say what knowledge it is which moves in my mind, and which derides me, now that I try to talk as to our marriage, our true marriage. I mean, that I have indeed come home. My home is wherever you may be. I mean, that I have faith in you, Leota, and in your very gallant, so stupid care for me, and in your absurd, your idiotic staunchness, now that not any other sort of assuredness remains anywhere, in these bad days. O woman, but you ought to blush with great shame now that you have dragged down so graceful a talker as was Don Luis de Velasco into such stammerings!"

Standing, she rubbed her hands together, with a queer wrenching gesture. Her shoulders were huddled.

She said: "You went away. You have not come back. You will not ever come back. I have what remains of you; and that remnant of my hurt boy is mine to keep. Nemattanon, they have hurt you. And I cannot punish those fine gracious people who have hurt you! Let us not speak of that. We have each other. That alone matters, Nemattanon, where nothing else matters at all. Nemattanon, but I do understand you.

Proud thoughts are marching in my mind, and I cannot get them out of my thinking into words."

He answered that, from a station between tenderness and flippancy, by saying:

"Our emotions, as it were, beggar description. So let us dismiss trying to describe them, my dear wife. Here is my cane, the One Reed. It is the prop, it is the proof even, of my roving divinity. See, now, I break it. I throw it into the fire without unloosing the four paragraphs of elegiac eloquence with which I might— I really do believe, my darling,—impress even my own wife rather favorably. I say only that I shall not leave you again. But until winter comes, I must remain with these Jesuits. I must make sure of their comfort, I must be their lackey"—he added grindingly—"for some while as yet."

"As yet!" she echoed, unpleased; and Leota, becoming rigid, then asked, with the asperity proper to a correctly reared and religious person,—

"Why do you need to be putting a slight upon Quetzal, and to be acting with open disrespect to your own divine father, by letting these heathen people live any longer?"

"Ah, but, my dear," Don Luis explained, "there cannot be as yet any question of dealing with these heathen people properly, now that they have sent letters to Menéndez asking for aid and supplies. Menéndez moves too quickly. Instead of waiting for next spring and fair weather, as any other seaman would do, it is quite possible he may get help to these pagan priests before the winter begins. He may reach us, not inappositely, during the Mad Moon, before snowfall. Should his soldiers and the guns of his soldiers not find the good Fathers as yet kindly treated, and prospering in their holy mission, the results would be unpleasing, for all Ajacan."

Now, the tale does not say whether or not the wife of Don Luis passed over this repeated phrase—this "as yet"—with a tactful silence or whether she, more simply, saw fit to dismiss it because of matters which, to a good housewife, were of actual importance. The tale records only that Leota said:

"Oh, very well then! And since you did not take the trouble to let me know you were coming, there is nothing whatever in this house except some ham and some maize bread and some eggs—"

"Why, but, my dearest! but I like eggs, and I like ham, quite well enough for my supper—"

"Yes," says Leota; "and then have you groaning and tossing about all night long, with that digestion of yours! for ham is so much poison to you, Nemattanon, at supper! and have you not any sense at all, Nemattanon?"

"I have had at any rate enough good sense," says Don Luis fondly, "to return to the well-remembered and shrill, caustic candors of our home-life. For you, my recriminative darling, you now address an appalled dastard who was once an all-conquering prince and the pet of two continents. During my travels, you must let me inform you, I have given away the great rich Province of Florida as a free gift; and I am told, upon sound authority, that the gods of Sinai and of Bethlehem as yet await my next doings with a trepidation perhaps not unnatural. Meanwhile, my own true wife, I have learned from you that my supper is rather more important. Let us by all means have the eggs without any ham."

★ 34 ★

HENCEFORWARD all prospered with the Jesuits; and
Don Luis set about aiding his Christian friends faithfully, with a not ever failing thoughtfulness, and with
unfaltering industry, in the advance of their holy work.

So complete became his devotion that, for this
while, abstaining from any resumption of domestic ties
and from his wife's company, he was now at pains to
conduct the priests yet further inland, by way of the
present-day R. F. D. route between Farnham and
Emmerton, to the banks of the Rappahannock River.
In this more sheltered place, so the Prince explained, he
could hope to make his reverend Fathers in God a bit
more comfortable during the winter. And here his
tribesmen provided the missionaries, very liberally, with
fish and game and fruit and nuts and corn, in addition
to a vast deal of reedwork house-furnishings and mats
and blankets.

Don Luis saw to the erecting of a spacious and
sturdy home for his friends to occupy; and this stout
log building (as the tale is related in the Northern
Neck of Virginia) stood just above Wilna, where Farnham Creek enters the Rappahannock, near the later site

of Sharps Post Office. Professional historians, it is true, have argued sharply against Sharps; for many of them assert the building to have been farther up the river, in a half-dozen or so other places. About that possibility I do not know any more than they do.

One end of the mission house was devoted to the priests' living quarters; the other end was fitted up as a chapel. Here the good Fathers performed, every day, the offices of the Church of Rome; and so remarkably did their evangelizing thrive that the devout Jesuits marvelled to see how very plainly the benign influence of Heaven abetted them. All Ajacan, it would seem, delighted to receive instruction as to a sound Catholic's pleasing future, beyond the transient inconvenience of death. And besides that, to hear about the main tenets of the True Faith, or about the misdemeanors of pre-eminent saints (prior to conversion), or about the loyalty due by the entire West Indies to the King of Spain on account of the infallibility of Alexander the Sixth, appeared, not merely to edify, but even in some sort to amuse, a great many of these gently smiling, quiet, grave, waiting savages.

The priests began to lay up a store of rustic luxuries, such as walnuts and chestnuts and chinquapins, as well as persimmons and a sweet-flavored root (not unlike, so they say, a yam) which at this time grew freely in the low moist lands that later on became the Northern Neck of Virginia. About more substantial foods they had no need to concern themselves—as Don Luis had been at pains to reassure his revered protégés —inasmuch as the Ajacans had put aside safely, in each of their storerooms, in every one of their villages, a sufficient supply of potatoes and of turnips and of dried corn and of peas and of beans, along with enough smoked meat and fish, to feed everybody with abundance.

It followed that, although in this idyllic land the Jesuits did not loiter among unsuitable luxuries, yet they were free from discomfort. They had excellent food, and sound shelter, and everyone's friendship. Day by day they were making converts to the proper service of God and of his Catholic Majesty, Lord Philip. For this reason, above all, were the hearts of these pious and patriotic clergymen uplifted with a holy joy, and their hopes were nourished with fine expectations as to next spring, when the soldiers would land with artillery, because then, said Segura, a selective draft (such as in Mexico had got handsome results) could be enforced among the young men of Ajacan, so that, by the survivors, a more suitable sort of church might be erected in each village.

Even Agomek, the dark priest of Quetzal, had begun to attend the mission services, and to display an encouraging fondness for the Jesuits' serving boy, who was called, I must here tell you, Alonso Olmos. In fact, Alonso was now teaching to Agomek his catechism.

This proved a prolonged task, which caused the two of them to spend many hours alone together in the woods; but in a number of informal smiling conclaves, the glad fact had been settled, by the Jesuits, that the conversion of Agomek was nowadays near at hand, as an all-staggering blow to the power of Quetzal.

When the first snows of winter set in, and when it was certain that no ship coming from Florida could now reach Ajacan before next spring, then Don Luis quitted the mission house; the people of Ajacan brought to the Jesuits no more food; and upon the gaunt cold western bank of Farnham Creek, so the tale declares, all the offices of the True Faith were conducted, henceforward, without a congregation.

Now the three Indian boys who had come with the Jesuits into Ajacan had disappeared; and only the young Spaniard, Alonso Olmos, remained to serve them. Now storms became more frequent, as well as far more vigorous. And now a northeast wind had begun to rage, unceasingly, without any relenting, and with an interminable fierce screaming, like that of fiends who inflict agony because of their own agony, across endless fields of deep snow.

The Jesuits were alone in a ferocious, frozen, implacable wilderness. They had left to them, in the mission house, not any food except a few persimmons and dried roots, some two bushels of mixed nuts and a half-barrel of biscuits, to intervene between God's champions and a death through starving in that cruel winter season which, every year, the inhabitants of the Northern Neck of Virginia stay doomed to survive as they can best manage.

★ 35 ★

Don Luis went to the House of Quetzal, which in the snow-covered forest clearing displayed with an uncommon vividness the harsh red and yellow of its coloring. The four images that guarded this holy place wore each upon its head a white, pointed cap of snow; and a coating of snow lay also upon the back of the green-and-silver dragon and of the black-and-gold leopard.

Agomek opened the door; and he faced darkly the pensive slow smiling of Don Luis de Velasco.

"How does your schooling thrive?" says the Werrowance—"fond student of the catechism!"

"It is not utterly unrewarded," said the priest, "inasmuch as I have learned to love at least one of our Spanish neighbors."

Don Luis answered, "You are a foul, gross, very lustful goat; and your main need is gelding."

"Perhaps," returned Agomek. "Meanwhile I enjoy my native gifts thankfully; and Aloncito is far more beautiful than are any of the boys of Ajacan."

"You filth!" said Don Luis.

He spat upon the snow in disgust. Then he went

235

into the House of Quetzal, where the main hall was now both warmed and lighted, ruddily, with a glowing fire.

And at first glance, nothing seemed to have been altered. Quetzal still sat looking downward into the magic mirror in which, it was reported, the God of Ajacan could see at will all the past, the present, and the future. He lifted very bright grave eyes toward his son, without moving otherwise.

Yet Quetzal had changed. Although in his unblinking eyes gleamed inveterate youth, now Quetzal was older looking; the aggressive straight line of his shoulders had curved downward; and under the white gold-embroidered robes his body seemed shrunken.

Don Luis said, "Hail, father! and how do matters go with you?"

The Lord of the Ninth Wind answered that with composure, and quite as if they had parted only yesterday; yet he spoke also with affection, saying:

"My very dear son! but all fares exceedingly well, now that you have returned into Ajacan. For my powers fail me; the weather gets out of my control; I cannot even keep a pestilence properly in hand nowadays. So I must go into Tapallan to renew my youth; and until I have come back—among, of course, supernal splendors and at the head of celestial cohorts—it is you, my own Nemattanon, who must maintain the old ways of Ajacan."

"Ah, but no, my dear father," Don Luis replied

with firmness; "I cannot permit you to ascend into heaven as yet; for we have nowadays a special want of protection by the son of the great White Cloud Serpent. Now that I have seen something of the wide world of Europe, and of the patriotism and piety which direct its obscene cruelties, I know that without the aid of your wisdom,—and except only for the mightiness of the Charm of Belshaddar," Don Luis added, slowly— "our people are doomed."

Quetzal stayed silent for some while. He asked then,—

"Have these East-people not taught you, Nemattanon, that I am an evil spirit? and that those who honor me must broil forever upon unquenchable flames?"

"It is a fact, sir, now you mention it, that they may have alluded, in their irresponsible way, I mean— and just in passing, of course—to some such insane slander—"

"Yet what—you soft-speaking lying Nemattanon, —what if that report were the truth?"

"Even then, sir," the Werrowance replied, with a sort of embarrassed firmness, "I would owe to you loyalty. Even then, the people of Ajacan would remain my own people; and at no cost will I consent to see them enslaved and robbed and tortured, like the people of Mexico and of Florida, and of every other part of the west into which these servants of Jehovah have entered."

"But you, Nemattanon, you have come home bringing along with you, so they tell me, no less than eight of these servants."

"Yes, my dear father: because for me to be travelling with foolish companions proved the one way in which I could escape from the snares of Christianity by showing myself a wise Christian."

"Do you not pity their condition, Nemattanon, now your unhappy priests perceive that you have betrayed them?"

The grave Werrowance replied with unaffected sorrow.

"I dare not pity them. Instead, I envy these fanatics; and I wish that I could have been created with a mentality so limited and a delusion so dauntless. These dear brave men are abandoned in what seems to them a wilderness, for no one of our people goes near the chapel since I left it. They are starving there: like the shipwrecked Lutherans of Ribaut, so now the trapped Catholics of Menéndez are forced to gather herbs and wild berries and roots for their food. They suffer always from the cold. They live in hourly expectation of death. They have not any gleam of hope. Daily they prepare, through spiritual exercises and through penances, against the dark moment when I come to destroy them. Yet they remain calmly exultant over the fact that they have been found worthy to suffer for what they term the True Faith. Every day, so noble is their insanity that they pray for my soul's salvation, because they consider I have been deceived by a devil."

Quetzal weighed that. He took up the birch-wood cup beside him, and he sipped at its contents, in very much the manner of Menéndez, pensively.

"Perhaps, Nemattanon"—was the divine verdict— "perhaps you are treating these East-people with an excess of harshness."

The face of the Werrowance was iron.

"I think not, my dear father, inasmuch as toward these Europeans I exhibit a European tenderness. I deal with them in the same calm spirit of forbearance which Laudonnière exhibited toward the women and children of Seloy. I have left them to starve. That is all. I have been as careful as were the Lutherans to keep my hands clean of bloodshed."

"Such carefulness is mere quibbling," says Quetzal.

It was a circumstance which to Don Luis appeared so inconclusive that he replied:

"Yet since when, sir, did quibbling become an un-heroic accomplishment? It is the supreme art of all heroes who last long enough to get public applause. And besides that, my conduct is well grounded upon mathematics. Plain elementary arithmetic assures me it is better that a few Spaniards should suffer and be destroyed than that all Ajacan should suffer and be destroyed. So I must imitate Segura; I must imitate my namesake, the Viceroy; I must imitate Laudonnière and

Ribaut; I must—oh, but above all—I must imitate
Menéndez. You conceive, sir, each one of these gentlemen, in his dealings with the people of America, has
held to his sense of duty; and in dealing with the East-
people, I too shall hold to my sense of duty. I have
observed, with my own eyes, how these Europeans
treat us Americans, as well as how they treat one another. Their motives are, no doubt, excellent; but when
once they obey the ideals of patriotism, then their
actions become pernicious. They compel me also, in
brief, to become a patriot, by ridding our own dear
land of their enormities."

"Well," Quetzal granted, with his customary tolerance, "there is no bond upon me to defend the sour
fruits of the East-peoples' civilization, or the blight on
it which they call their religion. Do you act as you see
fit, my own dear son. Yet by my advice, you would be
so benignantly un-Christian as to send to these wretched
Jesuits a supply of food, for here is poison with which
to season their food."

Don Luis de Velasco was now holding in his hand
just such another small bottle of clear liquid as (he
remembered) Pedro Menéndez had refused; and Don
Luis thought about the relief to his naturally kind-
hearted disposition which might be got out of this
bottle. He asked then,—

"Would their death agonies be terrible?"

"Not terrible at all, my son; for this is excellent

poison. I myself extracted it from the root of the trumpet vine and from five other ingredients; time and again, since I became God of Ajacan, I have used it as a sedative for heresy: so that I well know its praiseworthy results. There is no remedy for this poison; it kills assuredly; but it kills without pain."

Don Luis, upon hearing this comforting reassurance, shook his head.

"I might use it, at the last pinch, should they insist upon living until the Month of Crows; yet I should do so with unwillingness. I doubt if it would be right of me to destroy these great-hearted zealots without torturing them a bit further. I desire, sir, to retain their esteem; and they might think me ungenerous did I not permit them to attest their faith, rather more amply, through a death so unpleasant as to entitle them beyond any question to the crown of martyrdom and a fairly earned legacy of not ever ending bliss."

"It is my opinion," Quetzal said, "that one ought not to encourage these heathen absurdities."

"Still, one ought to be kindly," said his son; "and these missionaries tell me that, by intermeddling with the religious beliefs of a foreign country with so slight tact as to get themselves murdered, they acquire instantly, in the eyes of their own peculiar God, some special merit, through having preached about Him unconvincingly. It would be the part of an unfriend, I submit, to deny to their last hours the opiate of this, after all, inexpensive delusion."

Thus speaking, Don Luis put into the pouch at his hip the small vial of poison; and he left Quetzal seated beside the charmed mirror thoughtfully sipping at his drink. The tall Werrowance put on once more his heavy robe of painted buffalo-skin. He went to his own home, where Leota informed him that dinner was getting cooked to a cinder; that in all probability nobody ever would learn to consider her comfort; and that, more-over, three of those heathen East-people were dripping melted snow on her clean floors.

★ 36 ★

DON LUIS DE VELASCO found waiting for him Father
Quirós, as well as two of the Jesuit Novices, John Baptist Méndez and Gabriel de Solís. At a time when they
were near starved, it had been for these three an un-
comfortable journey (as Quirós granted, with his usual
placid smile), through the winter forest, over the frozen
creeks and the endless snowdrifts. But at the Spanish
mission the last morsels of their bush- and tree-roots
were now being parcelled out: so Father Segura had
sent them, first, to demand of the Prince of Ajacan that
he resume his allegiance to the Church of Rome, sub-
mitting his wicked body to the proper penances; and
second, to implore, in the name of God, food.

"After all," said Don Luis thoughtfully, "Menéndez gave food to the Frenchmen at Matanzas."

He fed them with profusion. Then, as the four
men sat over their dessert, beside a great glowing fire,
he leaned back in his reedwork chair, and he continued
to regard his guests thoughtfully.

I must here tell you that, to these Jesuits, the
Prince of Ajacan seemed almost a stranger, for their
patron of yesterday was no longer, in any respect, a

fine Spanish gentleman. Instead of gay silks and velvets, the Prince wore about his body only a breechclout of fringed deer-skin; his tall soft boots of white leather had been replaced by moccasins; and upon his head you saw a bright fillet of beads adorned with an eagle's feather.

Such, then, was the pensive savage Werrowance who remarked, with disfavor,—

"My dear Quirós! this affair becomes awkward."

"It is possible that we Religious," said Quirós, "could light upon an adjective rather stronger."

"It had seemed to me best," Don Luis continued, "to leave your fate to Divine Providence. So I quitted you in order that the wishes of Heaven might be fulfilled without any interference by me; and for that same reason I have prompted my Ajacans to render no further aid to your party."

"Even in the dead of winter!" said Quirós, reproachfully.

"Our winters are always rather dreadful," the Prince granted with sympathy. "And besides that, food was fairly scarce, even among us; whereas you had not any food at all. Yet, my friend, the Church which you adorn teaches that God and the Blessed Mother will always guard and protect good men against earthly evils,—among which I had made bold to include cold and starvation."

"What do you mean, my Prince?"

"I mean only that reflection told me— But these cakes have merit. It is one of my wife's favorite recipes. Do you youngsters try them!" the Prince urged the two Novices; and he resumed affably:

"Reflection told me, I repeat, that if you and your party, Quirós, were persons of distinguished virtue, then the Jehovah Who, by your account, overlooks all human affairs would see to it that His Christians survived the winter at any rate as comfortably as did the heathen of Ajacan. Why, but as a matter of course, He would send to you His ravens, or His manna, or something of that nature. He might even have managed to give you, as I do, these excellent cakes instead of working a more parsimonious miracle with tree-roots. To the other side, if you died of cold or of hunger, without the intervention of a miracle, it would be shown—said reflection —that your goodness was not pre-eminent."

"Each one of us," replied Quirós, "is frail and very full of imperfection."

"I dispute that," said Don Luis, shaking his high head with regret; "for I grant the miracle has happened. I consider it to be proved that each one of you is advanced, to a rather inconvenient degree, upon the road toward sainthood, because otherwise the God of Spain would not have defended you, as He has quite plainly done, now for three months."

"Your compliments are most generous, señor; and yet"—Quirós added—"they cause me to remember that

by ordinary the road to sainthood is through martyrdom."

"Yes," said Don Luis; "and that, my friend, is the
cause of my discomfort, precisely. You cannot well become martyrs unless I have you killed; and I do not
like the notion of killing you."

Then young Méndez spoke, with the generosity of
a high-born Ubedan, saying:

"Señor, we are willing to be fair in this matter.
We do not insist upon your killing us."

"Most certainly it is not you, my good John
Baptist, who demand of me any action so brutal. It is
the obstinacy of your hard-headed Jehovah, in declining to let you freeze or starve, which prevents the one
pleasant solution of this affair. I dislike, I repeat, bloodshed; I do not like killing defenceless persons"—Don
Luis quoted, smilingly;—"yet I cannot permit any
Christians to live in Ajacan."

"You brought us here, señor," says De Solís.

"Yes, Gabriel," says Don Luis benignantly; "for if
I had not done so, I would have brought myself into
Cuba and into the over-ardent attention of the Inquisition. I would have got myself, instead of you, into quite
serious trouble. And since human nature is what it is,
upon even the best Scriptural authority— However! let
us dismiss, for this while, the somewhat low-minded
cynicism of Jeremiah and of Jesus and of Paul and of
Solomon and so on, as concerns human nature."

"You blaspheme!" said Quirós. "It is an offence which puts God upon His mettle, my Prince, and which causes Him, for the sake of His honor, to smite with both fists."

"Hah, but surely you perceive my awkward position?"—the Prince quoted, with a continuing affability. "I had seen how the more enlightened races of Europe deal with Americans, when once you have got among us any foothold. And so I intended to save my people from grief, and from life-long slavery, and from a grinding, slow, merciless ruin. I meant to retain for my people the small, common pleasures of human living so long as I myself lived. Very well, then! It was unfortunate that these pleasures, howsoever trivial they might be, and no matter how commonplace they may seem to you, did, in this special instance, have to be paid for— But will you not have one of these figs?" Don Luis added, smiling reminiscently upon his trapped guests. "They are quite excellent. Figs are good for the stomach."

Quirós said: "I have no more appetite, thank you. I am perhaps biased in a transaction which involves my being murdered. Yet the price which you yourself, señor, would have to pay for killing us appears to me a great price."

"To me, Quirós, it appears an exorbitant price," Don Luis answered with candor: "for should I dispose of your party in the abrupt fashion which patriotism seems to demand of me, why, then in due course I may have to face the wrath of your God, Who has well shown His power by protecting you; and I do not cordially fancy the thought of hell fire."

"Why then, señor, need you provoke it? It would be more rational, I submit, for you to repent of your wicked conduct; and to be duly absolved by his Paternity, Segura, who, I am certain, would not impose upon you any insufferable penance—"

"You think, Quirós, that should I deny to Father Segura the privilege of becoming a martyr, he would be broad-minded about his loss, and not treat with extreme harshness my parsimony?" Don Luis asked.

—To which the tonsured gray-fringed head of Father Quirós nodded assent, in a sort of gracious, tutorial arrogance. One did not have any choice except to admire the overbearingness of these Christians toward their circumstances. One wished, almost wistfully, one could understand these fanatics . . .

"And I think also, my Prince," says Quirós—without holding back at all from his spiritual duty to reprove the unwisdom of sinners—"that now your pension has been continued, it would be more rational for you to resume living in civilized ease, whether in Spain or in New Spain, as an honorable hidalgo; to practise at the same time the bright amenities and the unexigent virtues of the polite world, among conditions a vast deal more luxurious than you can well hope to find in your native Ajacan; and thus by-and-by to expire with a reasonable hope of eternal bliss, after a not too prolonged stay in Purgatory."

Inasmuch as one could not understand these fanatics, one could but humor them ... So the Prince said:

"Truly, Quirós, all these are weighty considerations. They provide sustenance against both time and eternity."

"They are irresistible considerations, señor; for you have merely to abandon the notion—which you confess to finding distasteful, and which I, you must let me tell you without mincing matters, regard as irreligious —of murdering us poor servants of Heaven. You will thus make certain your comfort, alike in this world and in the next world. In such circumstances, I do not see, I confess, how you can well hesitate."

"Nor do I see that, either," said Don Luis, with a sudden, resolute and candid contrition. "I hesitate no longer. Inasmuch as your God has shown His power, I must now evince my respect for it. Go in peace, my friends, with your hearts at ease and with your bellies satisfied. Do you rest assured I shall straightway visit your mission house, both to make plain the extent of my repentance and to bring food for all you Religious."

—Whereupon, with the dignified, the approving, but the not too effusive kindliness which is due to a returned prodigal, Father Quirós arose, satisfied.

"There is joy in heaven, señor, at this instant; and I shall consult with his Paternity, the all-reverend Segura, as to the penances required of you."

In this manner did it come about that the three Jesuits left Don Luis' home well fed and highly elated by his resumption of correct principles. When they had gone a little distance, Don Luis cried out his orders. In the same instant the twelve Ajacans whom he had placed in ambush discharged their arrows, and they killed Quirós and De Solís at once. John Baptist Méndez, although badly wounded, got away into the woods.

They traced him easily enough by the trail of blood he had left, and they found his slim young body, distorted but rigid, under a holly-bush. They stripped the three priests of all clothing; they removed from each carcass the scalp and the male members; and then burned the remainder.

★ *37* ★

THE STORY now tells about what happened, upon the following morning, near the present site of Sharps Post Office, a little westward of where Farnham Creek enters the Rappahannock River. For all these events we have the report of an eye-witness, in the testimony of the boy, Alonso Olmos; and with a discreet amount of compression, I record his statement.

On Candlemas Day (says Alonso), when all were at their devotions before dawn, as was our custom, we heard a call at the door and a noise of people gathered about the house. Brother Gómez opened the door. Outside were many Ajacans, with their captain and leader, Don Luis, at their head. All were smiling, and each West Indian carried a bundle of food, which he brought in and laid down at the feet of Father Segura.

Don Luis said that his tribesmen had come to bring peace offerings, and to end our troubles. This was excellent hearing, Segura said; and he asked next where were Quirós and the two Novices (I mean, Méndez and De Solís), for we were greatly distressed and feared some evil had befallen them. They will be with you, Don Luis said, and you with them, in no long while.

251

How long? says Segura. Why, but within one stroke of Time's scythe, says the Indian Prince: and that reminds me, he said likewise. Do you lend us your axes and your hatchets, so that we may go into the forest and cut fuel. In this way we will make this bleak place more comfortable before you see them again, for the bodies of dear Quirós and of his two fine lads are cold.

The good Segura said they could take all (that is, all the axes and hatchets), and that two of our community, namely Brother Sancho Zeballos and I, would go along to help in bringing back firewood. So did Don Luis get into his own possession the axes and the hatchets with which we might have defended ourselves against attack.

The house was ringed about by Indians who stood ready, with their bows and arrows, to shoot anybody who tried to escape. Don Luis put on the garments which he had stripped from the corpse of Father Quirós, so that you could not doubt this wolf wore the skin of the slain sheep. He came back into the house with nine, or it may have been ten Ajacan warriors, after he had assigned to each one of these West Indians a special victim, so that all the Religious might be destroyed instantly, and no priest could go to the assistance of another.

When Father Segura saw Don Luis, who had left us wearing only a breech-clout and upon his head a tall feather, return in the robes of a Jesuit, then Segura's thick eyebrows went up, but he stepped forward smiling. I saw his mouth open. I remember he had lost two upper teeth. Before he had time to speak, Don Luis struck him down with the borrowed axe that this second Judas carried, and the Indian Prince rained blow after blow upon Segura's arms and legs and body, leaving all covered with wide wounds. So, with a pelting downpour of agony, did he repay the innumerable kindnesses which that virtuous priest had showered upon him and many other persons.

While Don Luis was thus showing his gratitude to his father in God, the other Ajacans, like ravenous wolves, fell upon gentle lambs who did harm to none and good to everybody. They killed Brother Gabriel Gómez and Brother Pedro Linares, chopping at these Religious until the groaning bodies became raw sausage meat. They entered the kitchen, where they found the Novice, Cristobal Redondo, who in person and soul and disposition and voice, was an angel rather than human. He was humming with contentment, it so happened, the *Dies Iræ,* as he went about preparing the food brought by the Ajacans as a breakfast for his already murdered brothers. Seeing those wild beasts, and bleeding from the wounds that they inflicted upon him without warning, he cried out for help. They hacked him into pieces. In the chapel, where two of us sought refuge at the altar, they came leaping about, and laughing happily, toward Brother Sancho Zeballos and me; and one of these Indians split open Zeballos' head with an axe before they hewed it off from his body.

They left me unhurt, because of a priest called Agomek, who served Quetzal, and with whom [*the rest of this sentence has been deleted*]. Agomek said it was the will of Quetzal for them to kill only the missionaries. When I saw my friends dead and their bodies mangled, then with great grief of soul I requested these wicked savages to let me die also, because I would rather die with Christians than live alone among unbelievers and barbarians; but in spite of my pleadings, they would do me no harm. Don Luis said that from and among the élite of Spain he had learned it was not praiseworthy to murder people until after they were more than fifteen years old. I do not know what he meant.

Now, since these enemies of our Holy Faith had killed my brothers in Christ, who desired so ardently, and who had exerted themselves untiringly, to bring to this heathen tribe a right sense of duty toward the King of Spain, along with some knowledge as to their Creator and Heavenly Father, I begged the Ajacans to let me have food, because I was young and very hungry. I asked them also to give a decent burial to the hacked and mangled corpses. And that bad Indian, Don Luis de Velasco, who was the author of all this devilry, although hardened in error and in every sort of wickedness, was so moved by the sight of their starved bleeding bodies as to give way to compassion. He called them martyrs. He spoke very nobly as to their virtues, citing both Holy Writ and a heathen called Cicero. His voice shook, and in his dark horrid eyes you could see tears.

At his command the Ajacans dug a great trench, and after they had dealt infamously with the bodies of my brothers, they laid in this trench all that remained of my brothers, side by side, placing in the right hand of each corpse a crucifix. The Indians buried Father Segura first, and then the others in the order of their age. Agomek took me away with him to be his bed-fellow.

Thus far, from out of the dead past, and with a rather touching, helpless simplicity, speaks Alonso Olmos.

★ 38 ★

THE TALE now records how Menéndez came up the
Potomac River with three ships; and how, in addition
to his sailors, Don Pedro brought with him thirty soldiers, along with a good supply of food, of wine, of
clothing, and of yet other necessaries, for the Jesuits.
When he observed the clergymen, whom he had
travelled so far and with such great haste to protect
from inconvenience, all dancing merrily and all gaily
turning somersaults upon the left bank of the Coan
River, his surprise became noticeable. He saw then
that these antic-mongers were eight men of Ajacan
wearing the torn and blood-stained robes of the Jesuits.

"We are the heathen priests who brought heresy
into Quetzal's land," these Ajacans cried out to the
Spaniards; "and we have been treated suitably. Do you
other East-people now come and be treated likewise."

Don Pedro landed his thirty soldiers, in three small
rowboats; and the Ajacans, very wisely, ran away into
the forest as fast as their heavy robes permitted. He
marched inland; and although his eight deriders escaped,
the Spaniards caught six other Ajacan men upon
the site of the Northumberland County Bank, and five

more in and about the play grounds of the present High
School of Heathsville. From these captives, Don Pedro,
through the loquaciousness provoked by a judicious
amount of torture, got the truth as to the fate of the
Jesuits. He was not pleased. He ordered that all his prisoners should be baptized instantly, by Father Juan
Rogel, who accompanied the Adelantado as his chaplain; and released two of them.

The other nine he marched back to his ships; he
had these men carried aboard; and he ordered all these
forcibly acquired converts to the True Faith to be
hanged at the yardarm, allotting three of them to each
caravel, just offshore, between Walnut Point and the
summer resort which is now called Lewisetta, in payment for the destruction of the eight Jesuits and of the
boy Alonso Olmos.

That Don Pedro had thus strayed into an excess of
justice, he conceded, without quibbling, when Luis de
Velasco came out of the forest unarmed and waving a
white bit of cloth; for the Indian Prince brought with
him this same Alonso Olmos, so that the boy might be
returned to his parents in Seville. Along with them
came Alonso's preserver, that kindly priest called
Agomek, with an inspiring and edifying intention.
Agomek, by this time, so fondly cherished Alonso that
Agomek had resolved to become a Christian, and to go
with his dear lad oversea, rather than be compelled to
break off their friendship.

Father Rogel, they say, wept with an unhidden delight over this so notable brand snatched from eternal burnings, because the conversion of a heathen priest—who had once been steeped in all manner of abominations, but was now letter perfect in his catechism—was for the True Faith a supreme triumph.

While Agomek was being baptised, four Spaniards fetched the Prince of Ajacan into the open tent facing the Potomac River, where Menéndez sat at ease sipping the smooth wine of Xeres. He arose with punctilious courtesy, as when one hidalgo addresses another hidalgo.

"I appear," says the Adelantado, waving toward his improvised gallows offshore, "to have hanged nine of your people when eight would have been better arithmetic. I render you my apologies."

Don Luis answered, "Since you now intend, I imagine, to destroy every one of my people, it hardly matters."

"Not in the long run, of course," the Adelantado agreed; "yet Christian persons ought to kill with exactness and honor each other refinement of war. So do you be seated, my son, now that you approach under a flag of truce and are my guest for this while. We can fight later, when I have come back with enough guns to ensure your destruction."

"I thank you for my reprieve," said the Prince of

Ajacan, as he sat down, and filled a cup, which he tasted consideringly. "And upon this Amontillado I make you my compliments. It is excellent. It promotes frankness, now that for this last while we sit together over our wine—just as we did upon the deck of the *San Andrés* when I saved your life, and just as we did outside the fort of San Juan de Pinos when you threatened my life." The Prince said then, with a sort of half-shame-faced tenderness:

"We two have played a long strange game, Pedro Menéndez; and our game is ending, now and here, in this small tent, forever. That is a reflection over which I incline to become sentimental."

"Hah, but yet again," said Menéndez, smiling amicably enough upon his godson, "the occasion is urgent; and we lack time to display emotion."

Don Luis said: "I had seen the fate of a conquered people in Mexico; in Florida I had seen the fate of a conquered people; and so, Pedro, I was resolved, utterly, not to have my own people, here in Ajacan, thus enslaved. Do you let me assure you that I killed your priests with regret; they were great-hearted and virtuous persons whose nobility I loved, and whose delusions I envied. You had compelled me to bring them into Ajacan. That was your error; for we both knew they came into Ajacan to teach and to promote subjection to the power of Spain. So I did as you would have done. I destroyed them, just as you destroyed the Huguenots who came into Florida to teach subjection to the power of France."

"I served Spain. I obeyed the will of God," said Menéndez stolidly.

"Indeed, dear Pedro, but in your every action you obey, with a fair hope of some final celestial profit, the will of Spain's ruthless, rather horrible God. Yet this Jehovah, you must let me remind you, is not my God. My God is old and frail; it may be that he is not a blaspheming devil, as you declare, but only—so I have sometimes thought—a shrewd human impostor. In brief, I disbelieve in my God, at bottom. My certainties are not many, nowadays. Even so, I do still believe in loyalty; I believe in an honorable avoidance of discomfort; and I believe in the freedom of my own thinking. My thinking tells me—when I would far rather be reaching other conclusions—that this Quetzal, in common with a depressingly large number of other persons, is more great and more important than I am. I have a smug turn for phrase-making. I can deride neatly. I can imitate a number of the more noble emotions quite well enough to impress my hearers. But Quetzal can create. He has created a people, a people who live with contentment and without any toplofty notions as to their duty to police other peoples. That, Pedro, is my meaning."

"And your meaning, my son, escapes me," replied the calm champion of the True Faith.

"Why, then, Pedro, do you let me put my poor argument *ad hominem*—as we scholars phrase it. The power goes out of Quetzal; he is not able any more to reward his servants; he abates in that strength which has protected me, always, with wisdom and with love. In the end perhaps—just as your Jesuits told me at our first meeting, Pedro,—all his tricked worshippers must go down into everlasting fires, to burn there eternally. Ought I to have deserted my people and my God on that account—because a bald blinking Hapsburg, who controls Spain, stood ready to bribe me with a large pension, and because your priests told me that a short-tempered blood-thirsty Jew, Who controls all heaven and all earth, stood ready to bribe me with wings, and with a harp, and with a surfeit of milk and honey?"

"You begin to play with words, Luis—"

"No, Pedro: it is merely that my argument continues *ad hominem*. My argument reminds you there was once a Captain of the West Indian Fleet who faced ruin rather than accept any bribes. It is true that the bribes offered to this captain were temporal; and his probable gain remained guesswork. Here the bribe was assured; here the bribe was, it might be, eternal. Here, in brief, the bribe was far larger; and it was guaranteed —so all your priests assured me—not by a document sworn to before a notary, but by the omnipotence of Heaven. It would thus have been for me a most profitable investment, to have made terms with your God, in whose brutal mightiness I do believe, upon the whole, more firmly than I believe in the parochial poor powers of Quetzal; and so perhaps I would have done well to let my people work out their own doom, in the bewildered misery of hurt animals, while I curried favor with Jehovah."

For a moment Menéndez was silent. He arose. He paced the ground; and in the instant his back was turned, the hands of the Prince of Ajacan moved swiftly above Don Pedro's wine cup. There was not any special need for hurry, though, inasmuch as Don Pedro stood for some while gazing out over sunlit Ajacan and the great River of Swans. That is what the West Indians then called the Potomac.

Now, there is no country, when once its sharp cruel winter is over, more beautiful or more noble than is the Northern Neck of Virginia, nor any river which in majesty excels the Potomac. Menéndez, appraising these matters, at this instant, in the opulent fulltide of summer, had in his brusque mind no shadow of doubt. All this great province belonged rightfully to King Philip; and Menéndez meant to see that his King obtained it. For Menéndez to do that, was the duty of an hidalgo.

Even so, the lean zealot had begun to wonder if it were quite so clearly the duty of the Ajacans to yield, and if it would not indeed have been currish of the Ajacans to surrender piously, at his righteous demands, all this superb country without making any wicked resistance? What would Pedro Menéndez de Avilés, for example, have done in the place of this dark treacherous scoundrel, his own godson, just behind him? The answer made by Don Pedro's heart was repudiated by his conscience with an orthodox haste. It remained, none the less, the true answer. The captor of Fort Caroline, the contriver of the Matanzas massacre, knew perfectly well what he himself would have done. . . .

Menéndez said harshly: "You play with words. Your words have in them the truth. It is not permitted any man to forsake his own people for a bribe, not even though that bribe be his soul's saving. Such was my belief in Caloosa when, for Spain's sake no less than for the furthering of God's kingdom, I blasphemed—beyond hope of pardon, it may be—against the great sacrament of marriage. Such is still my belief."

Don Luis said: "So you too—O most magnificent Señor!—you do not deny that, as an American, I ought to keep faith with America above all, and among the ruins of all minor loyalties. Your verdict heartens me, somewhat, Pedro, as to an affair which I have now in hand. Pedro, O my most dear, most stupid Pedro! the god I serve, and the country that I serve, are both doomed to perish before long; but they shall not perish, nor shall their power be lessened—I hope—through any default of mine. Let us drink to the better health of my steadfastness."

Menéndez turned; and you saw, incredibly, upon his gaunt weather-beaten cheeks, tears. He said:

"I drink, rather, to our dead love, my son; for henceforward we two must be enemies. Before the year is out, I shall be returning with a fleet huge enough to enable me to conquer and to punish all this part of America in the name of my own God and of my own country. And then, Christ aiding me, I must cut your throat, my own dear son in Christ, with these two hands."

Don Luis touched his wrist.

"Your Christ is not aiding you at this instant with very much vigilance. And I too, I fail in my duty. In that cup, Pedro, is the poison of Quetzal."

"So!" said Menéndez.

He put down the uplifted cup without any display of excitement. Still standing, he drummed on the table, thoughtfully. He frowned then, in cold rage; with treachery he was familiar enough; but that any opponent should have dared to spare the life of Pedro Menéndez, almost as if a Menéndez were insignificant, Menéndez found to be unendurable. Dignity, in brief, had suffered; and just so (Don Luis thought fleetingly) must the hidalgo Cortés have looked at that Vasco de Lerma who had been so impudent as to rescue an hidalgo without proper respectfulness.

"You poor chicken-hearted silken traitor!" the Adelantado said; "you halfman! you had managed all

handsomely. Now you spoil everything. If in that cup
there is poison, it was your business to let me drink."

"I grant that, Pedro," the Prince said, with proper
humbleness; "for only your death can protect Ajacan.
You had well taught me, when we last sat together
over our wine, that a well-bred person will do, at all
times, and at no matter what costs in the way of double-
dealing, that which aids the welfare of his own land. I
accepted your teaching. I had quite honestly meant to
kill you because of your teaching. Yet at the last pinch,
I could not go through with it. You see, Pedro, I remain fond of you."

"That did not have anything to do with your
moral obligations," Menéndez returned inflexibly. "I
can but repeat, señor, it is not permitted any man to
forsake his own people."

"Very illustrious sir," said Don Luis, "should you
insist upon it, then I will kneel down, here in this damp
sand; and even at the risk of rheumatism, I will implore
your pardon, with every required sort of breast-beating,
for not having got you to Purgatory in time for supper."

Menéndez answered with a restrained storminess:
"I have reared you as my son. And I find you a half-
hearted defender of your land and of your people,
even of your God, when you might have saved all by
putting out of living just one person. I am disappointed
in you; you milk-hearted savages of America do not

display the civilized instincts of patriotism; and that much, Don Luis, I must tell you with candor."

"You gentlemen of Europe are a shade difficult to please," the Prince replied, in the while that his dark gaze rested fondly upon this unbelievable person, "when you indignantly resent not having been destroyed, by us backward Americans, in a rational and appropriate manner."

"That," said the Adelantado, "is as it may be; that is not the point; and moreover, I have not the time for that. I consider only the circumstance that I do not condone in anybody a holding back in correct behavior. And so, señor,"—the offended hidalgo added, bowing with cool ceremony—"I bid you farewell. I cannot permit the ties of affection to mislead me into overlooking your incompetence."

They parted then, upon terms which remained formal.

⋆ 39 ⋆

IN THIS manner did the Spaniards go out of Ajacan; and it was just after their leaving that Quetzal went away too, in circumstances which were talked about rather widely, in every part of his former kingdom. His worshippers heard, with appalled interest, how a spider, about the size of a six-month-old calf, had come down out of the sky, dangling upon a strand of her web, and had talked, for some twenty minutes, or it might be a bit longer, with the God of Ajacan, in the House of Quetzal; and how, when they had ended talking, a thunderbolt struck and consumed the House of Quetzal, in the same instant that Quetzal began climbing up the celestial cobweb, hand over hand, toward his future home in a particularly bright star.

All the while he was climbing, he dispensed prophecies as to the continued strength of his people and as to the ruin of any person who annoyed Ajacan; and the gist of some yet further remarks, like a stern postscript, told about the bright future of the devout, and the terrors which would befall heretics, when the Lord of the Ninth Wind, made young again, had come back to his chosen people, in those western lands to which

Nemattanon was now going to lead them. The religious effect of this striking miracle proved so salutary as to increase the weekly burnt offerings, of fruit, of grain, and of flowers, which the Ajacans gave to Quetzal, during five whole weeks.

Even so, the story declares that, for general consumption, this miracle had been embroidered. What really happened, so the tale says, is that when Nemattanon came to the House of Quetzal, he found the place deserted looking, and the door untended, now Agomek had departed. In the main hall was an open grave; and beside it, sipping pensively from a birch-wood cup, sat Quetzal.

Nemattanon said, "Hail, father! and how do matters go with you?"

"Quite well enough, my son, now that you have rid Ajacan of the Jesuits."

"Nevertheless, sir," said Nemattanon, as he sat down in the chair of audience, upon the other side of the open grave, and tactfully did not ask any questions about this grave,—"nevertheless, my good friend Menéndez assures me that he will return, during the Hunter's Moon, to cut my throat and to lay waste these lands."

"It is possible, Nemattanon, that for this once, Menéndez may not be able to keep his word."

"All things are possible, sir, in a world which, to my finding, is swayed by insanity; yet in an affair of this delicate nature, which concerns the one throat I possess, I would prefer, I admit, complete certainness."

"Do you reflect then, my son, that it was perhaps not unpleasing to me that my own priest, staunch Agomek, should have given up serving me in order to go into Spain with Menéndez."

"Oh!" said Nemattanon; and he added with contrition,—

"I had underrated your abilities, sir."

"Yes," Quetzal granted; "for Agomek has intelligence. He has also that small bottle which your friend Menéndez would not accept from me as a gift."

Nemattanon sighed; but he said nothing.

"And so," Quetzal went on, as he waved toward his charmed mirror, "so I have seen herein that which leads me to dismiss Menéndez from all our future affairs. I think he will not return to annoy Ajacan. I think the Spaniards have gone out of Ajacan forever."

"Yet I, sir," Nemattanon said rather sharply—because it troubled him, even now, to know that he would perhaps not ever again see the Pedro Menéndez whom he both loved and disliked—"I believe that one Spaniard still remains here, in the person of the Vasco de Lerma who ran away from the anger of Cortés, and who passed himself off as a god among some Indian tribe or another."

"Vasco de Lerma?" says Quetzal blandly. "Why, but yes, to be sure! The name is not unfamiliar to me;

and he was, as I recall it, a rather charming young rascal, a most talented liar. You, my Nemattanon, you remind me of him, sometimes."

The God of Ajacan reflected, drawing together his white shaggy eyebrows. He sipped at his drink serenely. Then Quetzal said:

"Put it, my son, that I am neither a god nor a demon, but only a man such as you are, and such as was this Lerma. When I came into Ajacan, I found here a leaderless barbarian people living in savage discomfort. I gave to them a leader. I gave to them a fair portion of bodily comfort. I taught them to avoid the high-minded and heroic, wholly idiotic nonsense of intermeddling with any other peoples' affairs. I put upon them, for a protection, the Charm of Belshaddar—which is a quite sound bit of magic, I can assure you, so long as everybody believes in it. I gave to them, in short, the refining and the sedative influence of law."

The Lord of the Ninth Wind drank yet again, and now more freely, from out of his birch-wood cup.

Then Quetzal said: "Nor did I deny to them the inspiring influence of religion. They had need of a god more amiable than is black Maskanako or even—be it said with all proper respect—than is that Jehovah Who in any sort of theological debate considers leprosy or an earthquake to be a fair argument. So I became that god. I gave to my people reassurance as to what would happen to them after death, under my ever-loving care.

In brief, I gave to my people strength and contentment. I taught them—if not quite, as another Teacher
has urged us, to take no thought for the morrow—at
least not to be worrying about to-morrow any too constantly. I lied to them, it may be, as to affairs about
which no mortal person anywhere has certainness; yet
my inventions have satisfied my people. So do you let
them satisfy you also,—even you who have invented so
many splendid stories about Ajacan for the benefit of
half Europe."

"Indeed, sir," Nemattanon answered moodily, "but
I do not at all criticize your blasphemous improbity.
You have well served our people, with your high-
hearted pleasure-giving lies. And so, our people are
happy, as yet; they live—the more thanks to your un-
bridled mendacity—in a healthy and sane manner; they
neither envy nor annoy other peoples, as do all the nations of Europe: and yet, through no fault of our people, our people are doomed."

"Even so, my but too imaginative son, they do not
suspect it; they have learned not to worry about to-
morrow any too constantly; and for the rest, we are all
doomed."

From out of this truism Nemattanon did not seem
to get any large delight.

"Ah, but I, sir," says he, "I have seen with my own
eyes the strong nations of Europe who need new lands,
and who lust after the imagined gold of the west. I

know about the terrible piety of the Catholic priests
and of the Lutheran pastors, which cannot ever stay at
peace so long as the west remains what they call heathen.
Before very long, just as has happened in Mexico, and
then yet again in Florida, the adventurers and the missionaries will be coming into this part of America to
take over the lands and to save the souls of our people.
Whether they come out of Spain or England or France,
the results will be equal. They will wholly destroy our
people."

"What people is perpetual, my dear son? Let me
commend to your attention that horrible mausoleum
which is called history. I grant you that our people will
be overpowered and destroyed, cruelly, in order that the
fanatics and the blackguards who are now coming out
of Europe, in about equal numbers, may possess America and create in it a new nation. Yet very little of their
thieving will be completed in your day; nor need even
the beginnings of it occur within eyeshot. You have
only to lead our people westward, into the mountains,
and beyond the mountains, where not any Christian
marauders will be coming for long years."

"My father, do you abandon us?"

"What choice have I," said Quetzal, "now that my
staunch staid Agomek has digged my grave here before
he deserted me? and now that"—the God hiccoughed
slightly as he laid down beside him an emptied cup—

"now that I have made ready to go into Tapallan to renew my youth."

He leaned back in his chair; and across the open grave, the old gentleman regarded his son genially.

"You rogue," says Quetzal, "do you not comprehend it would be a bad setback for the rather picturesque religion of Ajacan should its God happen to die like a mortal person?"

"Indeed, sir," Nemattanon agreed, "but a shocking event of that nature would beget the impiety and scepticism which you have not ever permitted."

"Just so," says Quetzal; "and for this reason, now that I have become infirm and age-stricken, it is you, Nemattanon, who must take up my task of deluding these well-meaning but all-credulous Americans into contentment. For my own part, I have to round off my career as a deity, and I have to keep firm my earthly work, by disappearing, as is customary for divine persons. You will then need only to attend to my ascent into heaven with the full force of your imagination; after which, I daresay, everything will go nicely enough."

Nemattanon answered that with the correct amount of indignation and of horror,—

"But you condemn me, sir, to a lifetime of continuous lying!"

"You have had some practice," Quetzal remarked dryly. "For the rest, my unfortunate, fine-speaking and far too tender-hearted son, you know the ways of these Europeans. They come at first as a small company of guests who trust to your hospitality. They bring gifts; they speak handsome words, with complete sincerity; and it has been the all-human mistake of America to admire the bravery of these foreign blackguards and to requite with affection the loving-kindness of these foreign fanatics. You must not ever make that mistake. It is because of their virtues that such men are dangerous. It is their virtues you must learn to abhor. This much I told you when the Spaniards first came; and this much you also can now perceive. You must deal with your trustful, and friendly, and undefended guests as you dealt with the Jesuit missionaries. You must see to it that treachery devours them at one gulp. In this way alone can you protect our people for yet a while longer."

Nemattanon answered: "I shall obey you, sir, with that infamy which is proper among demagogues; for I now know that the Shaman of Caloosa was not talking nonsense. To-day it is indeed laid upon me to raise up my war-cry against the Gods of Sinai and of Bethlehem, and even in the same moment that I give to them belief and fear, yet to fight always against these true Gods with a futile lying until, at long last, death leaves me silent. I have no joy in this task; yet I shall not fail you, my most horrible dear father, in the protecting of the nation you made."

"You become the complete patriot," says Quetzal. "That is gratifying. And it does come hard at first, I remember, to kill foreigners for the sake of a notion so plainly foolish as is patriotism; yet habit will toughen you in homicide. Very well, then! with your future thus utterly settled, my dear child, I can now go into Tapallan with a contented mind. Do you let me sleep. I shall not awaken."

He spoke the truth, because in a little while the God of Ajacan moaned restively in his sleep, and he so died, killed by that merciful remedy which, throughout so many years of his deification, he had utilized to cure heresy.

So was it made plain to Nemattanon that his begetter, whether or not this Quetzal had once been called Vasco de Lerma, was neither a local god nor an evil spirit, but an old, feeble, and very brave bit of mortal wreckage. His father had been, in brief, a most impudent, swindling impostor, who had labored untiringly for the sake of, just as he now died to protect, his amiable swindling.

Inasmuch as this special sort of philanthropy could not easily be made clear to its beneficiaries, the kindly Werrowance of Ajacan did not at once advertise it to every one of his people. Instead, he buried Quetzal's frail body in the grave which Quetzal had caused to be digged; and he set fire to the House of Quetzal.

After concluding these filial duties, Nemattanon

made up his story, concerning the star and the spider and the thunderbolt, so that the people of Ajacan could know Quetzal had ascended into heaven, not in any fit of pettishness, but lovingly to watch over them, always, and so as to protect their national welfare against the whole visible world.

In Ajacan, by the more thoughtful, a god with this enlarged outlook was declared to be a great gain, both in convenience and in tribal dignity.

★ 40 ★

So DO WE come to the ending of this story about mortal beings who once lived in flesh-and-blood bodies; and who in consequence were fated to find, by-and-by, for all their pleasures, and for their griefs, and for their aspirations, the same opiate.

I will first tell you about Don Pedro Menéndez de Avilés. From Ajacan he passed oversea to Santander, upon the Bay of Biscay, in which rough waters Lord Philip had gathered a vast fleet. At Santander had assembled three hundred ships and 20,000 men, made ready to serve under the unconquerable hero who, now that he had got Florida, was about to bring likewise, it was rumored, all the north parts of America into the fold of the True Faith and under the tax collectors of Spain. The Royal Council met at Santander to receive Don Pedro with such stately rejoicings, such gun salutes, and such noble pageantry, as had not ever before been witnessed in Lord Philip's kingdom; and Pedro Menéndez in due form was appointed to be Captain General of all Spain's navy, so that henceforward there was not any country in the world but lay at the disposal of Pedro Menéndez de Avilés.

Upon that same afternoon Pedro Menéndez was

attacked by indigestion; it turned to a fever; he received the sacraments; and he died. Upon that same evening, about moonrise, the priest called Agomek threw an empty bottle into the Bay of Biscay.

Such then, at Santander, was the dark curt ending of the very illustrious Cavalier, Pedro Menéndez de Avilés, once a pirate and a jailbird, but afterward Adelantado and Conqueror of the Province of Florida; the founder of our civilization such as it is; Commander of the Holy Cross of La Çarça; Commander of the Order of Santiago; Captain General of the Ocean Sea; and Commander in Chief of the Invincible Armada, which Lord Philip, King of Aragon, King of Castile, and so on, had assembled against the north parts of America and all the heathen rebels therein—among whom was Quetzal, Lord of the Ninth Wind, that dead blasphemer, served even after his death by staunch Agomek, faithfully.

About Antonia no more is known. I am certain only that, whatever may have been her lot prior to the time of her burial, she contrived to get out of her surroundings complete comfort.

I will now tell you about the ending of Nemattanon. It is related that, with his entire people, he went out of the Northern Neck of Virginia; and that they travelled westward. The Monnakans, the Kecoughtans, and the Powhatans, with yet other uncivilized tribes, came back into the Northern Neck to wander about at random, in search of food and of stray chances to kill one another, and to live, with discomfort, in tents builded of poles and tree-bark. The dreadfulness and the good deeds of Quetzal faded out of remembrance. All the fertile country between the Potomac River and the Rappahannock River became, yet again, a wild fierce jungle, now that the Ajacans had gone out of it, just as they went out of history, into the vast, vague glittering fable-land of the West, travelling toward Cibola and Quivera and the diamond mountains of Appalachia and still other noble realms of Faëry.

Not any more was ever recorded as to the Ajacans with the certainty of an historian. But people say, in the Northern Neck of Virginia, that Nemattanon led his tribesmen up into the Blue Ridge Mountains, and beyond Charlottesville, and so came to a well-sheltered pleasurable land like a hollowed-out crevice in the Alleghanies. This is believed to have been in the present Rockbridge County, near the head of Bratton's Run, where afterward the Rockbridge Alum Springs prospered in levity. And the tale says that in this valley, for a good long while, they lived undisturbed by any of the Europeans who were now flocking oversea, in always increasing numbers, toward America.

Here, in his mountain kingdom, the Werrowance of Ajacan preserved the old ways of Ajacan sedately; he welcomed every party of Europeans who came to teach him a superior manner of living; he feasted them; and he then killed them. In this way did he keep firm the happiness of his people for a while longer.

That all his people were doomed, Nemattanon alone knew; and inasmuch as he hid his knowledge—even from that rheumatic and gray-haired and forever fault-finding, very dear woman who had once been Leota—he might yet be able to make their contentment and their faith in the unexampled future of Ajacan outlast his lifetime.

—For the God of the Christians, it appeared, was the true God. The power of Jehovah was making stronger and yet stronger the insane brutal people of Jehovah in a collapsing world wherein the Nemattanon who postured as a demigod was quite certainly an impostor; nevertheless did the lies of Nemattanon keep sleek and happy his people for a while longer. They bored him insufferably; and yet they were his own people. He could not break faith with them, by telling the truth.

So his people lived peaceful and honest and well-ordered lives, because of the lies of Nemattanon; and his people died, in due course, without fear, because of the earnestness with which he assured them how very soon they would reawaken, in the form of bright, glorious, happy humming-birds, in the heaven which is called Tapallan. How this nation perished is not known; but they took with them the sustaining comfort of their delusions from out of the north parts of America, leaving room for quite other delusions.

EXPLICIT

Editorial Note

So ends the history of the first settlement of white men on the soil of Virginia. The walls of the Capitol at Washington might well be adorned with a painting of a scene that occurred almost in sight of its dome—the founder of St. Augustine, the butcher of Ribault, the chosen commander of the Invincible Armada, as he stood surrounded by his grim warriors, planting the standard of Spain on the banks of the Potomac.

—JOHN GILMARY SHEA

EDITORIAL NOTE

MY PROTAGONIST I have made bold to call the first
gentleman of America, inasmuch as he was the first
native-born inhabitant of the present United States to
endure the influence of civilization and culture, of
travel and of polite refinements in general. That, with
such aids, he should reach an end so opprobrious as to
become, not merely a high-minded and wholesale murderer, such as seems commonplace nowadays, but that
really blameworthy monster, an American who preferred the requirements of his native land to the needs
of foreign empire-builders, was an outcome which
expediency demands I should here lament, even in the
same instant I refuse to distort history. I can tell only
what did happen, rather than what ought to have
happened, to the first gentleman of America.

That I have not told you all which is recorded
about Nemattanon, remains—a bit tantalizingly—just
possible. It is known, I mean, that near fifty years after
the events hereinbefore set forth, a very old man came
out of the west, into the early established Colony of
Virginia, saying all his people were dead. Captain John
Smith relates that the English nicknamed this vaga-

bond "Jack of the Feather," because he commonly
went about adorned with a feather; and that old Jack,
"for his courage and policy, was accounted amongst
the Salvages their chiefe Captaine, and immortall from
any hurt could be done him." Smith adds that the
Indians called the vainglorious stranger "Nemattanow."

This Jack of the Feather (Smith continues) was
the main cause of the Great Massacre of 1622, in which
almost but, through mischance, not quite all the English were killed; and at the very beginning of which,
Jack of the Feather was shot and captured by two
servant boys,—and so died, in a rowboat, near Berkeley
Hundred, on his way to jail. His last request, of his
lackey captors, was that he should be buried in secret,
"amongst the English," so that the Indians might continue to believe him a divine personage impervious to
bullets.

I would very much like, in the cause of irony, to
declare that this was indeed the ending, in a crude
small fishing-boat, upon the cheerless, coffee-with-milk
colored, ice-caked James River, of my protagonist, the
first gentleman of America, the grandee of Spain, the
son and grandson of pagan deities; yet nobody can be
certain. Smith gives the name as "Nemattanow"—
although he does record this name but once, it is true,
"as writ by M. Wimp," in an era of liberal-minded
orthography and of not puritanic spelling.

All in all, I elect to assert nothing as to this time-

obscured "Jack of the Feather." I introduce him as a
sardonic possibility.

For much friendly help in putting together such
variant legends of Nemattanon as yet survive in oral
tradition, I needs now extend my thanks to the follow-
ing benefactors: Professor Augustine Cockrell of Coan
Hall Academy; Miss Susan Cockrell of Ophelia; Cap-
tain Edmund Crabbe of Heathsville; Rev. Dr. J. Jett
Eskridge of the Avalon Independent Presbyterian
Church; Mrs. Adeline Ball Gaskins of Wicomico
Wharf; Captain Gilbert Gaskins of Callao; Francis X.
Goldberg of Horse Head; Judge Alpheus L. Haynie
of Farnham; Dr. Howard Haynie of Glebe Point;
Captain Richard Hull Haynie, Sr., of Burgess Store;
Captain Omohundro Haynie of Fleeton; Miss Hope
Hudnall of Morattico Manor; Captain Henry Hull
Jett of Sunnybank; and Father Ignatius L. McDon-
nell, S. J., Ph. D., D. D., of Lewisetta and Totuskey.

In reporting that the doomed Jesuits disembarked
from González' ship (of which the name stays unknown to me) at what, in 1571, was the head of the
Coan River, and that they then travelled overland to
meet death upon the western bank of Farnham Creek,
I am running counter, I know, to more skilled, and

to far more considerable, historians. A number of these would have it that the party ascended the Potomac much farther, perhaps even to Aquia Creek; and in that case, the log chapel wherein Christ Jesus first got any formal recognition from the first families of Virginia must have been erected about where Falmouth now stands, like a death-watcher, over the sand-strangled remains of the Rappahannock River.

Now, this is possible; I prefer not to deny this, outright; yet I do say that, to my mind, it is a theory which demands some adroit juggling with the figures left to us by Quirós and by Rogel and by Carrera, as well as an arbitrary assumption that these figures, while in the requisite places exact, are, in a number of inconsistent or self-contradictory statements, mere pardonable errors. It is a theory which likewise increases the dimensions of Aquia Creek, as that creek existed toward the end of the sixteenth century, to the verge of incredibility.

I think, in brief, the best available evidence as to all these points is now furnished by the Potomac River itself. The Jesuits came, we know, to the former home of Don Luis, upon the south bank of the Potomac; and this home, we know furthermore, stood at or about a place reached by the first party of Spaniards under the impression they were still navigating an arm of the ocean, toward China. It is not conceivable, I submit, that any ship could sail up the Potomac as far as Aquia

Creek without its crew's observing that for a good while they had been between the visible banks, and were following the bends, of an unmistakable river.

In short, I believe that the first party of Spaniards landed, as this book records, and as any rational explorers would have done, upon Hack Neck, or at utmost upon Mob Neck; that the second party went on a bit farther, to the Coan, which was the first tributary they could enter to a distance of "six leagues"; and that Don Luis murdered them, beside (as we know) the Rappahannock, in the neighborhood of Sharps. If I be wrong in any one of, or indeed in all, these beliefs, I cannot see that it gravely matters.

Nor do I think I have very much violated veracity through my acceptance of the story of Nemattanon in that special form which I have got together in the Northern Neck of Virginia. Nemattanon, it is possible, may in the flesh have been not quite the all-accomplished personage who figures in the legend which I send to you from out of my gleanings in Lancaster and Northumberland. It is a cry of some farness, for example, from the Nemattanon of this story to the more temperate appraisal of Dr. Gonzalo Solís de Merás that the Indian Prince "had been six years with the Adelantado: he was very crafty, a good Christian, with very good understanding, called Don Luis de Velasco."

Politeness, to say the least of it, is here unstressed by enthusiasm, in the bosom of Ribaut's murderer. Yet the remarks of Fulano Suárez, which I have quoted earlier, in the twelfth chapter of this book, would most amply seem to sustain the legend.

The specific mention of "six years," let it be said here, reminds me that in expanding and retelling this legend, I have now and then been troubled by my own carefree, but compulsory, treatment of the Julian Calendar. The Spaniards (I mean) first came to Ajacan in 1561; and Menéndez died in 1574: yet I do not think that anybody, off-hand, would suppose this story to cover a period of thirteen years. That during this story an appreciable amount of mortal nonsense slips by beyond correction, you are given to understand; but, always, just how much time may have elapsed between one event and some other event is left unconcernedly unsettled.

Now, this, of course, is a trait common to folklore. A tale which becomes preserved orally is very soon disburdened of exact dates, if but through the human unwillingness of its but human narrator to memorize any such dry-as-dust features. That, one imagines, is why all proper folk-tales tend to begin with "Once upon a time" and to end with an equally non-committal "forever after." In any case, one observes, in most legends, that the time-element stays thriftily unresolved, so as not to clog the tale's progress; and as I admitted at outset, this book is, fundamentally, a legend.

In brief, I have tried to record the story of Nemattanon more or less as one tells it in the Northern Neck of Virginia. That it has been revised and verified in the light of more formal chronicles, a Bibliography attests; nor very certainly, in its present form, does the legend contradict any sound historian with a more acrid freedom than is habitual to these same historians when they differ among themselves. My point here is but that this story, being folk-lore, does condense history, and it accelerates history, in the manner of any other local fireside tale, of which the double purpose is to incite a half-hour or two of indulgent attention and a good night's sleep.

I turn now from Nemattanon to one with whom this chronicle has concerned itself almost equally—to Pedro Menéndez de Avilés. The story of the American-born Don Luis de Velasco had lurked to the back of my mind, as a not impossible theme for romance to develop, since 1912, or about then, when I first ran across Shea's account of Don Luis in *The Indian Miscellany*—a great many years before I knew anything at all about the local mythology of the Northern Neck of Virginia. About the "Melendez" of Shea's version my ignorance was then not a whit less extensive. Nor even when, at a rather deferred long last, I set about the actual writing of this story, in the autumn of 1939, was my knowledge as to Pedro Menéndez more than a tattered and chance-woven, small rag of hearsay, despite the five winters I had spent in St. Augustine. It was a deficiency which had to be remedied.

Through the benevolence of Mr. and Mrs. Edward W. Lawson, those kindly curators of the St. Augustine Historical Society's headquarters, and through what I can but describe as the great-hearted prodigality with which Professor A. J. Hanna, of Rollins College, supplied me with books from out of the College Library, I made progress. I made, in fact, a bewildering progress, because of Menéndez' steadily crescent improbability.

A while later, Mrs. Dorothy Dewhurst Parker, of St. Augustine, very graciously put at my disposal the noble collection of Floridiana formed by her father, the late W. W. Dewhurst, who himself wrote an excellent history of St. Augustine; Mr. Watt Marchman, Curator of the Florida Historical Society, laid open to me the fine library of his organization: and I was thus enabled to read happily some thousands of pages relative to the great Adelantado—with whom, in the mean time, chance had acquired for me contact more startling.

Toward the end of the January of 1940, I noted, in the guide-book called *Seeing St. Augustine* a casual statement that the "headboard of the casket of Pedro Menéndez de Avilés, founder of St. Augustine, was presented to the city in 1924, and rests temporarily in the City Hall until another display place can be provided."

Now, over this item, I would willingly, as people do in books, have pricked up my ears if only any such feat were possible for mere humankind. Completely was this item, to me, news of an undiluted newness, for all that I had visited the City Hall, over and over again, to procure a dog license and yet other necessaries. I now went toward the City Liquor Store, where St. George Street is crossed by Hypolita Street, and is made desolate by that vacant block in which, once, the Magnolia House flourished and was burned to the ground. Passing by the City Liquor Store (with a brief nod of recognition to the younger Mr. Rogero), I entered the City Hall, it so happened, on a fair Saturday afternoon, when the city offices were closed; and the yellow, red-trimmed building was deserted but for a thin, coffee-colored and most polite official in charge of the elevator. Of him, therefore, did I inquire as to the headboard of Pedro Menéndez; and he answered—somewhat dubiously, I thought—to the effect that "if you have the great kindness to come along with me, sir, I think I know about where it used to be."

With wonderment as my companion, I entered

the elevator; and so reached the third storey, where my dark escort led me, past various unoccupied and closed, but duly labelled Departments and Courts and Clerks' Offices, to a door marked, non-commitally, 310. He unlocked it. We in this way entered a twilit place which I can only describe as a junk room, inasmuch as it seemed overflowingly occupied by dilapidated benches and desks and chairs and window-shades and large photographs and rain-rotted awnings, and with I know not what other waste furnishings—all long past usefulness, all heaped together at random, and all grayly covered with dust. I think I gaped; for no headboard was visible anywhere; nor very certainly, was it in such hugger-mugger conditions I had looked to revere the city's most intimate relic of its founder.

I noted then that my conductor, having passed to the south end of the room, was there engaged in operations which reminded one of a terrier in search of a rat, now that he rooted down, industriously, into what seemed to be a pile of torn camp-stools, and of framed photographs of civic pageants, and of yet other photographs of the fauna known as Aldermen dating from about the second administration of Grover Cleveland. Removing these top strata, he thus excavated, as it were, no headstone commemorative of Pedro Menéndez, but an uncommonly long, and narrow, and a portentously black, coffin.

"Here, sir, it is," he said; "but I ain't certain if the gentleman is still inside it or not."

The quiet City Hall, for the moment, seemed to me a peculiarly lonesome place in which to be finding, without any least warning, a coffin; and I approached it with a vague feeling of having strayed into a murder mystery story.

This casket (I observed, first of all) did not have the traditionary broad-shouldered form of a coffin: it was, rather, a long, thin rectangular chest. I found it to be uncheeringly adorned with three skulls, each one of which gripped, with bared teeth, a pair of cross-bones; and upon one side of the coffin there was a great deal of gilt lettering. Even to my infirm Spanish, and despite the room's dim light, this lettering revealed the fact that here was the coffin in which Pedro Menéndez had been placed in 1574. And as I found out later, it had lain, unseen, just where I found it, for a good while.

When the body of Menéndez got harborage in the third church niche to contain it—at his native Avilés, in 1924—then his remains (along with the remains, found in his coffin, of an unexplained infant, in whose composing, I would like to think, he and Antonia collaborated) were taken out of this coffin; and were put into the more cosy funereal urn which formed a part of the ambitious memorial, at long last, accorded to

Don Pedro, in the Cathedral of Avilés. At this season, both the coffin in which the never-resting Adelantado had been compelled to rest for two hundred and fifty years (or at any rate, ever since his body was brought from Llanes to Avilés in 1591) and the headboard of his former tomb, in the Church of St. Nicholas in Avilés, were presented to the city of St. Augustine in America. A delegation of pre-eminent Floridians went oversea to receive, and to bring back with them, these relics, among much pageantry and a nation-wide Associated Press display; whereafter the headboard was sent to Stetson University, and the coffin was put aside—by-and-by, at least—in the junk room of the City Hall. The entire affair, in brief, was conducted in strict accord with our American notions of honoring the heroic, with a processional from adulatory rambunctiousness toward quick oblivion.

Quite clearly did mature citizens of St. Augustine recall the week-long ceremonials which had greeted the coming of these relics; yet no living person—it was rather bewildering—no person living until 1940 seemed to have any notion as to what had been done with the coffin to receive which all St. Augustine had ramped *en fête* in 1924. The headboard, which my guide-book had assigned to the City Hall, was known to be, in mere point of fact, on view at Stetson, that perhaps unique university where so much knowledge alike inhabits, and has been developed by, hats: no human eyes, so nearly as I could discover, had ever rested upon the coffin of Menéndez during some dozen years.

Even at the City Hall, my dark guide to this coffin could only tell me that he had "just heard somebody or other say it was in there."

I am afraid that afterward I became a nuisance to the citizens, as well as to the winter residents, of St. Augustine upon the topic of coffins. A Virginian, you see, is not taught to be rational about relics.

—For which reason did I now speak, at large and without remission. Your city takes, I would point out, a well-justified pride in its antiquity, an antiquity rather carefully fostered. I love your city, as being by long odds the most picturesque and most kindly city in the United States of America; for that same reason do I resort to your city, winter after winter. In your antiquities I revel—and not merely in those of them which are authentic. The historic Fountain of Youth, from which Ponce de León drank, for example, I visit with a not ever failing delight in the embarrassment of the good-looking girl guides when they recite their so outrageous, so carefully memorized taradiddles; I regard with a proper reverence, and with not more than a half-dozen reservations which stay civilly tacit, The Oldest House; whereas toward The Former Mansion of the Spanish Governors between the Years 1597 and 1763 I cherish an almost proprietary feeling on account of the interest with which I saw it being builded during 1937.

Yet what—I would resume—what is the most ancient, the most interesting, and the most amply authenticated, of all the antiquities of Old St. Augustine? You do not know. *O tempora!* I stated; and as a rule I added, *O mores!* for that same great treasure is the coffin of the most magnificent Señor Pedro Menéndez de Avilés. And where have you put upon display, at a moderate entrance fee, this all-priceless relic? That also, your expression tells me, you do not know. His coffin at this instant reposes, under a pyramid of old photographs and of broken camp stools, in the junk room of your City Hall.

Thus did I speak, over and yet over again, to the nobility and gentry, and to the antiquaries, and to the newspaper people, and to the priesthood, and to the City Fathers, of St. Augustine; and having ceased my relation, I repeated it. I was even invited, you must let me boast, to address the Chamber of Commerce. In no other city, and not ever else in all my lifetime, has that happened to me.

Well! but the people of St. Augustine listened to my indignation, because of one reason or another. So the casket was removed from the City Hall a while later in 1940; the ownership of this casket was trans-

ferred from the City of St. Augustine to the Catholic
Church; and the coffin of Menéndez to-day lies in
state at the very beautiful Chapel of Neustra Señora de
la Léche.

Since, as I have told you in my twentieth chapter,
this structure graces the spot whereon Menéndez first
landed in St. Augustine—and where he then claimed
the whole of North America in the name of that special
religion for which the decisive proof depends on an
empty sepulchre—the fact that some three hundred
and seventy-five years later, Don Pedro should have
come just thus to be honored, in this special chapel,
cannot but seem, to the considerate, a quite stalwart
stroke of romance. It is a post-mortem feat (I submit)
which partakes of the Adelantado's lifelong implausi-
bility.

Let me record too in this place that, for once, a
befitting amount of reverence was not denied revenue.
More than sixteen thousand tourists gave their "vol-
untary offerings" in order to view this casket during the
first three months of its publicity; I lack later statistics;
but I do know the relic so far retains interest that the
erection of a special shrine to contain it is now planned.
And I will unblushingly to record that it was I who
re-discovered the forgotten casket of Menéndez, as
well as I who stirred up a sufficiency of indignation, of
remorse, and of thrift, among the people of St. Augus-

tine, to bring about the removal of this coffin from out of a junk room into a chapel.

It still stays to me a matter of frank wonder that I should have thus become, though but temporarily, a public-spirited citizen, a benefactor of the Catholic Church, and a sound financier also, through enacting the public scold.

Yet I dwell upon this incident less out of vainglory than because I like to feel that in a tangible way I have helped to honor Pedro Menéndez. In the book you are now holding, I have not, at any rate, maligned him; but I know I have fallen a long way short of according to him justice. Nobody, I console myself, can hope to do justice to Pedro Menéndez nowadays, for the sufficing and the rather dreadful reason that he is not any longer a credible person.

He remains, it is true, reasonably famous. He is remembered in particular for the Matanzas massacres, about one of which I have told you at some length; and both of which have evoked, now nearly for four centuries, a vast deal of horrified virulence and a fair number of abashed extenuations, according to the historian's religious leanings.

These massacres were, beyond question, brutal. Yet nobody, to my knowledge, has as yet suggested any rational method by which Don Pedro could have spared the Frenchmen. He could not leave an army of declared enemies at large in his Province of Florida; he could not hope, without defying both mathematics and human nature, to convey them to St. Augustine as his prisoners; nor for that matter, did he have at St. Augustine either the food or the accommodations needed for his prisoners. So he killed his prisoners out-of-hand. His conduct in this affair is simplicity's self; and has its present-day analogues.

But to my finding, the man's conduct upon three other occasions has a simplicity which is simply not any longer credible. I mean, his sending into Cuba of his best two ships, out of five ships, immediately before risking battle with fifteen French ships; I mean, the attack upon Fort Caroline, which involved an abandonment of St. Augustine at an instant when he had no least notion as to the whereabouts of the French fleet; and I mean, also, his bigamous marriage with Doña Antonia—a marriage into which the man entered unspurred by fleshly desires, and for which, as a sound Catholic, he expected to be punished with prolonged torments, if not indeed with eternal torments. That he did every one of these things, we know. It is his motive which is not any longer credible, nowadays.

His motive was that Don Pedro believed in the existence of God and in the omnipotence of God, as well as in the nobility of serving God with a completeness which did not grudge any sacrifice whatever to

God. If God so willed it, then God's champions would conquer the heretics at any and all odds; and if God so willed it that, in exchange for the salvation of many souls, the soul of Pedro Menéndez should be damned forever, why, in that case, Pedro Menéndez—he, at any rate—stood ready to applaud the bargain as being an excellent bargain.

He believed alike in the existence and the all-guiding wisdom of God; and he loved God utterly. It is that which nowadays makes Pedro Menéndez incredible. And it is that which leads me into parading the fact that I in some slight degree have helped to honor the memory of Don Pedro Menéndez de Avilés. I admire the man profoundly; and I envy him.

For another matter, I desire to express in this place my equally whole-hearted admiration for the Catholic priests who first preached in our two Americas their Faith. (It is a pleasure to record, in passing, that Father Rueda made an excellent town priest, and died in Santo Domingo, at an advanced age, universally loved and respected; as to the later doings of his confrère in mutiny, Father Anton de Campos, this modest chronicle does not speak.) The clergy did impress, into the service of their Church, the native Mexicans, just as I have told you in the tenth chapter of this book; but then with how far less of lenientness had these devotees impressed themselves! They were heroes—or to phrase it exactly, these bold athletes of God were daredevils—who did not merely live for the True Faith; they sought to die for it also, not with mild resignation, but with an active and vivid delight; nor did it ever occur to these Religious that any rational person might have elected for a course of conduct less thorough-going. They enabled, I mean, the natives of Mexico to die in the service of Mother Church, not as a punishment, but as an inestimable privilege, to enjoy which, through the favor of Heaven, they likewise nurtured hope, wistfully.

And I mean too that in their methods of preaching the Gospel to the heathen peoples of the West Indies these missionaries were equally forthright. They desired converts; and if one could most readily get these converts through the help of jingles and of jigging music and of kickshaw trinkets, one was none the less making converts to Christianity; one was saving imperilled souls.

To Father Luis Cancer de Barbastro of the Dominican Order—who, as Dr. Michael Kenny reports, correctly, "was in character and career one of the greatest as well as noblest that ever set foot or shed his blood upon our soil,"—the Catholic Church was first indebted for the composition of a catechism in rhyme, and an outline of Sacred History set to music, in the language of the Indians, among whom both *opera* proved highly efficient.

Father Cancer's methods and general outline of argument have been indicated in my fourth chapter. I add here that this protomartyr in the attempt to conquer North America for Christ came into the West Indies about 1535, attended by a male quartet; and that he journeyed unprotected among the Indians, for some fourteen years (even up to the day of his martyrdom, near Tampa, Florida), conducting divine services at which—with, as the rule, a gratifying number of encores—his quartet "gave to the eager tribesmen a complete performance, to the accompaniment of bells and timbrels and crude tribal instruments, reciting in simple melody, to hungry ears, the whole story of man's origin, redemption, and destiny."

One really does regret that matters of this nature cannot always be made understandable, thus easily and thus pleasantly, nowadays.

Poynton Lodge
June, 1941

Bibliography

Alas, we now know what they are, these Wapsinis, who came out of the sea to rob us of our lands. They came with smiles. They were well received. They were allowed to dwell with us as friends and allies. They were traders, bringing fine new tools, and trinkets, and cloth, and beads. And we liked them and the things they brought, for we thought them good. But they brought also fire-guns and fire-water, which burned and killed.

—*Translated from the Lenape,* BY JOHN BURNS

BIBLIOGRAPHY

Abbey, Kathryn Trimmer, *Florida, Land of Change* (Chapel Hill: 1941).

Averette, Mrs. Annie, editor and translator, *The Unwritten History of Old St. Augustine, Copied from the Spanish Archives in Seville, Spain, by Miss A. M. Brooks* (St. Augustine: 1902).

Barcía, Andrés González de, *Ensayo Cronológico Para la Historia General de la Florida,* from which, in view of my invalid Spanish, Mr. Edward W. Lawson has been so kind as to translate the requisite material (Madrid: 1723).

Barrientos, Bartolomé, "Vida y Hechos de Pedro Menéndez de Avilés," in Genaro García's *Dos Antiguas Relaciones de Florida,* with which yet again Mr. Lawson has aided me (Mexico: 1924).

Bernal Diaz del Castillo, *The True History of the Conquest of Mexico,* Translated from the Original Spanish by Maurice Keatinge, Esq., 2 vols. (New York: 1927).

Bourne, Edward Gaylord, *Spain in America* (New York: 1904).

Brown, Alexander, *Genesis of the United States,* 2 vols. (Boston: 1898).

Bulletins and Year Books of St. Augustine Historical Society and Institute of Science.

Bulletins of the St. Augustine and St. Johns County Chamber of Commerce.

Bulletins of the Tappahannock Chamber of Commerce.

Coloma, Luis, *The Story of Don John of Austria,* translated by Lady Moreton (London, New York, Toronto: 1912).

Connor, Jeannette Thurber, translator and editor, *Colonial Records of Spanish Florida, Letters and Reports of Governors and Secular Persons,* 2 vols. (Deland: 1930).

Corse, Carita Doggett, *The Key to the Golden Islands* (Chapel Hill: 1931).

Corse, Carita Doggett, *The Fountain of Youth and Ancient Indian Village and Burial Ground* (St. Augustine: 1937).

Dau, Frederick W., *Florida Old and New* (New York: 1934).

DeVries, Gerben M., *Chasco, Queen of the Calusas*, which is given as a translation from Ms. of Padre Luis, O. S. F. (privately printed: no place: 1922).

Dewhurst, William Whitwell, *The History of St. Augustine, Florida* (New York: 1885).

Edwardes, Marian, & Lewis Spence, *A Dictionary of Non-Classical Mythology* (London, New York: no date).

Eubank, H. Ragland, *The Authentic Guide Book of Historic Northern Neck of Virginia* (Richmond: 1934).

Federal Writers' Project, *Florida, A Guide to the Southernmost State* (New York: 1940).

Federal Writers' Project, *Seeing St. Augustine* (St. Augustine: Sponsored by City Commission of St. Augustine, 1937).

Firestone, Clark B., *The Coasts of Illusion* (New York: 1924).

Florida Historical Quarterly, Vols. I—XIX (Jacksonville, Tallahassee, St. Augustine).

Gaffarel, Paul, *Histoire de la Floride Française* (Paris: 1875).

History of Neustra Señora de la Léche y Buen Parto and Saint Augustine, published by the Cathedral Parish of Saint Augustine (St. Augustine: 1937).

Hodge, Frederick W., editor, *Handbook of American Indians North of Mexico*, 2 vols. (Washington: 1910).

Hughes, Thomas, *History of the Society of Jesus in North America* (London: 1917).

Kenny, Michael, *Pedro Martínez, S. J.* (St. Leo: 1939).

Kenny, Michael, *The Romance of the Floridas* (New York, Milwaukee, Chicago: 1935).

Laudonnière, René de, "The Description of the West Indies in general, but chiefly and particularly of Florida," p. 303 *et seq.*, and 'The second voyage unto Florida, made and written by

Captaine Laudonnière, which fortified and inhabited there two Summers and one whole Winter," p. 319 *et seq.*, in Richard Hakluyt's *The Third and Last Volume of the Voyages, Navigationes, Traffiques and Discoveries, &c.* (London: 1600).

Le Moyne de Morgues, Jacques, *Narrative of Le Moyne, an Artist who Accompanied the French Expedition to Florida under Laudonnière, 1564, Translated from the Latin of De Bry,* with Heliotypes of the Engravings Taken from the Artist's Original Drawings (Boston: 1875).

Loth, David, *Philip II of Spain* (London: 1931).

Lowery, Woodbury, *The Spanish Settlements Within the Present Limits of the United States,* 2 vols. (New York: 1905).

Margry, Paul, *Découvertes et Établissements des Français dans l'ouest et dans le sud de l'Amérique Septentrionale* (Paris: 1886).

Mendoza, Francisco de, Vicar of Florida, in *Archivo General de Indias,* Seville, a long and remarkably candid letter written from St. Augustine, 6 August 1567, to Menéndez, and forwarded by the Adelantado to the King of Spain: concerning the late mutiny and the conduct of Father Anton de Campos. This document has not ever been published—in full, at any rate,—nor is it likely to be.

Merás, Gonzalo Solís de, *Pedro Menéndez de Avilés, &c.,* translated and edited by Jeannette Thurber Connor (Deland: 1923).

Northern Neck News, Vols. 56—63 (Warsaw, Va.: 1934-41).

Parkes, Henry Bamford, *A History of Mexico* (Cambridge: 1938).

Parkman, Francis, *Pioneers of France in the New World* (Boston: 1894).

Prescott, W. H., *History of the Conquest of Mexico,* 3 vols. (New York: 1843).

Prescott, W. H., *History of Philip II,* 2 vols. (New York: 1855).

Reynolds, Charles B., *Old St. Augustine* (St. Augustine: 1886).

Reynolds, Charles B., "The Fakes of St. Augustine," in *Mr. Forster's Travel Magazine,* for January 1921.

Reynolds, Charles B., "*The Oldest House in the United States,*" *St. Augustine, Fla., An Examination, &c.,* (New York: 1921).

Ribaut, Jean, *The Whole and True Discouerye of Terra Florida, &c.,* translated and edited by Jeannette Thurber Connor (Deland: 1927).

Riudaz y Caravia, Eugenio, *La Florida, au Conquista y Colonización por Pedro Menéndez de Avilés,* Vols. I & II, from which, through consideration of a before-named deficiency, Mr. Edward W. Lawson has put into English the needed parts (Madrid: 1894).

Robinson, Conway, *An Account of Discoveries in the West until 1519 and of Voyages to and Along the Atlantic Coast of North America from 1520 to 1573* (Richmond: 1848).

Shea, John Gilmary, "Ancient Florida," the fourth chapter in Vol. II of Justin Winsor's *Narrative and Critical History of America,* 8 vols. (New York: 1905).

Shea, John Gilmary, *History of the Catholic Church in the United States,* Vol. I (New York: 1886).

Shea, John Gilmary, *History of the Catholic Missions among the Indian Tribes* (New York: 1857).

Shea, John Gilmary, "The Spanish Mission Colony on the Rappahannock," p. 333 *et seq.,* in *The Indian Miscellany,* edited by W. W. Beach (Albany: 1877).

Smith, John, *The Travels of Captaine John Smith,* 2 vols. (Glasgow: 1907).

Sparke, John, A Gentleman of the Voyage, "Sir John Hawkin's Second Voyage to the West Indies," p. 31 *et seq.* in Vol. I of *Voyages and Travels mainly during the 16th and 17th Centuries,* edited by C. Raymond Beazley, 2 vols. in An English Garner, 12 vols. (London, New York: no date).

Spence, Lewis, *The Civilization of Ancient Mexico* (London: 1911).

Spence, Lewis, *The Gods of Mexico* (New York: 1923).

Spence, Lewis, *The Myths of Mexico and Peru* (London: 1913).

Squier, E. G., "Historical and Mythological Traditions of the Algonquins," p. 9 *et seq.*, in *The Indian Miscellany*, edited by W. W. Beach (Albany: 1877).

Telephone Directory, St. Augustine, Fla., January 1940.

The St. Augustine Record, Historical Restoration Issue, in Six Sections, Including Comics, July 4, 1937.

Tyler, Lyon Gardiner, *The Cradle of the Republic* (Richmond: 1906).

Tylor, E. B., *Anahuac, or Mexico and the Mexicans* (London: 1861).

United States Geological Survey, *Topographical Maps of the United States*, the Heathsville, Kilmarnock, Tappahannock, and Morattico Quadrangles for the State of Virginia (Washington: 1917-1918).

Verrill, A. Hyatt, *Romantic and Historic Virginia* (New York: 1935).

Wilstach, Paul, *Potomac Landings* (Indianapolis: 1921).

Wilstach, Paul, *Tidewater Virginia* (Indianapolis: 1929).

Zweig, Stefan, *Mary Queen of Scotland and the Isles*, translated by Eden and Cedar Paul (New York: 1935).